Disconnected

A NOVEL

A.K. Adler

Published in the United States by Luft Books, New York.
www.luftbooks.com

ISBN 9780985976835

Cover designed by Morgan Dodge.

Visit www.akadler.com for more information on the writing of A.K. Adler.

For My Adorable Monster.

Through the swollen slit she saw only two things that mattered.

HER LAST MOMENTS, AT THE LAST PLACE SHE'D SEE

REBECCA OPENED HER eye. Through the swollen slit she saw only two things that mattered. The face of the man she loved. And the gun he was pointing at her.

This wasn't going to end well for little Becky Tyler. This wasn't going to end well at all.

It seemed important to Rebecca that she got up. That she faced him as an equal. There was no cavalry coming. Or, if there was, it would arrive too late to make a difference. She was going to have to do this herself.

But she hurt all over. She hurt so very much. Even breathing hurt. Breathing! That couldn't possibly be a good sign. She tried to push herself up with her good hand. Her head spun with the effort and she slunk back down.

Maybe she'd just continue to wallow in the dirt. After all, if she did get up, what was to stop him from just kicking her back down again? It would be a lot of effort—a lot of pain—for no result.

Easier just to stay on the ground and wait for the inevitable.

No, god-freaking-damn-it!

She was going to stand up and face him. She wasn't an animal. If he was going to shoot her, he was going to have to see her bloodied, swollen face as he did it.

She rose to one knee. Then pushed up to her feet. She staggered a little as a fresh wave of blackness threatened to swamp her.

She inhaled a pair of deep, sharp breaths.

The blackness retreated. She turned to face him.

He still had the gun fixed on her. She tried not to look at it.

"Mark," she said. "If you have any feelings at all for me, please don't do this." Her voice cracked a little. "Please. We can come up with another way to make this work."

"Babe," he said. "You know I love you. I've never loved anyone as much as I've loved you—"

"You only hurt me because you love me, right?" Her face throbbed.

He shook his head. Disappointed. "Don't turn me into a cliché, Bec," he said. "You know that's not what this is." He stumbled for his next sentence. "This wasn't part of the plan. I don't want to do this."

"But you're going to."

He nodded. Looked up at the sky for a moment, before turning back to her. "Yeah," he finally said.

Rebecca's heart raced.

It couldn't end this way. She and Mark belonged together. Not *this* Mark, obviously. This Mark was a ridiculous parody of the man she'd fallen in love with. She didn't know where he'd come from. She didn't want to know. She just wanted her Mark. The witty doofus who'd (almost literally) swept her off her feet when they first met. The man who'd stolen her heart. The man with whom she belonged. Rebecca and Mark. Mark and Rebecca. It was a pairing the universe itself had endorsed. They belonged together. Theirs was a connection that (again, almost literally) transcended time.

It didn't end with a bullet.

Did it?

She took another deep breath. Fresh pain filled her chest.

She closed her eyes.

As she did, a sense of… relief? Acceptance? Peace? Understanding? A sense of something washed over her. She saw clearly how this was going to end.

Everything would be all right.

"I love you, Mark," she said. Her voice a whispered wheeze. "I love you so very much."

She opened her eyes. Looked up at him. Took one last deep breath. Sucked in the pain. Flashed a bloodstained smile.

"Do it," she said.

"I'm so sorry," he said.

She snorted a half-laugh. Yeah. Whatever. She felt a disgusting combination of snot and blood running out her nose. She wiped it with her good arm.

So much blood.

"Just do it," she said.

"I love you," he said.

And pulled the trigger.

SPACE

CHAPTER ONE

She was butt-ugly. There was no getting around it.

"Weird Al is not for dancing."

"The devil horns are the giveaway."

She probably had a boyfriend.

A WEDNESDAY AFTERNOON SEVERAL MONTHS EARLIER

SHE WAS BUTT-UGLY. There was no getting around it.

Her name was Sharon. She was twenty-eight. She was sharp. She was funny. She worked in an accountancy firm that 'paid her well enough to justify the brink of tears boredom'. She wrote coherently and with almost no spelling errors (apart from the unavoidable 'irresistable'). She knew a startling amount about Duran Duran.

She also had a face like one of the uglier Cabbage Patch Kids.

Mark knew he had to escape from her. He just wasn't sure how. But that was why he had Jodie.

He unlocked the front door of his apartment and walked in, dropping the key into its bowl. He picked up the phone. The dial tone told him he had a message. He ignored it and speed-dialled Jodie.

"Hey," said Mark. He removed his tie.

"Marcus Aurelius," replied Jodie. "What's up?"

"Sharon."

"Sharon?"

"The internet girl."

"The funny one?"

"Yeah."

"The one whose turn of phrase charms the pantaloons off you?"

"Uh, yeah."

"What about her?"

"I got a photo."

"And?"

He kicked his shoes off. "She's not pretty."

"How not pretty?"

Mark paused. "You know those pig creatures who guarded Jabba's fortress in *Return of the Jedi*?"

"Oh."

"Yeah," said Mark. "Worse than that." He took his jacket off and threw it over the chair.

"Oh," said Jodie again. "The poor girl."

"Poor girl? What about me?"

"You look nothing like a pig creature. I don't care what anybody says."

"Yes. Your hilarity is as hilarious as ever."

"You can't get past the looks?" asked Jodie.

"No," said Mark. "And yes, I know that makes me the shallowest person ever."

"Yes. Yes it does."

"I mean, I know I'm no—" Mark flailed a hand. Jodie intuited it.

"Insert latest celebrity male hunk here," she said.

"Exactly."

"No. No you're not."

"Thank you. But I'm not… misshapen."

"Not grotesquely so."

"And I just don't see the point of dating somebody I don't find physically attractive."

"Aren't ugly people with great personalities the worst?"

"Yes they are."

"You'd think they'd have the common decency to be wretched people."

"It would prevent turmoil. You're ugly. *And* you're a foul person. I therefore choose to dismiss you."

"What about this? Since she's ugly, but not considerate enough to have a foul personality, that very thoughtlessness makes her a bad person."

"Because she's not awful, therefore she is?" said Mark.

"Exactly."

"Hmmm…" He opened the fridge door and recoiled. Something reeked in there. No doubt the squid. He grabbed a beer and shut the door. The squid was a problem for another time. "So how do I get out of this?"

"Next time don't reply unless the girl has a photo posted."

"Oh, good. Retrospective advice. That always helps. You got any way of telling me that three days ago?"

"It's a lesson, Marcus. You make mistakes. You learn from them."

"I thought this was why I had you."

"What? You think I'm going to prevent you from making mistakes with the whole internet dating thing?"

"Ideally."

"Oh, you will have fun. What's her nickname again?"

"LossaLove."

There was clacking at the other end as Jodie logged on to the dating site.

"Yeah," she eventually said. "It's a good profile. She's a funny girl. But, y'know, no photo."

"The lack of a photo didn't necessarily mean she was a horrific monstrosity."

"It's a clue."

"Thank you again, Miss Retrospect. How do I get rid of her?"

"You have to write back a few more times. You can't stop straight after she sends a photo."

"Why not?" said Mark.

"Um, because it's just too shockingly cruel for words."

"Can't I be cruel to be kind?" he asked. "I'm sure I've heard that somewhere."

"No," said Jodie. "You're gonna be kind to be kind."

"Fine," said Mark. "Whatever."

"After a couple of kind emails," said Jodie. "You can pull the 'I've met somebody else' gambit. That's always a safe escape route."

"Okay."

"You'll have to take your profile down for a while. Can't have her seeing you still up there when you've supposedly just met somebody."

Mark sighed again. "How long did you persevere with this nonsense before you met Rich?"

"Couple of years."

"Gawd." He took a sip of beer. "How is the big Dick, anyway?"

"He's fantastic. Don't forget his birthday party's this Friday."

"How could I possibly?"

"Be nice."

"I am nice. He's the one who's weird around me, remember?"

"He's only weird around you because you're weird around him."

"Oh, good. Chickens and eggs."

"Go away and email your pig-woman."

"Will do."

"Be nice."

"Yeah, yeah, yeah."

He hung up.

He took another sip of beer and remembered he had a phone message. He pressed Speed Dial 0.

"You have one new message," the phone told him.

"Hi," came a woman's voice. "It's Rebecca."

Rebecca? He didn't know any Rebeccas.

The message continued. "From last night?"

Ah. That helped. Or, y'know, would have, had he met a Rebecca last night.

"The one who so brazenly spilt wine on your jacket?"

Mark looked at his jacket. No wine stain. No Rebecca. No last night. He let the wrong number continue.

"Anyway… Um. Maybe I could take you out to dinner to make up for it. Don't worry, I'll still pay for the dry-cleaning as well. I may be the world's most monstrously oafish person, but I'm no cheap-skate. Call me."

An intriguing offer. But not one he felt he could take up. He'd learned his lesson about getting involved with faceless women.

Also, he didn't have her number.

He pressed a button on his phone.

"Message deleted," it said. "You have no more messages."

Jodie walked the phone back to the kitchen and hung it up.

"Who was that?" said Richard, looking up from the lamb pieces.

"Mark."

"Yeah?"

"He's upset because on his first foray into internet dating, he's landed himself an ugly one."

Richard snorted. "Hardly surprising."

Jodie raised an eyebrow at him.

"Obviously not you," he said. "That goes without saying."

"Say it anyway."

"Obviously not you."

Jodie lowered her eyebrow. "Okay," she said.

"*You* are stunningly gorgeous," said Richard. "It's just that others on the internet… well, aren't."

Jodie nodded.

"And you can't always tell from the photos," he said. "There are some highly misleading camera angles out there."

"This one didn't do that."

"No?" Richard scooped the lamb into the wok.

"This one didn't even provide a photo."

This time, Richard raised *his* eyebrow. "Now I have no sympathy."

"None?"

"Not one bit," he said. "You never respond to profiles that don't have photos. That's just asking for trouble."

Mark sat down at his computer. Might as well get it over with. He fired up his browser and logged into the email address he used for the online dating. Perhaps it was paranoid to keep those emails separated from the others, but—

Ding! "Hey you!"

God. The instant messenger. It had automatically logged him in and declared him to be at his computer. He hated this freaking thing.

The message was from Sharon. Of course. Damn, blast and double damn.

"Hey," he typed back. "What's up?"

Gotta be nice, right?

Sharon started typing again. The instant messenger told him this. It was excellent at poking its e-nose into other people's activities.

Ding! "Not much. Just hanging around at home, surfing ye olde web."

Before he could reply, he saw Sharon was typing some more.

Ding! "What's up with you?"

This was bad. Any second now she was going to try to discuss her photo or a date or something equally awkward. How was he supposed to escape? He took another sip of beer.

"Just logged on to download some stuff from work," he typed. The lie came easily enough. He typed on.

Sharon started typing as well. Oh good. Now there would be some out of sync instant messaging. That was always fun. He stopped typing. So did she.

A pause and she started again.

Ding! "That sucks like a Suckulon Sucks-Thousand."

He started up again. "Yeah. Got a stupid report due tomorrow. Probably going to be on it for a while."

Ding! "That sucks like a Suckulon Sucks-Thousand." Copy-paste.

Ding! "Again."

Mark typed on. "Yeah. I'll email you tomorrow."

"Okay. Bye!"

"Bye!"

Nice. Nice. Nice. Jodie would be proud of him.

He selected his status. Changed it to 'Busy'. He should set 'Busy' as the default. Prevent such close calls in the future. He did so while he thought of it. Busy, busy, busy. That's what he'd be from now on.

He alt-tabbed over to Sharon's email. He double-clicked on the photo attachment. It opened in Photoshop. Yeah. It still wasn't good. He clicked on some auto settings. Auto contrast. Auto colour. Auto balance. They all made her look a little different. None made her look any better.

He sharpened the image. That made it worse. He undid that and blurred. Blurring helped. He blurred some more. And again. Sharon's face was now a generic fuzz. A generic, slightly chubby fuzz. He selected the image and squeezed it thinner. Much better.

Yep. He was, indeed, the shallowest person ever.

He closed Photoshop, refusing to save his changes. He went back to her email and replied to it without enthusiasm. He saved it. He'd have to send it later if he wanted to preserve the facade of being too busy to chat.

He grabbed the phone and ordered some ribs for dinner. He got the serious man. It was always either the serious man or the chatty girl. The serious man always took his order like a robot, asking the same questions each time, oblivious to the regularity of his calls. The chatty girl was much friendlier. She recognised his number. Always sounded happy to hear from him. Always asked how he was. Always wished him a good night. Always sounded genuine in that wish.

He was a little sweet on the chatty rib girl.

This made him not just the shallowest person ever, but also the saddest.

He hung up and logged on to the dating site. Did a search for girls with photos. Went to work.

THURSDAY AFTERNOON

Mark arrived home. What a day. He threw his keys in the bowl and hit the speakerphone button on his phone. There was the 'you have messages' dial tone again.

He speed-dialled zero and listened to the message.

"Hey, it's Rebecca. I, uh, I wish you'd kissed me too. C'est la vie. Anyway, thanks again for last night. I can't remember when I've had such a fantastic evening. I still don't know how you knew about my predilection for tulips, but they're beautiful."

Mark rolled his eyes as he kicked off his shoes. The message continued.

"Uh… I was thinking, if you're not doing anything, maybe you'd like to come around for dinner tonight. I'll make some proper pasta and maybe we could watch *Brazil?* Gimme a call."

He tore his tie off and deleted the message.

"Message deleted," his phone said. "You have no more messages."

He speed-dialled Jodie. Richard answered.

"Rich," said Mark.

"Hello?"

"It's Mark."

"I'll get her for you."

"Hey," said Jodie, as she took the phone. "Wassup?"

"I'm grumpy."

"Okay. But I get to be Bashful."

"I logged on last night," said Mark. "Replied to Sharon. Because, y'know, don't want to be too shockingly cruel for words."

"You're a good man, Grumpy Brown."

"Then I scoured around the girls with photos. I figure if I'm going to tell Sharon I've met somebody else then it would be ideal if I didn't have to lie about it."

"That *would* be ideal, yes. And you're renowned for your idealism."

"So I scour."

"And?"

"There's SmileyKylie."

"SmileyKylie," echoed Jodie. "Is SmileyKylie smiley?"

"SmileyKylie *is* smiley. If the one photo she's provided is to be trusted. She has a big, toothsome grin."

"That sounds smiley to me."

"She's got large, brown eyes. Frizzy, auburn hair. Pleasing to the eye."

"Sounds like a catch. A big, smiley catch."

"Of course, her profile was littered with 'LOL's and 'OMG's and the like."

"Oh," said Jodie. "You don't need that."

"No. But then there's BellOfTheBall."

"She sounds promising."

"BellOfTheBall has a cute, dare I say, elfin face."

"Elfin?"

"Elfin."

"Not many ugly elves."

"Exactly. She lives in St Ives."

"That's close."

"She's a couple of years younger than me."

"Perfect."

"We share several favourite books and movies."

"I feel like I should be preparing a bachelor party."

"Yee-eeeah…"

"What's wrong with her?"

"Spell 'belle'," said Mark.

"As in 'belle of the ball'?" said Jodie. "Oh."

"Exactly."

"Well, that's… sad."

"Extremely sad."

"Normally, I'd defend the spelling. Because I know you can be harsh."

"I can be harsh. That's correct."

"But if it's part of the nickname, you should at least check the spelling."

"That was my thinking, yes," said Mark. "So I moved on to ReadyForFun."

"R-E-A-D-Y?"

"Yes."

"F-U-N?"

"Yes."

"F-O-R?"

"Yes."

"Not the number 4?"

"If it had been the number 4 I'd have had no choice but to vomit all over my monitor."

"I can see that. So what's ReadyForFun's story? Is she ready for—"

"Fun? She is."

"Excellent."

Pause. "ReadyForFun is a pleasantly neutral girl," said Mark.

"Pleasantly neutral?"

"She's an average of every other profile out there."

"Oh. I remember those."

"She's looking for somebody to be friends with at first and then, who knows?"

"I see."

"She wants somebody who makes her laugh."

"Does she like going to the beach?"

"She does. She also likes movies."

"I see."

"And hanging out with friends."

"With a bottle of red, perhaps?"

"I don't think she clearly spelt that out. But I think it's safe to assume. She also likes all kinds of music."

"Not heavy metal, though."

"No. Nor country. She parenthetically vetoed those two."

"Of course."

"I fell asleep reading her profile."

"I'm not surprised."

"So I sent Kisses to all three."

"Oh," said Jodie. "Okay."

"What the hell."

"That's the spirit."

"I spend all day today checking my emails regularly, waiting for a response."

"And?"

"Nothing."

"Nothing?"

"Nothing. The only personal email I got was from Sharon. Some funny, chatty anecdote about the time she'd battled a deck chair on a Pacific cruise. And you know what?"

"What?"

"Two days ago I would have enjoyed her tale so much more."

"Because you would have pictured her locked in deck-chair battle, looking like—"

"Insert latest celebrity babe here," said Mark. "Exactly. Now the tale just makes me sad."

"Because you are the shallowest person in the world."

"Yes. Also, she sent through her phone number."

"Oooh. That's not good."

"I'm going to email her tomorrow and tell her I worked late tonight and so I couldn't call. I'll also explain about Richard's party tomorrow night. That will buy me time until Saturday."

"Good thinking."

"But I have to get out of this soon."

"A phone call won't be that bad," said Jodie.

"Do you want to make it?"

"Not at all."

"I just wish one of these other girls had replied. I feel like emailing them all and pointing out that I wasn't all that interested in any of them."

"Probably not a productive move."

"They're nothing special. They were just the only vaguely plausible options among several thousand duds."

"You can be such a Casanova when you put your mind to it."

"This is why I'm grumpy."

"Because you can be such a Casanova?"

"No. Because of the annoying women who don't email me and the ugly one who does. And I haven't even told you about this fool woman leaving me wrong number messages on my machine."

"I'm sure it's quite the tale. Unfortunately, while you're grumpy, I'm hungry, and my handsome husband has just placed my dinner in front of me. So I'll leave you with your pig woman and your trio of vaguely plausible, non-replying options and your wrong number woman and see you tomorrow."

"Yeah."

He hung up. Dinner sounded good. There were leftovers in the fridge.

"Why is he grumpy?" asked Richard, after Jodie hung up.

"The usual Mark stuff. World not revolving around him and falling effortlessly into place."

"His life is hell."

"So he'd have you believe."

There was a pause.

"Why is he a Casanova?" asked Richard.

"What? Oh. He, um, he wants to email women to tell them he doesn't think all that much of them."

Richard frowned. "Really?"

Jodie laughed. "I guess he hasn't quite got the hang of this internet dating thing." She took a sip of water. "Y'know, after dinner, I might have a surprise for you."

"A surprise?"

"Uh-huh."

"For me?"

"Uh-huh."

"A birthday surprise?"

"Maybe," she said, her voice a teasing singsong.

"Will I like it?"

"I think, based on previous experience, you might like it rather a lot." She arched an eyebrow at him.

"After dinner?"

"After dinner."

"All right. Let's eat," said Richard.

Mark opened his fridge and searched for dinner. The remains of last night's ribs smothered the foul octopus smell. He grabbed the ribs and dumped them on a fresh plate. There was also a cob of corn. He picked it up and considered it carefully.

What the hell.

He put it on the plate as well. He opened the microwave door and deposited the meal inside. Clocked in a safe two minutes and hit 'Start'.

Why had nobody replied to him? His profile was personable. Witty. Charming. Nicely self-deprecating. With a photo.

If he was a girl, he'd respond to such a profile. Weren't they always going on about the sense of humour thing?

His microwave beeped at him. He opened the door and reached for a plate.

Ow! Hot. Two minutes had clearly been too long.

He grabbed a beer instead. Wandered over to his computer.

He checked his email. Still no responses. Damn their eyes.

He checked his instant messenger. He was still 'Busy'. Just as well, because Sharon was back. Did the girl have a life away from her computer? Wondered Mark, sitting at his computer. Yes, yes. Glass houses. Stones. And so forth.

He logged back on to the site and checked his profile again.

While it was loading, he grabbed the ribs and brought them back to the computer. He tore a rib from the rack. Sucked all the barbecue sauce goodness off it.

His profile had loaded. He cast another eye over it.

Damn. There was some good stuff here. How were these woman resisting this? They had to be crazy.

He put the rib bone back on his plate. Sucked his fingers clean. Went for the next one.

Jodie finished tying the suspenders in place. She looked up. Caught a vision of herself in the mirror. Dear god. He'd better appreciate this.

"Are you ready?" she called out. This was not a flattering outfit.

"Never been readier," came the reply.

Jodie stood. Pressed the top down. She looked ridiculous. She felt ridiculous. She clearly *was* ridiculous. She grabbed the ridiculous feather duster and strode out to the living room.

"God help me," said Richard. His mouth gaped.

"You like?"

Richard nodded. Fast. Many times. "Oh, I like."

"Now, Mr Flannery," said Jodie. She'd begun to feel a little less ridiculous. It was astonishing how men worked. Richard was the smartest, most sensitive and caring man she knew. But shove a French maid outfit in his face and he turned into a sex-crazed teen again.

"Yes?" said Richard.

"Is there anything in particular you would like me to polish?"

FRIDAY AFTERNOON

Mark threw his keys in the bowl and hit the speakerphone as he kicked off his shoes. Another message dial tone. He speed dialled MessageBank and removed his tie.

A man spoke. "It's just… well, me. Calling to… Shit!"

Mark looked up at the phone. He pressed a button and listened to the message again.

It didn't change the second time around. He pressed another button.

"Message deleted," his phone told him, before starting the next one. It was Wrong Number Rebecca.

"Hey sexy," she said. "I don't have any classes this afternoon— so I'm sitting in my bubble bath all alone… naked… wet… waiting for you. Come over as soon as you can."

Mark's eyes opened wide. He'd received 'thanks but no thanks' responses from BellOfTheBall and SmileyKylie. Sharon had also sent through another irritatingly entertaining email. And there was continuing silence from the not-as-ready-as-she'd-advertised ReadyForFun, Which meant Wrong Number Rebecca now officially qualified as his most promising female correspondent, just ahead of Chatty Rib Girl.

This was far too sad to even think about.

He pressed a different button on the phone.

"Message saved. You have no more messages."

Mark made his way to the shower. Turned it on. Undressed. Clambered in. Time to get ready for Rich's party. He didn't have an overwhelming urge to be there. But he couldn't think of a good reason not to show. So it looked like he was going to have to go.

He wasn't good at parties. Too many people. Too much noise. He knew that, in theory, they were fun places to be. But he always found himself overwhelmed and would just end up in a quiet corner somewhere. From there, he'd watch the clock until it was a fitting time to leave.

He knew this was not normal. Every profile on the dating website made this clear. Everybody loved to party. Let their hair down. Go to nightclubs. Go to bars. Dance. Go crazy. Have wild times. Rock on. And so forth.

Every time he saw this, his heart sank a little more. Was it so odd to prefer talking to an interesting person one-on-one, somewhere quiet and relaxed? He understood that all the partying and wild-time rocking and fun-having was some theoretical shortcut to sex. But he'd never understood how that worked either.

Sharon had not been interested in the wild, fun-having party-times. That had been part of her early appeal. And she had turned out to be… well, Sharon.

Maybe he was the male equivalent of Sharon.

He turned the shower off rather than linger any longer on the thought.

He dried himself and began a search for clothes. The bottom half was easy. He picked up his jeans. Smelt them. They were fine. He thought about ironing them.

Jeans were a pain to iron. He pulled them on.

Back to the bathroom for the deodorant. Sprayed it on. Couldn't have himself odorising up the place.

Now, the tricky bit.

Shirts were troublesome. It was so easy to misjudge the shirt requirements. Long sleeve. Short sleeve. Collar. No collar. V-neck.

Round neck. Pattern. Plain. Buttoned. T-shirt. There were too many choices. And he invariably chose the wrong one.

He looked through his wardrobe. Nothing grabbed him.

Screw it. A T-shirt would do. He opened his T-shirt drawer. Grabbed the one on top. He held it up. A little wrinkly. Not too bad. Nobody would notice with his jacket on, anyway. Looked like he could forgo the ironing-board again.

He pulled the shirt on.

Was it a sneaker night? Or a boots night?

Boots were always safe. He grabbed them and his work socks. One final nasal check (socks were okay for some more wear). Done.

Okay. Ready to go. He checked his watch. He still had half an hour to kill.

He decided to check if ReadyForFun had responded. He logged on to his computer.

She hadn't.

Richard brushed his teeth. Jodie emerged behind him and pointed to the bathtub.

"Ice. Soft drink. Beer. Wine," she said.

He spat. "You've already checked them," he said.

"I'm double-checking."

Richard wiped toothpaste spit from his chin. "You're *over*checking," he said. "Everything's done. The party will be fine. Your organisational skills are not in doubt."

She hugged him from behind. "I know," she said. "I just want everything to be perfect."

"It will be."

Her face pulled away from him.

"Did you put aftershave on?"

"Yes."

"Not enough. I can barely smell it."

"I don't like too much."

"Lift your arms."

He did so. Jodie sprayed scent all over him. "Much better," she said.

"If you're looking for something to do, you can always iron my shirt."

"Nice try," she said. "Iron your own damn shirt."

"I'm just trying to help," he said. "Be nice."

"I am nice."

"If you don't want to iron my shirt, you could always go remove the Weird Al songs from the playlist. You're only going to skip over them when they come on anyway."

"You put Weird Al in the playlist?" she said. "Weird Al is not for dancing."

"It's the same music as the original song. If the original song is fit for dancing, then so is the Weird Al version."

But she wasn't listening. She'd already made her way to the living room to exorcise tonight's music.

He went back to brushing his teeth. Jodie had many fine qualities. But her appreciation of quality musical parodies was not one of them.

FORTY MINUTES LATER

Jodie answered the door. It was Mark. He held a six-pack and was dressed as stylishly as one could hope.

"Marcus Aurelius. You're late."

"I did my best."

"You did well. It's a good foundation for us to build on."

"Am I the first one here?"

"You're not," said Jodie.

"Boo-yah!" Mark gave a punch of triumph.

"I knew you could do it." She looked him over more closely. "No present?"

"Was I supposed to bring one?"

"It *is* his birthday."

"I know. But I just thought… you know. Dick and I don't exchange presents."

Jodie sighed. "Whatever. Come in."

"He can have the six-pack."

"I'll pass on his behalf. Let me put these in the bathtub." Mark grabbed one and left the rest with her.

"There should be a book that explains this stuff," said Mark, following her to the bathroom. She immersed the remainder of his six-pack in the bath ice.

"That explains about birthdays and the associated giving of gifts?" said Jodie.

"Yeah."

Jodie turned and raised an eyebrow at him.

"What?" said Mark. "Dick and I have never given each other a birthday present before. How was I supposed to know this party signified the beginning of such a trend?"

"It's surely one of the more impenetrable social riddles of our time."

"This book I'm proposing would also explain how even though a party invitation says to show up around 8:00, that's not at all when you should aim to be there."

"We told everybody else 7:30."

"Really? Everybody else is forty-five minutes late?"

"Not everybody. Come on." She led him down the hall.

"Rich," said Mark, reaching out for a handshake. "Happy birthday."

"Thanks." He introduced him to the couple who had beaten him here, and broken his longstanding 'first at the party' streak. "Mark's just started internet dating," said Richard.

"Isn't that how you and Jodie met?" said the woman, whose name Mark had already forgotten.

"That's right," said Jodie, handing Richard a beer.

"How's it going?" said the equally nameless man to Mark.

"It's going well," said Mark.

"Yeah?" said Richard.

"Yeah."

There was a pause.

"Mark's a bit swamped with choices at the moment," said Jodie. "He's got three or four girls he's emailing and then there's some woman leaving messages on his answering machine or something." She looked over to him. "What's her story?"

"She got lucky."

"Oh."

"What?" said the nameless man.

"Got a message from her just before I came over. Sounded like she'd just had herself some sex-u-al in-ter-course."

There was another pause.

"Good for her," said Richard, eventually. He raised his beer in toast. Mark clinked and they both swallowed.

"Anyone want another one?" said Mark.

THREE HOURS LATER

"You having fun?" said Jodie.

"Fun?" said Richard.

"Yeah."

He pondered for a drunken second and a half. "Yes," he decided.

"You look like you're having fun."

"You do?"

"You do."

"I do?"

"Yes."

"I'm a little bit drunk," he said. He held his thumb and fingers apart to show exactly how much.

"The devil horns are the giveaway."

"What?"

"The devil horns." Richard looked at her. Blank. "The horns on your head."

Richard felt his head. He found the horns in question. "I forgot about them."

"Have you had anything to eat?" asked Jodie.

"Sausage rolls."

"We didn't have any sausage rolls."

"Sushi. Sushi rolls."

"Okay. Maybe I'll get you something else to eat."

"And another beer, please."

"Of course. Anything else, your majesty?"

"A kiss."

"You're lucky it's your birthday, mister."

She kissed him.

"Have you seen Mark?" she said.

"Out the back talking to Holly about being a dog."

"Oh."

"I don't think you're following me," said Mark. "We're talking about a legitimate puzzle here."

"Uh-huh," said Holly.

"A dog has no shame. A dog will express delight at seeing you. A dog will not play games with you. A dog will——-"

"Dogs play games."

Mark stopped. His train of thought had fallen to pieces. He tried to repair it. "A dog will love you and not— Wait. What?"

"Dogs play games all the time. It's pretty much what they do."

"Ah," said Mark. He understood Holly's point. "Ah," he repeated.

"I'm going to get another drink."

"Excellent. Me too."

"You have a drink."

"Ah."

"I'll be back."

She wouldn't be.

As Holly left, another woman walked over to Mark.

"I get what you're saying."

"Hmmm?" said Mark.

"About dogs. Dogs are so open and loving. They don't hide how they feel. And everybody adores them in return. And yet if a human tries that, they're usually treated with complete disrespect."

"Exactly!" said Mark. "That was my point."

The girl smiled. "I'm Rebecca."

"I'm Mark." He smiled as a thought passed by. "You haven't been leaving wrong numbers on my answering machine for the past three days, have you?"

"I would be extremely surprised," said Rebecca. "I only had my phone put on yesterday."

"Well, some Rebecca is."

"I'll bring it up at the next Rebecca Meeting."

"See that you do."

She felt his jacket. "Nice jacket," she said.

"It's suede."

"Really?"

Mark shrugged. "I have no idea. Clothes are not my milieu."

"'Milieu'?"

"Is that not how it's pronounced?" asked Mark. Before Rebecca could reply, however, her ankle slipped beneath her. She reached out to avoid falling. In the process she spilt wine all over Mark's jacket.

"Oh my god," she said, regaining her balance. "I'm so incredibly sorry. I am the world's most monstrously oafish person! You can't take me anywhere."

She reached over to the outside table and grabbed some napkins. She dabbed his jacket with it.

"I have no idea what I'm doing with this, by the way," she confessed. "I'm so sorry. You're going to have to dry-clean this. Give me your phone number. Obviously I'll pay for it."

"You'll pay for my phone number?"

"I'll pay for the dry-cleaning." She smiled. "Just give me your phone number."

Mark did so. "Maybe you should give me yours as well," he said.

She smiled. "Should I now?"

"Well," said Mark. "You did just throw yourself at me."

"And your parents didn't warn you about girls who behaved like that?"

"No," said Mark. "I mean, they might have. If they hadn't, like, died when I was six."

Rebecca stopped dabbing. She held out her hand. "Hi," she said. "I'm Rebecca. When I'm not tripping over my feet, I'm shoving them into my mouth."

Mark smiled. "It's okay," he said. "Batman was an orphan. And Superman. I'm in good company."

"Okay," said Rebecca.

"Of course, my parents didn't rocket me to a new planet where I'd have a ridiculous array of superpowers while the Earth exploded behind me," said Mark. "So, y'know. Trade-offs."

"Good for the rest of us Earthlings, though," said Rebecca.

"I suppose."

There was a pause. Rebecca broke it.

"So do you want my phone number or not?" she said.

VERY EARLY SATURDAY MORNING

Mark shuffled inside. Threw his keys at the bowl. Missed. He pressed the button on the phone. No messages. Perfect. Maybe Sharon had given up.

That had gone well. Rebecca was awesome. They'd only been able to talk a little longer after the wine-spilling. Something about an early morning delivery of stools. He sure hoped she meant the kind you sat on. He'd thought about making that joke when she'd mentioned it, but had decided no. Jokes based around faecal samples could be tricky. Especially with somebody you'd just met.

Still. She was awesome. Even on fifteen minutes of conversation that was clear.

She probably had a boyfriend.

Of course she had a boyfriend. She was too cute. Too funny. Too awesome not to have a boyfriend.

The lucky bastard.

Mark undressed. Masturbated with purpose. Went to bed.

TEN HOURS LATER

"Mark?" said Katrina.

"Sure," said Rebecca. She shifted the phone to her other ear and grabbed a pen. She began to doodle. "Why? What's wrong with him?"

"Nothing. I don't even really know him."

"So why did you say 'Mark?' like that?"

"Like what?"

"Like 'oh, my god, woman, are you insane?'"

"It wasn't like that."

"It was a little like that."

"You just surprised me."

"Why?"

Katrina sighed. "He's just not my type, that's all."

Rebecca waited for elaboration. Katrina provided it.

"He just seems a bit… detached," she said. "Disconnected."

"I liked him," said Rebecca. "I thought he was funny."

"I suppose."

"He's cute."

"You think?"

"In a dorkish way."

"I suppose," said Katrina again. "You're not just feeling guilty because you spilt wine all over him?"

Rebecca laughed. "I would never ask a guy out because of some misplaced sense of guilt."

"Okay."

"Sure, I'll stay with them twelve months too long out of a misplaced sense of guilt. But I won't ask them out over it." She snorted a laugh.

Katrina forced a return snort. "You heard from Andrew?"

"Nope."

"Good."

"Yes," said Rebecca. She let the word trail away.

"It *is* good," said Katrina. "You don't need that asshole in your life."

"I know, I know."

"But?"

"But, damn, Kat. I need to get laid."

"Ah," said Katrina. "The plot thickens."

"I'm doodling as I talk to you, and all my stick figures are performing unspeakable acts on one another." This was not strictly true. She was doodling concentric circles. But the lie illustrated her point.

"That does sound like the act of a horny woman," said Katrina.

"I haven't had sex since we broke up. I need to have sex soon."

"So you're not interested in Mark so much, as in his penis."

"I'm interested in all facets of the man."

"But you'll start with his penis."

Rebecca shrugged. "A woman has needs."

There was a knock at the door.

"That'll be my stools," said Rebecca. "I have to go."

HALF AN HOUR LATER

Rebecca sat on her new stool. She looked at the phone number. She looked at the phone. She'd been alternating between the two for twenty-five minutes.

She looked back at the phone number.

"Screw it," she said, to nobody. She picked up the phone and dialled.

It rang. And rang. And rang.

Great. He wasn't there.

The MessageBank answered her. "You've reached Mark's phone," it said. "Talk to me."

And the tone.

"Hi," said Rebecca. "It's Rebecca. From last night? The one who so brazenly spilt wine on your jacket?"

Why was she going into so much detail? He'd remember her. She had made an impression. Spilling red wine all over a person would do that.

"Anyway… Um. Maybe I could take you out to dinner to make up for it. Don't worry; I'll still pay for the dry-cleaning as well. I may be the world's most monstrously oafish person, but I'm no cheapskate. Call me."

She hung up. Exhaled.

Did it.

The telephone converted Rebecca's message into electrons. In that form, it made its way down the phone line. It arrived at the MessageBank computers. There it was converted into digital form. This digital form was then saved to Mark's individual storage space of messages.

Somewhere in that process, and for reasons nobody would ever be able to explain, the message went back in time three days.

CHAPTER TWO

There was a girl last night.

Nobody could object to Jodie Foster.

Something very illogical was happening.

Are you sure he's not gay?

SATURDAY AFTERNOON

MARK WALKED IN and dumped the DVDs on the floor. He hit the phone.

No messages. Disappointing.

He called Jodie.

"Hey," said Jodie. "What's news?"

"There was a girl last night."

"There were many girls last night."

"I'm thinking of just one in particular. Her name's Rebecca. Tall, cute, nose freckles."

"I remember her. She's Katrina's cousin."

"Which one's Katrina?"

"You've met Katrina."

"I meet lots of people. Help me out here."

"You've met her many times."

"And yet she hasn't stuck in my memory. Give me a clue."

"Katrina works with Rich. She's the one with…" Jodie sighed. "Yes?"

"The one with the nose."

"Oh. Right. I know her."

"I know you do."

"So Rebecca's her cousin?"

"Yeah. She's just moved here."

"I gathered this." Mark paused. "Do you know if she has a boyfriend?"

"Probably not. She *did* just move here."

"True."

"And if she did have a boyfriend already here, he would have probably come along to the party too."

"Also true. You make good sense."

"You like this Rebecca woman?"

"She spilt wine all over me."

"A solid foundation for any romance I'd have thought."

"Exactly. She then patted me down with napkins. That made me go a bit funny inside."

"Dear god, Marcus. You need help."

"I know. And you're not offering any."

"What do you want me to do?"

"She said she'd call me. About cleaning my jacket."

"And?"

"And she hasn't."

"It's only been a few hours. She's probably sensibly passed out somewhere."

"Maybe. I dunno. We chatted for a few minutes after the wine-spilling until she had to go. I liked her."

There was a pause. "Great."

"Do you think it would be okay if I called her?"

"You have her number?"

"Yeah."

"She *gave* you her number?"

"Yeah."

"Then call her. That's what she wants you to do. That's why she gave it to you."

"I thought so. But I wasn't sure."

"You think too much about this stuff."

"But she did say she'd call me."

"Then wait."

"I don't want to wait."

"Then call."

Mark thought about his options. "I *will* call," he eventually decided.

"Does that mean this conversation is over?"

"Yes."

"Excellent. Good luck."

"Thanks."

He hung up.

Mark found Rebecca's number. He stared at the digits. Was he going to do this?

He looked over to his jacket. The wine stain was impressive, despite her napkin-dabbing.

He was going to do this.

He picked up the phone and dialled.

"Hello?" came Rebecca's voice.

"Rebecca?"

"Yes."

"Hi. It's Mark."

"Hey, I was hoping you'd return my call."

Return?

"I was hoping we could get together tonight. For dinner?" he said. He inhaled.

"Sure. Tonight would be great." Mark threw a little punch at nothing in particular. Rebecca continued to talk. "Do you know any good restaurants? Because my culinary knowledge is currently poor. Or are restaurants not your milieu either?"

Mark grinned. "That *is* how it's pronounced, right?"

"I have no idea," she said. "We can discuss it over dinner."

"I'll find somewhere convenient. What's your address?"

She told him. Mark clacked on to the web and found a nearby restaurant that Jodie had once recommended. After agreeing to this and setting a time, Mark hung up and punched the air once more.

Take *that*, SmileyKylie!

Rebecca hung up the phone. Walked over to the couch and flopped on it. That had gone well. It was moments like these that made the soul-crunching fear of asking somebody out worthwhile.

She speed-dialled Katrina. "We're going out tonight," she said.

"You don't muck about," said Katrina.

"It was his idea."

"Sounds like he's horny, too."

"Let's hope so."

"Where are you going?"

"Some place called 'Bravo!'. In Newtown?"

"Never heard of it."

"It's Italian."

"Yeah, still never heard of it," said Katrina. "Still, buon appetito."

"Grazie."

"And if you can't be molto goodissimo, then be molto carefulis-simo."

"Si."

"Ciao bella."

"Ciao."

Rebecca hung up. Now, what was she going to wear?

Mark looked around his apartment. Here was the thing. If he tidied up expecting that Rebecca might perhaps return here this evening, then cosmic law dictated there was no chance of her doing so.

On the other hand, if he didn't tidy, then they *would* end up back here. Because of the same cosmic law. And his sheer slovenliness would repulse her. And possibly cause her to storm home to vomit in disgust.

Cosmic laws sucked.

Of course, he knew this particular cosmic law didn't exist. Tidying his house and seducing women had nothing to do with each other. Any causality he'd previously noted was purely imaginary.

If he tidied the house this afternoon, that could not possibly affect whether she returned home with him tonight. All it could affect was her impression of him if/when she arrived.

So, he would tidy.

He went to work. First things first. He opened the fridge. That odour stenched forth again.

What on Earth was it?

He rummaged through a few plastic containers of leftover food. None of them were the culprit. Even the squid seemed okay. And it had seemed the most likely candidate for his fridge-rank.

Still, none of the containers held anything that would ever be edible again. He threw them all in the garbage bag. The odour remained in his fridge.

He dove back in. Found a microwave container sitting alone up the back. He pulled it out. There was no denying the stench clawing its way through the plastic wrap cover. Some kind of vegetable had liquefied itself.

Vegetables. Of course.

Typical. Useless bloody foodstuffs.

He pulled back the wrap.

Oh sweet Jesus.

He tipped the contents into the garbage bag. Threw the microwave container into the sink. Turned the hot water tap on hard.

He tied the garbage bag up. Ran it down to the community bins.

This girl had better be worth it.

A FEW HOURS LATER

Rebecca stretched back in the bath. She lifted her leg up. Cleaned the razor. Slid it down her calf. She cleaned the razor again. Repeated.

Eventually she moved to her armpits.

Then, finally, some much-needed pubic topiary.

There. Now if they were to do the deed, she could do so smooth of skin.

Of course, her fresh smooth skin and socially acceptable nether region meant there was now zero chance of any deed-doing. That was the cosmic law.

Mark was feeling déjà vu. Wasn't he just making decisions about shirts last night? How could he be back to making them again?

The house-tidying had taken longer than he'd thought. For a one-bedroom apartment, he seemed able to amass a remarkable amount of clutter. Still, all tidy now. This included moving two of the less female-friendly DVDs he'd hired that morning into his porn box. He'd left *Panic Room* out on display. Nobody could object to Jodie Foster.

He chose a long-sleeve, black and grey buttoned shirt with collar. Nobody could object to that, either. He assumed. He was more confident about Jodie Foster than the shirt.

He decided to iron it. That helped with the confidence.

SATURDAY NIGHT

Mark walked down the street. He pulled his mobile phone out of his pocket. Five minutes early.

He stopped.

Beside him was a florist. Mark looked at the sign. 'TULIPS! CHEAP!!' Mark wasn't sure the affordable tulips warranted three exclamation marks. But something nagged at him.

Tulips.

Who was talking about tulips?

He couldn't remember. He bought them anyway. Because, hey, who can argue with 'CHEAP!!'.

AN HOUR LATER

"How's your pasta?" he asked.

Rebecca pulled a face.

"Delicious?" guessed Mark.

"The other one."

"Awful."

She tapped her nose.

"I blame Jode," said Mark. "She recommended the place."

"She has terrible taste."

"You've met Richard then?"

"Ooooh. Harsh."

"I joke. I joke because I love."

"Of course," said Rebecca. "I dance because I love."

"That works just as well."

"How do you and Jodie know each other?"

"We used to work together."

"So you're a nerd too?"

"Of course."

Rebecca chewed. "Are you going for that 'nerds are the new cool' thing?" she said.

"Do you think it'll work?"

"Seems unlikely."

"It does, doesn't it?"

"You never know," said Rebecca. "What have you got for me? *Star Trek* references?"

"*Star Wars* references."

"Of course."

"But that's not all."

"No?"

"No. I have far more to offer a young lady than a deep and detailed understanding of the troubled mind of George Lucas."

"I would hope so."

"Sure. I also have comic books. Computer games. Chess. Magic."

"Revealing these tendencies gets you women?"

"Not at all," said Mark. "I barely even try any more."

"I've noticed."

"Thank you."

"So what's your favourite movie? And if you say *Star Wars* I *will* scream."

Mark paused. Too many to choose from. A name popped into his head. "*Brazil*. Terry Gilliam."

Rebecca fixed a gaze on him. "You, Nerd Boy, are beginning to scare me. You somehow guess my favourite flowers." She gestured to the tulips atop the table. "Now you share my favourite movie. Keep this up and I may just be able to look past your uberdork tendencies."

"Deal."

"I'd suspect you of inside knowledge, but you're about three people removed from anybody who could tell you this stuff." She paused. "Y'know, I have the Special Edition of *Brazil* on DVD. You should come around and watch it one night."

"I'd like that."

Rebecca smiled at him. "I might even cook you dinner."

"I'd... like that?"

"Oh, you'd like it, buddy."

Rebecca noticed her fork. "Why am I still eating this pasta?"

Neither of them could answer that.

AN HOUR LATER

As the waiter brought the bill, Mark reached for it.

"I'll get this," he said.

"I'm happy to pay my share," said Rebecca.

"You have large dry-cleaning bills in your future," said Mark, smiling. "I've got this."

Rebecca smiled back. "Thank you. I'll pay next time."

Next time? Mark liked the idea of a 'next time'. "Deal," he said. "Do you want to get a drink?"

"Sure," said Rebecca.

HALF AN HOUR LATER

Mark captured the attention of the barman. He turned to Rebecca and raised an eyebrow.

"Light beer," she said. Mark tilted his head in query. "I have to drive," she explained.

"Ah," said Mark. He turned back to the barman. "Two Cascade Lights." He turned back to Rebecca. Her head was matching his earlier tilt. "I'm watching my weight," he explained.

"There is nothing sexier than a man counting calories."

"It is the cornerstone of my raw animal magnetism, yes."

She laughed. Mark felt his heart race once more. The girl had a laugh to die for. Or, even better, to *not* die for and instead spend a lot of time with.

"You do realise that light beer is low in alcohol, not low in calories," she said.

"Yeah?"

"Yeah, it's not Diet Beer."

"Huh," said Mark. He rubbed his stomach. "That explains much." He smiled at her. She smiled back.

"You want to sit over there?" said Rebecca, gesturing to a table.

Mark shrugged. "Sure."

"Okay. I'll be back."

She dropped the tulips at the table, then disappeared for the bathrooms. Mark paid for the beers and made his way to the table. He put the beers down.

This girl was amazing.

Rebecca checked her makeup. All good.

Now. How was this going to work? She'd forgotten Mark didn't have a car. She'd offer to drive him home, but he didn't exactly live close. She didn't want to look desperate.

This also ruled out inviting him home with her. She wanted to sleep with him, but she wasn't just going to hand it to him. He'd have to work for it a little.

Damn.

Engh. He had a drink and a walk back to her car's worth of time. If he hadn't made a move on her by then, he didn't deserve to sleep with her tonight.

And if he did make a move?

Well, she'd jump that bridge when she came to it.

TWO HOURS LATER

They left the pub and started walking back to Rebecca's car. After a night of effortless conversation, words were suddenly hard to come by.

"I had a great night," said Mark.

"Me too," said Rebecca. Was he going to hold her hand?

There was a long pause as they walked on, hands not held.

"Want to do this again?" he said.

"Very much," said Rebecca. She let fly with her best smile. Was he going to kiss her?

"Great."

Another pause. He hadn't kissed her.

Damn it.

They walked on.

"That's my car there," said Rebecca.

"Okay," said Mark.

"Thank you for a great night," she said. She pulled out her smile again. Fixed her gaze on him. He couldn't possibly resist this.

"No, thank *you*," said Mark.

He *was* resisting this. He seemed happy with the evening. Happy with her. But he wasn't doing anything.

Maybe she was misreading this.

"Okay," said Rebecca. "Speak to you soon." She unlocked the car and got in. Mark raised a hand in farewell as she drove off.

Damn. Damn. Damn.

Mark walked to the station.

Why didn't you kiss her goodnight, you bloody fool?

The moment was right. They'd had a perfect evening, sparks flying all over the place, hitting other people, starting small fires and so forth.

And yet, at the moment of whatsisname, he'd chickened out. This was why he didn't have a girlfriend.

He picked up his mobile. She wouldn't be home yet. He called her home number. He didn't have her mobile number yet. He should have asked for that.

Nevertheless.

Her answering machine picked up.

"Hey," he said. "It's Mark. I'm just on my way to the station." He paused. Took a deep breath. "I sure wish I'd kissed you good-night." There was another pause. Was there anything else to say? "Thanks again for a great night. Speak soon."

He hung up.

Too little, too late.

AN HOUR LATER

Mark arrived home. It had only occurred to him after he left the message that he hadn't given her his mobile number either. So if she'd got his message, she couldn't call him back.

He could have left another message on her machine with his mobile number, but that truly would be stupid. Bad enough that he'd not kissed her goodnight and then left a message saying he wished he'd done so. He didn't know yet whether that message was a brilliant recovery or the final dollop of idiocy on a fool end to the evening.

But calling and leaving a phone message with his mobile number on it? He might as well leave a message saying 'Call me back tonight and affirm that you like me, despite my lack of goodnight-kissing'.

And that would be too sad. Even for him.

However, she did have his home number. She might have arrived home and left a message for him. She hadn't, of course. He'd spent the entire train ride convincing himself of that.

He still held his breath as he picked up the phone and listened for the dial tone.

A message.

He breathed out. Pressed the button for the message.

Brilliant recovery? Final dollop of idiocy? Time to find out.

"Hi," said the message. It wasn't Rebecca. "It's Sharon. Just trying to get hold of you and maybe organise a time to get together."

Mark cringed. Sharon left her number for him again, in case he'd misplaced it, or 'something'.

"I'll give you another call tomorrow," she said, before hanging up.

Mark couldn't wait.

SUNDAY MORNING

Rebecca took a deep breath in, picked up the phone and dialled.

She'd received his message when she arrived home last night. It had made her smile. It was clear he had no idea how to deal with women. She found this charming. Or, if not charming, less irritating than some other personality quirks he could have had.

And trying to compensate by leaving a phone message confessing his attraction to her? That was sweet and charming, too. In a clueless doofus kinda way.

He was worth a second chance.

She got the answering machine again. Did this guy ever answer his phone? She waited for the beep and left a message.

"Hey, it's Rebecca," she said. "I, uh, I wish you'd kissed me too." She blushed as she said it. "C'est la vie. Anyway, thanks again for last night. I can't remember when I've had such a fantastic evening. I still don't know how you knew about my predilection for tulips, but they're beautiful."

Stop jabbering, woman. Get to the point.

"Uh… I was thinking, if you're not doing anything, maybe you'd like to come around for dinner tonight. I'll make some proper pasta and maybe we could watch *Brazil*? Gimme a call."

She hung up. She blew an irritated breath into her fringe.

Whatever.

Once again, this message somehow ended up on Mark's MessageBank three days earlier.

Mark looked at the ringing phone. Rebecca?

No. Don't be stupid. It was Sharon. Sharon was the one who promised to call him back. Rebecca was the one who would never call him back after last night's idiotic series of events.

And he couldn't deal with Sharon this morning.

He let the phone go to MessageBank. After all, that was what it was for, surely.

It rang out.

He waited a few minutes. Long enough for Sharon to leave a message.

He picked up the phone. Huh. No message.

How dare somebody call and not leave a message. What was this? 1984?

He speed-dialled Jodie.

"How'd the date go?" was her first question.

"Don't want to talk about it."

"Okay," said Jodie. "What would you like to talk about?"

"Sharon called me."

"The pig woman?"

"Yeah."

"How did that go?"

"She called last night. Left a sad little message."

"I see."

"Tried to lay a guilt trip on me about not calling her. Then left her number again, in case I'd misplaced it or something."

"Oh dear."

"Then she called back this morning."

"And?"

"I let her go through to MessageBank. I think that'll be my policy for a while."

"What did she say?"

"She didn't leave a message. That's why I'm liking this policy."

"You could call her and tell her you've met somebody else."

Mark snorted. "Yeah," he said. "Or I could just screen my calls until she gives up."

"That is more you, yes."

"So if you call and I don't pick up, just leave a message and I'll call straight back."

"Understood," said Jodie.

"Besides," said Mark. "I can hardly tell her I've met somebody else after last night."

"Tell me about last night," said Jodie. "You know you want to."

Mark sighed. "I blew it."

"How so?"

"I didn't kiss her good night."

"That's hardly the end of the world."

"No?"

"Nah."

"But the moment was right. I should have kissed her," he said. "And like some cry-baby wiener boy, I let the moment slip."

"But this is a good thing."

"Me being some cry-baby wiener boy?"

"No," said Jodie. "You're going to need to work on that. But the fact the moment felt right. That's a good thing."

"Yeah?"

"You wouldn't have felt that way if she'd spent the evening chewing her fingernails, looking out the window, bored out of her mind, would you?"

"I suppose not."

"So unless you misread the pre-goodnight kiss portion of the evening, it sounds like you had a good date."

"Y'know, the pre-goodnight kiss portion of the evening *was* a good date."

"See?"

"A very good date."

"Excellent."

"But there's something else I should tell you about the post-non-goodnight kiss portion of the evening."

"Hit me."

"I called her phone and left a message telling her I wished I had kissed her."

There was a lengthy pause.

"That's a ploy I'd expect from nobody else," Jodie eventually said.

"Stupid, huh?"

"Not 'stupid', per se. Just, uh, atypical," said Jodie. "I'm trying to work out how I might have reacted to such a ploy from somebody I'd just had a very good date with."

"Cast your mind back."

"I'm casting," said Jodie. "I think I'd be… frustrated. On the one hand, happy to know you'd wanted to kiss me. But, on the proverbial other, annoyed you hadn't done so."

"Would you have called back?"

"I take it from your general melancholy that she hasn't?"

"Nope."

"Ah."

"I blew it?"

"Marcus," said Jodie. "If she's written you off just because you didn't kiss her goodnight, then you did misread the situation."

"Thank you."

"I'm just saying—"

"No, that's great. Because a feeling of self-confidence can be such a burden."

"Hush now," said Jodie. "If she had a great time on the date, she's not going to give up on you because you didn't kiss her goodnight. Especially since you later expressed an interest in her."

Mark didn't say anything.

"She'll call back. Patience, young Jedi."

"Patience. Prrrffrt."

Another long pause before Jodie spoke again. "Marcus?" she said.

"Yes."

"How do you know the call this morning was from Sharon?"

"Hmm?"

"If she didn't leave a message, how do you know it was her? How do you know it wasn't, say, Rebecca?"

"Don't say that."

"I feel I must."

"Rebecca would leave a message."

"How do you know?"

"She seems like a message-leaver."

"Uh-huh. Has she ever left a message for you before?"

"Don't try to confuse me with logic," said Mark. "No. She hasn't ever left me a phone message. But I did get several from Wrong Number Rebecca."

"Clearly just as good."

"Precisely. Rebeccas are message-leavers."

"Okay."

"Although," he said. "I haven't heard from Wrong Number Rebecca since Cute Freckle-Nosed Unkissed Rebecca showed up."

"That must save confusion."

There was a pause.

"Yeah," said Mark.

He paused again.

"I'll call you back," he said.

"What's his problem?" said Richard.

"The usual," said Jodie.

"How did he screw it up this time?"

"He didn't kiss her goodnight."

"Did she want to be kissed goodnight?"

"He thinks so."

"Yeah, but this is Mark," said Richard.

"True," said Jodie. "Who knows what's going on? I'm sure he'll work it out."

"You think?"

"No, you're right. He probably won't," said Jodie. "But we *will* get to hear all about it."

"Can't wait," said Richard.

Mark sat down and looked at the phone.

His brain nagged at him. It had been doing so since Rebecca spilt the wine on him. And increasing by the day. It was now relentless.

Something illogical was happening.

He thought for a long, long time.

Wrong Number Rebecca's first message had been about spilling red wine on him. Something Cute Freckle-Nosed Unkissed Rebecca did a couple of days later.

Her second message had been something about great dates and tulips. And cooking pasta. And watching *Brazil*. And she'd left that a couple of days before the Cute Freckle-Nosed Unkissed Rebecca date that had covered all those things.

This was a staggering coincidence. In fact, too staggering to be a coincidence. But if it wasn't a coincidence, then what was it?

Hmm…

It had to be a coincidence.

The phone rang.

He stared at it.

Perfect. If he answered it, it would be Sharon. If he didn't, it was Rebecca for sure. Damn cosmic laws.

He answered it.

"Hello?"

"Mark," came Sharon's voice. "We speak at last."

"Sharon?" said Mark. "Hi."

The cosmos hated him.

"I know how it sounds," said Rebecca.

"No, let me get this straight," said Katrina. "You have a perfect date. Sparks fly. Chemistry exudes. All is perfect."

"Yeah."

"You give him all kinds of signals that you like him and would perhaps consider taking him home to ravish your smokin'-hot bod."

"Yeah."

"And he responds with a hearty handshake goodnight and a follow-up phone call where he tells you how he wishes he had enough testicles to respond to your charms like a man."

"Not in so many words, but yeah."

"And you find this so charming that you hurl yourself at him again."

"Yeah."

"By his preferred medium of choice, the telephone answering machine."

"Yeah."

"I think your horniness has driven you insane."

"Very possibly."

"Are you sure he's not gay?"

"He's not gay."

"I'm just asking."

"He's not gay."

"Because there are other men out there, you know," said Katrina. "Heterosexual men who'd give their right leg to jump you."

"Surely at that point they'd be 'hopping' me."

"What?"

"If they gave their right leg, they wouldn't 'jump' me. They'd 'hop' me."

"Rebecca TYLER."

"I'm just saying."

"You can't make fun of amputees."

"You brought them up."

"I was speaking metaphorically," said Katrina. "I was trying to let you know you had alternatives."

"I see," said Rebecca. "But I like Mark. He's funny. Smart. Bi-pedal."

"Don't."

"I think he just panicked at the end of the night."

"If you say so."

"He deserves another chance."

"If you say so."

"But if he blows it tonight, I'm moving on to one of your amputee friends."

Mark hung up.

That had not been fun. It had taken ten minutes of inane Sharon chatter before he'd been able to tell her about Rebecca.

"Oh," she had said.

"I'm sorry," said Mark. "We only just started going out."

"No, I understand," said Sharon.

"I like her. I just don't feel right seeing two girls at—"

"No," said Sharon. "I understand."

"Okay," said Mark. He didn't know how to wrap this stupid conversation up. He just wanted to slam down the phone and end it. Only his sense of how much Jodie would disapprove prevented him from doing so.

"Good luck with it," said Sharon. "I hope everything works out well for you."

"Yeah," said Mark. "You too."

Sharon snorted. "Yeah." Then below her breath. "Whatever."

They'd then stumbled through what seemed like half an hour of awkward farewells, before he could hang up.

After hanging up, he logged on to the dating site and hid his profile. He didn't want to go through that again. Stupid awful pig-women.

Of course, since the phone call he'd just answered had been from Sharon, it meant the previous one could well have been from Rebecca.

This led him back to the nagging thoughts.

Cute Freckle-Nosed Unkissed Rebecca had not left a message for him this morning.

But Wrong Number Rebecca had left an applicable message for him three days ago.

Spookily applicable, really.

He strained to remember what Wrong Number Rebecca had said. She'd definitely mentioned tulips. And pasta.

And watching *Brazil*.

It couldn't possibly be a coincidence.

But if it wasn't, what did that mean?

It meant Wrong Number Rebecca wasn't leaving messages on the wrong number at all. She was just not playing the 'cause and effect' game by the proper rules.

This alternative was impossible.

It had to be a coincidence.

Except…

Had she mentioned something about wishing she'd been kissed in the message?

He thought she had.

It couldn't possibly be a coincidence.

So how was she doing it?

He rubbed his eyes. How did you leave messages referring to the events of dates three days in the future? It was impossible.

And yet… that second message three days ago had referred to her cooking dinner for him. Could he assume that was an invitation for tonight?

The third message.

He'd saved the third message for posterity. He picked up the phone and replayed it.

"Hey sexy," she said. "I don't have any classes this afternoon—so I'm sitting in my bubble bath all alone… naked… wet… waiting for you. Come over as soon as you can."

He sat back.

If Wrong Number Rebecca's second message was for him and this third message was also for him, then…

Then it seemed this second date was going to go very well indeed.

He played the message again.

It was an experiment worth undertaking. What was the worst that could happen? She could say 'of course, I didn't invite you over for dinner, you non-kissing lame-ass. Begone from my presence.'

That would be unpleasant.

But it would at least clarify where he stood.

He dialled.

"Hello?" she said.

"Rebecca?"

"Mark. Hi."

"Hi," said Mark. He tried to work out a way to phrase his next question. "Um, am I coming around to watch *Brazil* tonight?"

"I hope so. And the pasta. Don't downplay the pasta portion of the evening, mister."

"I wouldn't dare." A grin sprouted all over his face. He hadn't blown it at all. He clenched his fists in triumph.

"Good."

"When should I get there?"

"Sevenish?"

"Seven, really seven? Or seven as a polite code for a fashionably late 7:30?"

"Let's call it seven for really seven."

"I like your sense of precision," said Mark. "I'll see you then."

"Great. I can't wait."

"Me neither."

They hung up.

Mark played the third message again. This was going to be a good date.

SUNDAY NIGHT

"Would you like some more?" asked Rebecca. She stood up.

Mark looked up, mouth full. He nodded.

"You like?" she said.

"Mmmmm," he said. His nodding grew more frenzied. He swallowed. "Oh yeah."

She smiled and dished up some more ravioli from an ornate pot.

"Thank you," said Mark. Rebecca gave herself some more too.

"So much better than the restaurant's," said Mark.

"That was my primary aim."

"You succeeded admirably," he said. "For example, your ravioli lacks a certain… rubberish quality."

"That's my speciality. A certain lack of rubberiness." She swallowed some pasta and groaned. "Damn, I'm good at this."

"More wine?" said Mark. This polite conversation was driving him nuts. The unspoken non-kiss hovered over everything.

"Thank you."

He topped her glass. She smiled at him.

He smiled back and went to refill his glass.

Screw it. He put the bottle down and stood up.

Rebecca's gaze followed him.

He walked over to her and kissed her.

She kissed back. "Mmmm," she moaned.

He tilted his head a little more to prevent nose-bump. Her hand moved up to his hair and their tongues pressed deeper.

The positioning was awkward. She was sitting. He was stooping over. He probably should have thought of that before he'd made his move.

She clearly felt the same way. She moved her lips to his neck, standing as she did so. The move had a certain smoothness and grace that Mark was sure he would never have been able to pull off.

He ran one hand through her hair. The other moved down her side. He hesitated uncomfortably at her breast before deciding to move on.

Why didn't this ever come naturally to him? The girl was all over him. She wasn't going to object if he put his hand on her breast. It was not even something he should be thinking about. He should be just reacting naturally.

React naturally. Good advice. Except his natural reaction was to endlessly think about these things.

So, how did one resolve that particular problem?

Her tongue hit his ear. He moaned. No need to think about that.

His hand moved back up to her breast. He cupped it.

God. It felt so good. It had been so long since he'd felt a woman's breast. And, damn, if Rebecca didn't have fine ones. He squeezed it gently, enjoying its soft weight beneath his palm.

She moaned again and her mouth moved back to meet his. This kiss was hungrier. Their hands roamed over one another's bodies. Her hand cupped his crotch and delight swept through him.

He moved to her neck and kissed it. Her head tossed back and she let out another moan of pleasure. He ran a series of kisses down her throat as his hands moved up and ran through his hair. God, she smelt so good. His hands moved down to her butt.

He pulled her crotch in to meet his. She groaned again and brought her mouth down beside his ear. "Bedroom," she whispered.

He kissed her again and they moved, entwined, down the hall.

He started to move toward a door. He wasn't exactly sure where they were going. Since he was the one moving forward, this could prove an issue. He hoped Rebecca could manoeuvre backwards.

She had no trouble. She kicked the bedroom door open as they approached it. The two of them stumbled in and fell on to the bed.

Mark moved his attention back to her throat. He dropped a kiss there. She did smell good. His lips moved down to the top of her breasts, while she started undoing his shirt buttons.

She reached the last button and pulled his shirt off. It stuck on his left hand. He yanked it out and dropped the shirt on the floor. Her fingers caressed wispy chest hair and she gently kissed his nipples.

He reached for the bottom of her shirt. She raised her arms in the air and he pulled the shirt over her head.

Yowsers. It hadn't just been a long time since he'd felt breasts. It had been a long time since he'd seen them too. Even the sight of Rebecca's bra aroused fresh lust in him.

He lunged back at her breasts, kissing her cleavage. She moaned again. He reached his hands around behind her and fumbled with the bra clasp.

And fumbled.

And fumbled.

Stupid bloody bra clasps. He understood, in principle, how they worked. And yet, as ever, in the moment that mattered, they refused to detach.

Rebecca reached behind her back and undid the bra. It fell off.

Her breasts were beautiful. So very beautiful. He kissed one nipple, running his teeth across it slightly.

"God, yes," whispered Rebecca.

He didn't need any further invitation. While his mouth worked on the one breast, his hand moved to the other. He squeezed it. So incredibly soft.

Rebecca's hands moved to his belt. She unbuckled it, then undid his fly and tugged his jeans down. The jeans caught at his knees, and his erection poked out of his boxers.

She wrapped her fingers around it. Mark's eyes closed. Ecstasy. Indescribable ecstasy.

He kicked his jeans off. Rebecca helped, pulling at the legs. She then turned her attention to her own pants. Once she'd undone her belt, Mark tugged her pants off.

Wearing only boxers and panties, they returned for another kiss. A deep, passionate one. The lust was overwhelming. He loved the feel of her breasts against his chest. And the warmth further down was going to drive him mad.

She broke the kiss.

"I want you inside me," she whispered, before kissing him again.

Mark was happy to oblige. He pulled her panties down. She removed his boxers. They kissed again, fully naked for the first time.

Rebecca's hand fumbled for the bedside drawer. She pulled out a condom. She broke the kiss and bit the wrapper open, spitting the bitten portion away.

Mark had forgotten about the condom moment. Still the best way to add an unwelcome intermission to a romantic evening. He sat back and Rebecca leant up on one elbow.

She reached over to him and unrolled the condom down.

Finished, she looked back up at him with large eyes. They kissed. Softer, this time. Less ravenous.

She leant back, allowing him to settle atop her. She guided him inside.

"Gently," she said.

He did his best. And, for a short time, they were slowly pushing against each other, enjoying the fresh sensation of it all.

But soon gentleness subsided. Urgency increased. They thrust hard against each other. Finally, with mutual groans and shouts of approval, it was over.

They fell back on the bed.

"Oh, god," said Mark.

"You glad you kissed me tonight?" said Rebecca.

Mark smiled. "One of my better decisions," he said.

"Look at this," said Jodie. She walked over to Richard and shoved her breast in his face.

He looked up from his book. "What am I looking at?"

"This," she said. "Look. It's a hair."

Richard peered in. "So it is," he said.

"I shouldn't have a hair on my breast."

Richard shrugged.

Jodie sighed. "I'm getting old." She looked in the mirror and grabbed a handful of her bum. "Look at that."

Richard looked up from his book again. "What?"

"My bum. I shouldn't be able to grab a handful of it like that. I'm getting fat and hairy and old."

"Firstly, you're not," said Richard. "Secondly, even if you were, I'd still love you. Now come to bed."

Jodie sighed. She put her pyjamas on. Climbed into bed.

The pair of them read for twenty minutes before Jodie put her book down and turned off her light. "Good night," she said.

"Night," said Richard.

Jodie rolled over and quickly fell asleep. Richard read for ten more minutes.

MONDAY MORNING

Mark woke up. Why were women's beds always so much more comfortable? He was sure it had something to do with fabric softeners.

Rebecca poked her head around the corner.

"Hey, sleepy head. I'm just going to take a quick shower." She smiled. Her freckles danced with mischief. "Care to join me?"

"In a minute."

"Okay."

Rebecca disappeared. Mark heard the shower start.

He leant over to her bedside phone. He had to test this out. He dialled his number.

"You've reached Mark's phone," his MessageBank said. "Talk to me."

"It's just… well, me," said Mark. "Calling to—"

He suddenly remembered the man's message he'd heard three days ago.

That wasn't a man at all. It was *him*.

"Shit," he said.

He hung up.

It was true. Rebecca's phone sent messages back in time.

This was…

No words described what this was.

Rebecca called to him from the shower.

"Are you coming?" she said.

"No doubt."

He got up and joined her.

CHAPTER THREE

It's not some kind of venereal disease, is it?

"Fine. More marinara for me."

Who in blazes was Emma?

There's a naked man in my bathroom.

MONDAY AFTERNOON

REBECCA ARRIVED HOME early. One of the major advantages of being a casual teacher was the occasional free afternoon to spend as she pleased. The major disadvantage, of course, was the associated tiny income.

She called Katrina at work.

"Katrina Tyler speaking."

"Hello, Katrina Tyler speaking. This is Rebecca Tyler speaking."

"How'd it go?"

"It went well."

"How well?"

"*Very* well."

"And?"

"It was good," said Rebecca. "You know how it is the first time. One can't expect miracles."

"No. One. Can't."

"You seem adamant about that."

"Trust me. I know of the lack of miracles of which you speak."

"Anything you'd like to share?"

"Some other time. Tell me more about your night."

"No miraculous sex," said Rebecca. "But some strong efforts. I feel we have a fine foundation to build on."

"Excellent."

"He's a bra-fumbler, and a tad more obsessed with my breasts than I'd like," she said. "But we can fix that."

Rebecca went on to give Katrina the edited highlights of the last twenty-four hours. She was getting to the post-shower portion of the morning when Katrina interrupted.

"Sorry, babe," she said. "I have to go. The boss-man is calling me."

"Okay," said Rebecca. "Give me a call later."

"Will do."

Katrina hung up. Richard smiled at her.

"What's the gossip?" he said.

Rebecca decided to run a bath. She turned the taps on and rummaged through her essential oils. Lavender. Yes. In it went.

Bergamot. Yep. In with that one too.

Eucalyptus. No. It wasn't a gum leaf kinda day.

Peppermint. Mmmm, minty. Yes. In with it also.

She walked into her bedroom and undressed. She picked up the phone.

Should she call him?

No. It was his turn to call her. She'd done all the legwork so far. Sure, he'd jumped her mid-meal last night, but only after she'd put out a detailed series of clear-cut welcoming signals.

She was happy to help kick-start matters. Some guys needed a push along. But at some point, it would be nice if he stood up and took control.

Feminism. Equal rights. And the rest. Sure. No problem with any of that.

But there was still something to be said for the man taking charge in the romantic arena.

So, that was that. Decision made. She wouldn't call him. She'd wait for him to call her.

But she could still take the phone to the tub.

Y'know, in case he *did* call her.

She picked up the phone and headed back to the tub. She dipped her feet in and let herself get used to the temperature.

Just shy of scalding. That's how she liked her baths.

And showers, too.

She smiled, remembering how Mark had recoiled when he'd joined her in the shower this morning.

"Ow," he had said.

"What?" she'd replied. "Too hot?"

"No. I love me some second-degree burns. It's the perfect way to start the working day."

"Don't be such a nanna," said Rebecca.

"You shower with your nanna at these temperatures?"

She'd laughed at that. "Here," she had said. "Let me take your mind off the temperature."

It had been a perfect morning.

Mark was just so funny. He seemed to be made for her.

She lowered herself into the bath. Exhaled and smiled. She felt so relaxed. So happy with the new turn her life had taken. Working up the nerve to leave Andrew and move to the city had been the best move she'd made in a long, long time.

She closed her eyes and smiled some more as she reminisced further about the shower they'd shared.

She'd told Katrina the sex hadn't been miraculous. And it hadn't been. There was still a lot she had to teach him before they could aim for such unearthly heights.

But it had been pretty damn good. After six years with Andrew, it had been thrilling just to feel the touch of another man on her skin.

The newness of it all was part of the attraction.

Screw it. She couldn't wait for him to get home from work and call her. The sooner she got him back over here, the sooner she could start teaching him what she liked.

He'd be at work now. She'd call and see how flustered she could make him.

It'd be fun.

She picked up the phone.

Damn. His mobile number was on the pad on the bedside table. And the bath was too good to leave. She decided to just leave a dirty message on his home answering machine instead. Delayed flustering could be just as much fun.

She dialled his home number. No need to look that one up any more.

"Hey sexy," she said, when she got the machine. "I don't have any classes this afternoon—so I'm sitting at home in my bubble bath all alone… naked… wet… waiting for you. Come over as soon as you can."

She hung up. Smiled to herself. If that didn't get him sprinting over here when he got home, she didn't know what would.

She put the phone down beside the tub and sank into the bath, smile on her face.

Mark was at home. After he'd left Rebecca's apartment, he'd called in to work and declared himself sick. He needed to think too much to spend the day in the office.

He heard the phone ring. He went to pick it up, then thought better of it.

This was the bubble bath message.

He let it ring out.

He had no idea what would happen if he answered a message he'd been predestined not to answer. But he didn't think it was something he wanted to test.

He waited a few minutes then picked up the phone.

No message. Well, none in this time zone, anyway.

He called her back. Time to sort this out.

He got her machine. That was odd. Why was he getting her answering machine? She just called him. Was he also leaving a message in a different time?

"Hey, it's me," he said. "Uh, Mark. I thought you'd be there. Did you call a short while ago? Leave a naughty, naughty message on my machine? Because, if not, you've got competition." He went to hang up, then thought again. "You don't have competition. You're one of a kind."

God, that sounded lame. He decided to hang up before he messed the message up further.

Now what? What if his message had also gone back, or forward, in time? How confusing was this going to get?

Rebecca heard the phone ring. Typical. You put a mud pack on your face and the phone will inevitably ring. Her impulse was to ignore it. But what if it was Mark?

She dunked her hands in the water to clean them off. She shook them dry and reached for the phone. It fell on to the floor. Perfect. Wet, muddy phone. She picked it up and pressed 'Answer'.

Too slow. It went to the machine.

She stopped splashing and listened to his message.

"Hey, it's me," came the voice. "Uh, Mark. I thought you'd be there. Did you call a short while ago? Leave a naughty, naughty message on my machine? Because, if not, you've got competition." There was a pause. "You don't have competition. You're one of a kind."

Gawd, he was cute.

She called him back.

Mark's phone rang. He looked at it. Eventually picked it up.

"Hey, sexy," said Rebecca. "You got my message."

"I did indeed. And you got mine."

"It's a miracle of modern technology."

You have no idea, thought Mark. "How's the bubble bath going?"

"It's a bit lonely."

"Ah."

"What are you doing home?" asked Rebecca.

"Sick."

"I make you sick?"

"You give me fever."

Rebecca smiled. "What's wrong?"

"Seriously. I have a fever," lied Mark. "Just started feeling unwell on the way to work. So abandoned it and came home."

"Oh. Poor bear."

"So, as tempting as your offer is, I think I'm just going to go back to bed and watch *Jerry Springer*."

"That's probably sensible," said Rebecca. "Who has Jerry got on today?"

"I think it's the one where somebody cheated on somebody else."

"That's a good one."

"Yeah."

"Okay. You wrap up warm. Look after yourself. I might call you a bit later."

"Okay."

He hung up.

Picked up the phone again. Called Jodie.

Rebecca looked at the phone.

Shit.

That had not been the voice of a sick man. That was the voice of a man in total freak-out mode.

How could she be so stupid? She'd been way too pushy. Making all the phone calls, all the advances.

If she kept it up she was going to push him away.

Hell, he'd chosen to fake illness rather than return to ravage her. He must have been seriously freaked out.

Stupid fucking men. They were always pulling shit like this. What was so scary about liking somebody?

She dropped the phone with a clang. Sunk down into the bath again. Closed her eyes. Cried just a little.

"I hear you got lucky last night," said Jodie. She put down the notes from which she'd been reading and switched the phone to the other ear.

"How did you know that?"

"I have my sources."

"What kind of sources?" said Mark. Had Jodie received some message from the future as well? What in blazes was going on here?

"Rich told me."

"Who told him?"

"What is up with you?" said Jodie.

"Who told him?"

"Katrina," said Jodie. "Rebecca's cousin? The one who works with him? The link responsible for introducing you two lovebirds?"

"Ah," said Mark. That was a plausible, non-time-travelling explanation.

"Is that okay?"

"Yeah. Fine."

"Because you don't seem fine."

"There is something strange going on."

"I know. You had sex."

"Even stranger than that."

"What do you mean?"

"What are you doing tonight?"

"Why?"

"I need to talk to you. I need to show you something."

"It's not some kind of venereal disease, is it?"

"Ew. No."

"Because I don't need to see it, if it is."

"It's not a venereal disease," said Mark. "We were careful."

"Good to hear."

"Can you come over tonight?" said Mark. "It's important."

"Fine," said Jodie. "I'll come over straight after work."

"Thank you."

Jodie called Richard back.

"Hey babe," she said.

"What's up?"

"I might be a little late home tonight. Marcus has some emergency he needs to see me about."

"Emergency?"

"A Mark emergency," said Jodie.

"What is it?"

"I don't know. Probably some issue with her preferred brand of toothpaste or something."

Richard snorted. "Okay."

"What's for dinner?" said Jodie.

"Seafood marinara," said Richard.

"Yum."

"So don't spend too long sorting out young Marcus's latest turmoil."

"I'll be in and out before you know it."

"Excellent."

MONDAY NIGHT

"You're not going to believe this," said Mark the instant Jodie arrived.

"Hello to you too."

"Shh." He handed her a wine.

"Shh?"

"I have news."

"About your date?"

"Sort of."

"How'd it go?"

Mark exhaled and stared at her.

"Not well?"

"Hush." He made the lip-zipping gesture.

Jodie zipped her lip. She gestured to Mark to continue.

"I don't know where to begin," he said.

Jodie sighed. "So why do I have to hush?"

"Okay, okay." He sighed. "Rebecca, the girl I've seen the last three days is the same Rebecca who left me those wrong number messages."

"That *is* deep."

"No. You don't get it. She left those messages before I met her."

"Okay." Jodie fiddled with her wine glass. "That's a freaky coincidence."

"It's not a coincidence at all."

There was a pause. "I think I should confess now that I don't at all understand what you're trying to tell me."

"I would have been impressed if you had." He paused again. "As far as I can tell, when Rebecca calls me and gets my MessageBank, her message ends up three days in the past."

"I... still don't get it."

"Listen."

He played his MessageBank.

"Hey sexy," it said. "I don't have any classes this afternoon—so I'm sitting at home in my bubble bath all alone... naked... wet... waiting for you. Come over as soon as you can."

Jodie raised her eyebrows. "I'm not sure I needed to hear that," she said.

"That's Rebecca," said Mark. "She made that call this afternoon. I received it on my MessageBank three days ago."

"She left that message this afternoon?"

"Yep."

"And you're spending this evening talking to me about it?"

Mark smiled. "I'm keen for the ravaging. But I'm also keen to understand these time-travelling phone messages."

"You have unique priorities." Jodie took a sip of her wine. "Okay. Let's sort this out."

"Please."

"You're sure that's her?"

"Oh it's her."

"It's not just some woman who sounds like her? A wrong number or something?"

"Nope. It's her. I spoke to her this afternoon."

"And she left that message this afternoon?"

"Yep."

"And you received it three days ago?"

"Yep."

"Well, that *is* weird."

She sipped her wine again. Mark joined in with his beer.

"She also left the message apologising for spilling the wine on me three days before she did so."

There was a long pause.

Mark spoke again. "I also left a message for myself. I received it three days before I left it."

"You're serious."

"I could not make this up if I tried."

"You have a time wormhole in your phone?"

"Somewhere between hers and mine, yeah. So it seems."

"We're going to need more alcohol."

Mark headed back to the kitchen. He grabbed himself another beer and the bottle of wine. He topped up Jodie's glass.

"How does it work?" said Jodie.

"I don't know. But it's just the MessageBank. We talked real time and there was no problem."

"And it's one way?"

"Seems so. I called and left her a message. She got it straight away."

"So how does this work? If she calls you now and you pick up…"

"Then we talk normally."

"But if you don't pick up, she leaves a message three days in the past?"

Mark nodded. Jodie took another long sip from her glass.

"What if she rings you now," said Jodie. "But you don't pick up, but you also didn't receive a message three days ago?"

"I guess that means she hung up without leaving a message."

"You'd hope so. You don't want to muck around with time paradoxes. You've seen the *Back to the Future* movies. You know how much trouble Michael J. Fox got into."

Mark smirked. "Maybe Michael J. Fox's time-travelling was the source of his Parkinson's."

Jodie raised an eyebrow. "Oh, Marcus."

"What?"

"It's not funny to make fun of people with life-threatening diseases."

"Okay. Fine." There was a long pause. Mark spoke next. "Besides, Muhammad Ali has never travelled through time, so…"

Jodie raised her disapproving eyebrow again. Mark ignored it and continued.

"Y'know, to the best of our knowledge."

"Are you done?"

"Yep."

"Okay," said Jodie. "I'm going to forget you even mentioned Parkinson's."

"Fair enough."

"Because we can totally exploit this."

"Oh yeah," said Mark.

"But we need to be careful. Repeat after me: We will not rupture the space-time continuum."

"We will not rupture the space-time continuum."

"Nor invoke time travel paradoxes."

"Nor invoke time travel paradoxes."

"Lest Terminators destroy mankind and pave the way for the machines to take over the future."

"Yeah. Let's start working this out shall we?"

"Okay. Let me just call Rich."

Rebecca did her best not to look at the phone. Did her best to ignore it completely.

He hadn't called back. She'd blown it.

She put a Lean Cuisine in the microwave and set it going.

Seven and a half minutes.

Seven and a half minutes of not looking at the phone.

This was insane. She had to find something else to do. She flicked on the television. Some inane sitcom blared out at her. She flipped through the other channels.

Nothing. There was nothing of interest on any station. When on Earth were they going to hook up the Pay-TV? She'd pay a lot to be distracted at the moment. These people were missing an opportunity.

Music. She needed music. Where was her *Jagged Little Pill* CD? She flipped through the CD boxes and found it.

No.

Mark didn't deserve Alanis. Alanis was for the end of real relationships. Not some half-assed shagging session with some weak-willed weenie, too pitiful to make a—

The phone rang.

She pounced.

"Hello?"

"Hiya," said Katrina.

"Oh. Hey."

"Don't overwhelm me with your enthusiasm, there, Bec."

"Sorry. I just—"

"You thought I was Ma-ark." Her voice took a singsong tone.

"Yeah." Rebecca's voice was the opposite of singsong.

"What's up?" said Katrina.

"It's stupid."

"Tell me anyway."

"He hasn't— He didn't—" Rebecca stumbled on her words. She began to realise she couldn't clearly explain why she was so upset with him. "He's being weird," she finally said.

"In what way?"

"It's hard to explain," said Rebecca. "We had a weird phone conversation earlier today. I—" She exhaled. Irritated. "Something's not right."

"You *have* been moving quickly," said Katrina.

"I suppose."

"Maybe you should just take a deep breath and slow it down a little."

"You're right, you're right."

"Everything will work out how it's supposed to."

The microwave beeped. "That's my dinner," said Rebecca.

"Okay," said Katrina. "Go eat. Relax. Chill. Watch some television. Listen to some music. Take a bath."

"Will do," said Rebecca. "Thanks."

"I'll speak to you tomorrow."

"Sure."

Rebecca hung up. She tore open the wrapping from her meal and sat it on a plate.

She loved Katrina, and appreciated all her help in settling into the city. But if she had to listen to any more of her romantic advice, she was going to scream.

She turned on the radio.

Ignored the non-ringing phone.

Richard paused his computer game and picked up the phone.

"Hello," he said.

"It's me," said Jodie.

"Hey," said Richard. "You going to be home soon?"

"Maybe not as soon as I'd hoped. Is that okay? Mark's got something… important here."

"His new girl hasn't devoted her life to him yet?"

"Nah. This is something else. I'll tell you when I get home."

"Can't wait."

"I won't be too late."

"Fine. I'll see you then."

"This is important," said Jodie.

"Sure," said Richard. "What about dinner?"

"Maybe I'll get some McFood on the way home."

"So, you're not going to be home for dinner."

"It doesn't look good at this stage."

"Fine. More marinara for me."

"I'm sorry," said Jodie. "This is important."

"Apparently so."

There was a long pause.

"Okay," said Jodie. "I need to get back to sorting this out."

"Okay."

"Okay. See you later."

"Yep."

Richard hung up. He refused to let this annoy him. There was no need to be annoyed by Jodie's relationship with Mark. It was harmless. He knew that.

And yet, he *was* annoyed.

The fact he was annoyed by Jodie cancelling dinner to spend time with Mark was more annoying than the cancellation itself.

Meta-annoyances. He was dealing in meta-annoyances. This was obviously the most annoying situation he could possibly be in.

He unpaused his game. With a few swift mouse clicks, he'd marshalled a powerful Russian medieval army. He sent it off to crush the wretched Romans.

As he burnt their wretched villages, he felt a little less annoyed.

Jodie hung up. "Can I get another wine?" She finished off her existing glass.

"Sure."

"Okay," said Jodie. "Let's do this. First things first. We need to find out the exact time difference between message leaving and message receiving. We don't want to go leaving messages too early or too late."

"We will not rupture the space-time continuum."

"Exactly. Don't leave any messages from her machine for the next couple of days. But in three or so days leave one telling you what time you're leaving it."

"Will do."

"Just keep checking your MessageBank regularly. Make sure you... don't... Hmmm."

"What?"

"Check your MessageBank now."

"You just called Rich. If there was a message, you would have got the weird dial tone."

"I know," said Jodie. "Just check it."

Mark hit the speaker phone. The 'you have messages' dial tone sprung forth. He looked at Jodie. She smiled back.

He hit the phone and retrieved the message.

"Hey, it's me." It was him. "Synchronise your watch now. This call is being made at 8:41:07, 08, 09. I'll save you some calculatin' time. You're about 3 days, 71 minutes of time difference. You're also going to get in a little bit of trouble from Jode for saying that. Sorry about that. Damned if you do, damned if you don't."

Mark hung up.

"Am I in trouble?"

Jodie looked up from her watch. "Just a little bit, I guess. The 3 days, 71 minutes difference seems right by my watch. But we probably shouldn't pre-empt information that we work out ourselves. That's a little bit too close to messing with the space-time continuum for my liking."

"I promise not to do it again."

"Apart from when you leave this first message."

"Obviously. Because if I don't say it…"

"Yes. You'd be messing with the space-time continuum."

"Damned if I do, damned if I don't."

He sighed.

"This is starting to weird me out," he said. "I think I need another beer."

"You're only halfway through that one."

"Yeah. Nevertheless."

He disappeared to the kitchen again. Jodie topped her glass.

Mark returned. "How did you know there was going to be a message there?" he said.

"I think it's the decision to call."

"The decision?"

"As soon as you decide to call, that must set the chain of events in motion. Once you decide, the message appears at the appropriate time."

"Three days, 71 minutes before you make the phone call you've just decided to make."

"Right."

"The *decision* to call is the key," said Mark.

"I guess." She sipped some more. "You're not the only one weirded out by this."

TUESDAY AFTERNOON

"Hey, Miss Tyler."

Rebecca looked up. It was Libby, one of her students. "Yes, Libby?"

"It's seventh period."

"Yes?" Rebecca didn't get the point.

"You said we could go over *Emma*?"

Go over Emma? Who in blazes was Emma? What was Libby talking about? "Emma?" said Rebecca.

Libby held up her copy of *Emma* by Jane Austen. "*Emma*," she said.

"Oh, oh!" said Rebecca. "Right. Sorry. My head was somewhere else."

"Man troubles?" said Libby. Her brow furrowed in sympathy.

Rebecca smiled. Her concern was adorable. "Something like that," she said.

"You can't let them get to you," said Libby, calling on the wisdom of all of her sixteen years.

"True," said Rebecca.

"I remember when I used to go with Damon White. He used to make me so mad. Half the time he could be the sweetest boy in the school. The other half, he was totally retarded. Showing off for his dumb friends. Being a total tool."

Rebecca smiled some more. Libby didn't notice.

"Eventually I told him that I expected higher standards from my boyfriend, and if he couldn't live up to those standards then he'd have to go. It was his choice."

"And?"

"He chose to be a tool with his friends."

"Oh," said Rebecca. "I'm sorry."

"No," said Libby. "It's all good. Because I deserve somebody awesome. I'm an awesome person. And I deserve somebody equally awesome. Damon couldn't be that awesome, and that was sad, but c'est la vie." She pronounced it 'sest la vee'. She shrugged. No biggie.

"That's a very good attitude, Libby," said Rebecca. God, had she ever been that together at sixteen? She wasn't that together now. It was a little humbling to be out-matured by somebody a decade younger than her.

"I don't see the point in getting worked up by situations that you can't control," said Libby. She smiled and sat down at one of the desks. She thwapped the book onto the table. "So, what's Emma's problem?"

TUESDAY EVENING

Mark walked in the door and dropped the bag full of library books on the floor. He threw his keys into the bowl and hit the speaker on the phone. No messages. Okay.

He flopped on to the couch and reached over into the bag. He pulled out a book at random. Stephen Hawking's *A Brief History Of Time*. He picked it up and flipped through it, also at random.

He'd taken another day off work, putting in an award-winning sick call this morning. Then he'd headed to the library, where he'd borrowed every book that hinted at time travel, black holes, cosmology or the like.

And now he had to read them.

He flicked through the Hawking book again.

He'd read it later.

He dropped the book on the floor. Found *Back to the Future* in his DVD collection and put that on instead.

Research could take many forms.

TWO AND A HALF HOURS LATER

Mark looked at the phone. He tried to summon his courage. He'd gone over the plan with Jodie a few times now. His first mission was to leave the message they'd both heard him leave last night.

That meant he had to get to Rebecca's phone on Thursday night.

Neither of them knew what would happen if he didn't leave the message. It would certainly create some kind of paradox, but what effect that paradox would have on the universe was unknown. Somewhere between nothing and total destruction seemed the best guess.

So best to get over there and leave the message.

He picked up the phone and dialled.

The phone rang. Rebecca looked up. Mark?

Don't get your hopes up, you stupid girl. It's probably just a telemarketer.

She picked it up. "Hello."

"It's me," said Mark. "Mark."

"I know who 'me' is." It was him! "How are you feeling?"

"A lot better," said Mark. "Must have been a twenty-four hour thing."

"Hope I don't get it."

"Yeah."

"So, what's news?"

What's news? God, she could be lame.

"I was just wondering if I could maybe invite myself over on Thursday. Maybe bring over a DVD. Maybe catch up on that bubble bath I missed."

"You're a fan of bubble baths?"

"It depends on who I share them with."

"Sure. That sounds like fun. Do you want to try for seven, really seven?"

"Seven really seven sounds perfect. See you then."

"Okay."

She hung up. A gigantic grin covered her face. It was stupid that her emotional state already depended so heavily on whether he called. Libby would not approve.

But she couldn't deny that his call made her happy indeed. He *did* like her. He *had* been sick yesterday.

Life was good.

THURSDAY NIGHT

Rebecca turned off the tap. She dipped a finger in the water. Scalding. Perfect.

It was five to seven. Mark would be here shortly. The bath was ready, as bubbly as one could possibly expect. She had champagne cooling in the fridge, and chocolates at the ready.

She lit a candle. The scent of lavender filled the air.

Perfect.

She looked herself over in the bathroom mirror one more time. Her hair was still not right. The flick at the back made her look like something from a fifties beach party. She grabbed the brush and tried to fix it.

There was a knock at the door.

She put the brush down. Took another look at the mirror. The hair was better. Slightly.

Screw it.

She walked down the hall and stood in front of the door.

One more deep breath.

She exhaled. Opened the door.

"Hello," said Mark.

"Hiya. Come on in."

Mark did so. He handed her a bottle of wine. "You look gorgeous," he said. He moved in awkwardly for a kiss. Rebecca helped him along.

The kiss was passionate, but not frenzied. Rebecca let out a soft moan as it ended.

"I needed that," she said.

"Me too," said Mark. He smiled at her. Her heart beat a little faster. "How've you been?"

"Good. What about you? Feeling better?"

"Much better."

"Excellent. Let's hope I don't make you sick this time."

"Deal."

There was a pause. It bordered on the awkward. Rebecca tried to get rid of it.

"You ready for the bubble bath?" she said.

"Never been readier."

"Excellent. You get in. I'll go get the champagne and chocolate and will join you shortly."

She left him to undress in the bathroom and made her way to the kitchen.

Something was still up. The easy rapport they'd had on that first date had been replaced with an awkwardness. A tension. She hoped it was just nerves.

She opened the fridge. Replaced the champagne with Mark's wine. Grabbed the chocolates and headed back.

Mark looked at his watch. Two and a bit hours until the phone call was due. He took it off and placed it on his shirt. He kicked off his shoes.

He'd been nervous all day. Partially about seeing Rebecca. But mostly about getting this phone call made. He wasn't at all sure how he was going to get away from her and make it at precisely the right time.

He removed his socks.

He'd tried to comfort himself with the idea that he was predestined to make the phone call. Surely that meant an opportunity would present itself.

But he wasn't in any sense certain this was the way time-travel worked. He still suspected he had much work to do to make sure everything fit together properly.

He pulled off his jeans and boxers. He dipped a toe through the bubbles. It hit the water and he jerked it back.

Hot, hot, hot.

Rebecca returned with champagne and chocolate.

"Oh my god," she said. "There's a naked man in my bathroom." She mock-averted her eyes.

"I'd be in your bath*tub* if it was at a temperature that humans could withstand."

"But then you'd be all covered in bubbles and I wouldn't be able to check you out."

"So your scalding bath-water was part of an insidious plan?"

"Sure," she said. "You're kind of cute, just standing there all nuded up."

Mark covered his groin with his hands. "I am not a sex object for you to gawp at as you please."

Rebecca smiled. "Then, boy, have you come to the wrong apartment," she said. "Now, get in the tub, sex object boy."

Mark did so, wincing as his feet got used to the water temperature. He took one last subtle look at his watch as he sunk down.

He had two hours to come up with a phone call plan.

FIFTEEN MINUTES LATER

Jodie looked at her watch. One and three quarter hours. She wandered over to Richard. He was still being cold. When she'd arrived home the other night, he was in bed, asleep.

They hadn't discussed the reason for her staying late at Mark's place. He clearly wanted to ask, but was too stubborn to do so. For her part, she had no idea where to begin. Time-travelling phone messages? How did you explain that to a jealous husband?

So it remained unspoken.

"What's for dinner?" she said.

Richard didn't look up from his computer game. "Hmm?" he said.

"What's for dinner?"

"Thought we might order in."

She wasn't sure whether to let that one go. The pair of them had a fair and just meal schedule. They ordered in on Sundays. On all the other nights, they alternated cooking duties. There was flexibility in the schedule, but that was the general idea.

She decided to cut him some slack. After all, if Mark didn't make the phone call, who knew what would happen? For all she knew, the universe was ending in about a hundred minutes.

From that perspective, allowing Richard to get out of cooking dinner tonight was probably okay.

"What were you thinking?" said Jodie.

Richard clicked his mouse furiously. "Damn it!" he said. Something exploded on his screen. "Chinese," he grunted.

"Chinese sounds good," said Jodie. "Do you want me to order?"

A flurry of key-presses. "Sure."

Jodie let him go. He could have his tantrum. If the universe survived the next couple of hours, they'd sort it out then.

FIFTEEN MINUTES LATER

"More champagne?" said Rebecca.

"Sure," said Mark. He held his glass out. Rebecca emptied the remaining champagne into it.

Mark raised his glass in thanks.

"Want to wash my back?" said Rebecca.

"I'd rather wash your front."

Rebecca smiled. Her foot moved between Mark's legs and played with what she found there. "Maybe this bath has run its course."

"Well, the water temperature *is* now sub-boiling."

"Then it is clearly time to retire to the boudoir."

She stood and reached for a towel. She tossed it to Mark and reached for the other one.

Mark began to dry himself off. He took the opportunity to sneak another look at his watch.

He kissed the back of her neck. "My god, you're beautiful," he whispered.

Ninety minutes. Plenty of time.

EIGHTY MINUTES LATER

Jodie looked at the clock again. Ten more minutes.

"What's happening?" said Richard.

Jodie swallowed her chicken. "What do you mean?" she said.

"You keep looking at the clock."

"Do I?" She stabbed another piece of chicken with her fork. She didn't believe in chopsticks. She didn't see the point in increasing the difficulty level of one's meal. Eating was not a gymnastics routine.

Richard smiled. "Yeah. What's going on?" he said. "Is it something to do with Mark?"

"Yeah." She put her fork down and rubbed her chin. "But, it's… hard to explain what's going on with him this time."

"Try me."

She sighed. "I'll make you a deal," she said. "If everything goes well, I'll *show* you what's going on in a week or so."

Richard shrugged. "Fair enough. Do you want any more of this?" he said, holding up the pork.

"I'm porked out."

Richard served himself the rest of the pork. "And what if everything doesn't go well?"

"Sorry?"

"You said that if everything went well, you'd fill me in on Mark's latest escapades. What if everything doesn't go well?"

"Trust me," said Jodie. "We don't even want to think about what happens if everything doesn't go well."

"Wow," said Richard. "That's dramatic."

"Isn't it?"

TEN MINUTES LATER

Mark stole another look at his watch. It sat on the bedside table beside him. He'd brought it back during a post-coital toilet stop.

"You okay?" said Rebecca.

"Hmmm?"

"You seem distracted."

"I do? No, I'm just thirsty." He sat up in the bed. "Do you want a glass of water?"

"Sure."

"I'll be right back."

He picked up his watch and walked naked to the bedroom door.

"Cute butt," said Rebecca.

"Well, I never," said Mark. "Are you objectifying me again?"

"You bet."

"Excellent."

Mark made his way to the kitchen, stopping to grab the piece of paper from his wallet. He opened the fridge and removed the jug of water. He took another look at his watch. It was time. He reached over to the kitchen phone and picked it up.

A thought occurred to him. He sure hoped the MessageBank thing worked from the kitchen phone as well. He'd only tested it on the bedroom one so far.

Too late now. He had three, two, one.

He dialled his number in.

The MessageBank spoke to him. He spoke back, reading from the paper.

"Hey, it's me," he said. "Synchronise your watch now. This call is being made at 8:41:07, 08, 09. I'll save you some calculatin' time. You're about 3 days, 71 minutes of time difference. You're also going to get in a little bit of trouble from Jode for saying that. Sorry about that. Damned if you do, damned if you don't."

He hung up. Looked around for evidence of the space-time continuum falling to pieces.

Nothing.

He poured two glasses of water and headed back to the bedroom.

This was going to work.

CHAPTER FOUR

"Great day for small talk."
Luck? Prrffrt. Who needed it?
"I like the trailers."
Boy, Bec, you sure can pick 'em.

FRIDAY NIGHT

MARK OPENED THE door.

"Hey," he said.

"Hey," replied Jodie. "Guess what I've got?"

"Really?" said Mark. "Already?"

Jodie held up a folder, filled with papers. "I took most of the afternoon off work," she said. "But the legalities are all done."

She dropped the folder on to the table. Mark opened it up, picked up a contract at random and flipped through it. He stopped on a page and read a paragraph or two.

"I'll take your word for it," he said. He dropped the contract back into the folder.

"You nervous?" said Jodie.

Mark snorted. "Me? Never."

"I'm nervous," said Jodie.

"Well, you would be," said Mark. "You're not as experienced in the ways of time-travelling phone messages as I am."

"This is true." She gestured to Mark's impressive array of library books. "Did you find any answers in there?"

"I found the answer to insomnia," said Mark. "Does that count?"

"I'll take any answers at this stage." She picked up one of the books. Flipped to the index. "I remember reading somewhere that black holes can create localised time wormholes. You didn't find anything like that?"

"Uh, nope," said Mark. He'd only skimmed through most of the books. He'd started with the best of intentions, but Hawking's literary style had defeated him. *Stick to the heavy thinking and wheelchair-riding, Stevo. Leave the wordsmithing for others.*

Some of the other books had been less impenetrable. But they weren't actually penetrable. Mark had hoped one of the books might have had a specific chapter on time-travel and telecommunications. In retrospect, that may have been too optimistic.

Jodie dropped the book back in the pile. "I think we may have to assume we're pioneers in this field, Marcus."

Mark smiled. "You want a drink?" he said.

"I thought you'd never ask."

Richard sat in his car, his face frozen in an unconscious scowl. Friday night traffic was the worst. And what made it even less tolerable was that *The Bellows*, his favourite drive time radio show, had been moved to the breakfast shift. In its place were two moronic morons bantering moronically.

He'd tried flipping through all the preset channels. Nothing. There had been a reason he'd locked on to *The Bellows*. Everything else at drive time was awful.

The lights ahead turned green. He waited for the convoy of cars to turn. Was he going to make the turn this time? He'd already spent three light changes this side of the intersection.

The Toyota ahead of him moved. Come on, come on, come on. Let's go.

The Toyota went. Richard followed. The morons on the radio worked far too hard on a pun. God, he needed to get out of this traffic.

The lights turned orange.

The Toyota went for it.

He was going to go for it, too. He rounded the corner as the lights turned red.

The road stretched out in front of him. Now he was off the highway, the rest of the trip home was easy.

The morons babbled on. He couldn't wait to get home, settle in for dinner and enjoy a night in front of a DVD with his wife.

"How long?" said Mark.

Jodie looked at her watch. "Ten minutes?" she said. "Maybe fifteen to be safe."

"Now I'm getting nervous."

Jodie smiled. "It's a big day."

The phone rang. They both jumped. "Is this it?" said Mark.

Jodie looked at her watch. "Shouldn't be," she said. "The phone's going to ring in three days. It's just the message that should be coming through now."

"True," said Mark. He stared at the ringing phone. "Should I get it?"

"Hmmm… Safest to leave it," said Jodie.

They watched the phone ring out.

"Give it a few seconds?"

"Yup."

They looked around.

"So…" said Mark.

"Lovely day."

"Yeah."

"Great day for small talk."

"Boy, that weather, huh?"

"Good for the farmers."

"Got to keep the farmers happy."

"Long enough?"

"I think so," said Mark. He hit the MessageBank button.

Nothing.

"That's an anti-climax," said Mark.

Richard unlocked the door. "Hello?"

Nothing.

She was with Mark again. This was getting tiresome. He didn't know what was going on, but it was time to sort it out.

Jodie looked at her watch. "It's probably time. You ready?"

"Can I say 'as I'll ever be'?"

"Just this once."

Mark hit the MessageBank button. This time, his voice came back at him.

"It's 8:41pm and 31, 32, 33," said MessageBank. "The winning Lotto numbers are 3, 5, 9, 27, 28 and 33. Good luck."

"Marcus Aurelius. We just became millionaires," said Jodie. "Nothing's going to stop us now."

Rebecca picked up the phone again. She couldn't put it off any longer. When she'd arrived home, there'd been a message on her machine from Katrina, wanting to know how last night had gone.

Rebecca had been keen to find out herself. There had been something odd about the way Mark had behaved during the evening. She'd tried to call him, hoping to talk things out. But, just for a change, he hadn't been there. She hadn't bothered leaving a message this time. This was not a conversation to be had via MessageBank.

If he was screening her, then so be it.

But if she couldn't talk things over with Mark, she might as well do it with Katrina. She wasn't sure that rehashing the evening with Katrina was the most productive choice. Truth be told, she was tired of thinking about Mark and his oddities.

Still, she couldn't ignore Katrina's message either. She picked up the phone and called her.

"So?" said Katrina.

"So?"

"How did it go last night?"

Rebecca sighed. "He's still behaving oddly."

"Like how?"

"I dunno," said Rebecca. "He came over last night. We shared a bubble bath, some champagne, some chocolates…"

"And?"

"He was clockwatching the whole time."

"What?"

"Every five minutes, he was checking his watch."

"Did he say why?"

"No," said Rebecca. "I didn't bring it up."

"You should have."

"What would have been the point?"

"You could have pointed out to him what a self-absorbed dick he was being."

"It wasn't that bad," said Rebecca. Then immediately wondered why she was springing to his defence.

"It's just plain rude," said Katrina.

"Maybe he had something on his mind."

Katrina laughed. "I don't pretend to understand men," she said. "But I do know one thing. Nothing focuses their mind like a naked woman in the room with them."

Rebecca had no response to that.

"Whatever he was so obsessed with," continued Katrina. "It could have waited until after your evening together."

"I think he relaxed as the night went on," said Rebecca. "Maybe he's still nervous. He's shy."

She was still defending him. Why was she doing that? She knew Katrina was right on every score. And yet, she was defending him. She had issues. This was becoming more and more obvious.

"Shy?" said Katrina. "Give me a break."

"I just don't understand what the problem could be," said Rebecca.

"Whatever the problem is, it's not yours."

"What if it is?"

"Oh, hush! Don't you dare go taking the blame for his behaviour. We put up with enough of that nonsense when you were with Andrew. I'm not going to let you start up with that again."

Rebecca sighed. Katrina was overreacting of course. But what if she had a grain of a point? Could she really be following the same pattern of behaviour again? After going through all the shit she had to go through to escape from Andrew?

Was she really that stupid?

"So I'm not making too big a deal out of this?" said Rebecca.

"Definitely not," said Katrina. "These are the first signs of trouble further down the road. Best to nip it in the bud right now."

"You think?" said Rebecca.

"I know." There was a pause. "You are a sexy, beautiful woman. Why settle for a jerk who seems only vaguely interested in what you have to offer?"

Rebecca wanted to object again. 'Jerk' was a bit harsh. But, hell, maybe Katrina was right. Maybe Mark *was* a jerk. She had no faith in her ability to judge these things any more.

He was charming and funny and cute. But maybe he was a jerk as well.

What a bloody waste.

"I don't think he's had the easiest life," said Rebecca. "His parents died when he was just a kid."

"I've heard about what happened to his parents," said Katrina. "And yes, I can see how that could cause some issues. But his issues should not become your issues."

"No. I guess not."

"Of course not," said Katrina. "And if his issues are causing trouble already, then you're better off without him."

"I suppose."

"Please don't 'suppose' this," said Katrina. "It's my job as the older cousin to prevent you from falling into the same trap you did in the past. Mark is another Andrew. Get rid of him before he gets a chance to really hurt you."

Rebecca stopped herself from objecting once more. Calling Mark another Andrew seemed to be making a large leap. Mark was not being the suitor he could be, but he wasn't the irredeemable loser that Andrew had turned out to be. Was he?

It was uncharitable, but Rebecca was a little sceptical about Katrina's motives. Maybe her adamance about dumping Mark had just a teensy bit to do with the fact that Katrina was still single. Had been single for a long time. And might be a tad annoyed that her little cousin had come to town and hooked up in her first week.

She stopped herself from going any further down this line of thought. Katrina was just trying to help her overcome her clearly appalling taste in men.

"Okay," she said. "You're right. I'll end it."

"I'm sorry," said Katrina. "I know this sucks."

Rebecca suddenly found herself wishing for a fresh dose of the sixteen-year-old wisdom of Libby.

LATER THAT NIGHT

Jodie fumbled for her keys with her left hand. Her right hand held a pair of pizza boxes. A meat-eater and a seafood pizza. Richard's two favourites. Personally, Jodie had never understood seafood pizzas. Seafood was one kind of meal. Pizza was another. Why anybody ever considered combining them was beyond her.

Still, Richard liked seafood pizza. And she felt she owed him one.

She snagged her keys. She pulled them out and went for the lock. The pizza boxes swayed. She steadied them with the key hand.

"Shit."

The door opened. "You need some help?" said Richard.

"Thank you."

He grabbed the pizza boxes and went inside.

Jodie followed. "How was your day?" she said.

"Fine," said Richard. He peeked inside the top box. "Meat?"

"Seafood in the other one."

"Really?"

"Sure."

"So you *do* feel bad about spending most of the week with Mark instead of me."

"You got me," said Jodie. "But I think you'll forgive me on Monday."

"What happens Monday?" Richard put the pizzas on the table and went to the kitchen for some plates.

Jodie opened the fridge. Grabbed the bottle of Pepsi and poured them a glass each. "Monday, we become millionaires."

Richard put the plates down on the table. "What?"

Jodie handed him a glass. "In a little less than three days, we become millionaires."

"Thank you," said Richard, taking the glass. He drank most of it down. "How?"

"We're going to win Lotto."

"What?"

"Lotto," said Jodie. "We're going to win it."

"But we don't play Lotto. It's a… 'futile display of the inability to understand the fundamentals of probability theory'."

"Sure. If you don't know the numbers beforehand."

"What?" He frowned. "This is what you've been doing with Mark all week?"

"Kinda. Yeah."

"You've been working out some kind of foolproof Lotto system?"

"Kinda. Yeah."

"How do you know it's going to work?" said Richard.

"Trust me," said Jodie. "We know."

"It's not that I don't trust you," said Richard. "It's just… it's impossible."

Jodie just smiled.

"It's random. How can you predict which balls are going to come out?"

"We don't even try," said Jodie.

"Then how do you win the Lotto?"

Jodie smiled. Enough torturing of the husband. "What if I told you we just got a message from three days in the future, telling us what the numbers were going to be?"

Richard frowned in confusion. "You got a message from the future?"

"Yeah."

"Who from?"

"Mark."

Richard's frown deepened. "I still don't get it," he finally said.

Jodie smiled. She kissed him. "I'll start from the beginning," she said.

As Richard ate the pizza, Jodie told him about the MessageBank. The phone calls Rebecca had made to Mark before they'd even met. The phone calls Mark had made to himself to test whether the time-travel was for real. And, finally, the phone call tonight that revealed what Monday night's Lotto numbers would be.

When she finished, Richard put his slice of pizza down. "This is all for real?" he said.

"One hundred percent."

"On Monday night, we will use a time-travelling answering machine to help us become millionaires?"

"Exactly."

"I want to believe this," said Richard. "And I guess I do. It would, after all, be a very strange thing for you to just make up."

"That it would."

"But," he said. "I'm still going to wait until the numbers come up before I get excited."

"Very wise," said Jodie.

"Because, y'know, this is…"

"Crazy?"

"Exactly."

SATURDAY MORNING

Jodie and Richard pulled up in front of the news agency. Mark was waiting outside.

"Hey, Rich," said Mark. "I assume Jode's brought you up to speed?"

"Yeah," said Richard. "Sure."

"You got the numbers."

Mark tapped his pocket. "Aye."

"Then let's do this."

The three of them marched into the news agency.

"One Lotto ticket, please," said Mark.

"Do you want an Autopick?" she asked.

"Autopick?"

"The computer chooses the numbers for you."

"Ah. No thank you," said Mark. "Just a regular ticket you fill in."

"They're over there," said the newsagent. She pointed to an area devoted to the filling in of Lotto tickets. "You fill in a ticket over there, then bring it back here for processing."

"Thanking you muchly," said Mark.

The three of them left for the Lotto ticket area.

Mark picked up a ticket and pen. "Hmm," he said.

"What?" said Jodie.

"There are twelve different entries here," said Mark.

"What?" said Jodie. She grabbed the ticket and looked at it.

Richard smiled. "That's how it works, guys," he said. "You buy one ticket, you get to enter twelve different combinations of numbers."

"Well, that's stupid," said Jodie.

"So, do I enter the numbers twelve times?" said Mark.

"No," said Jodie. "We don't want to draw attention to ourselves. We just enter them once."

"Right," said Mark. He filled in the first box. Three. Five. Nine. Twenty-seven. Twenty-eight. Thirty-three. He looked up at Jodie. "What do I put in the other boxes?"

"Whatever you want."

"You can enter some variations on those numbers," said Richard.

"Variations?"

"Sure. If you enter four or more of them in a different box, that box will win one of the lower-level prizes. It'll flesh out our winnings."

"It's too suspicious," said Jodie.

"No it's not," said Richard. "Many people do this.

"Enter the same numbers in all the boxes?" said Jodie. "Why on Earth would you do that?"

"People like to use birth dates of loved ones," said Richard. "So they use those same dates in each game."

"So, they're biasing their picks to the sub-31 section of the game box."

"I suppose they are."

"And everybody else is doing the same?"

"Maybe not everybody else," said Richard. "But lots of people, yes."

"So we're probably going to have to share our winnings with one of these morons," said Jodie.

"We've got a 33," said Mark.

"Yeah, but everything else is below 31."

"True."

"Yeah," said Richard. "We'll probably share with a 33-year-old somewhere with a—" He grabbed the numbers and looked at them. "—28 year-old wife, born on the 27th of September. His birthday will be the fifth of March."

"I loathe this couple already," said Mark.

"This is why we should fill in all the boxes with the right numbers," said Richard. "We'll have twelve winning entries to Mr Thirty-Three's one."

"But if we do that we'll just draw attention to ourselves," said Jodie. "We need to think of the big picture, not just Monday."

"Monday's just the seed money," said Mark.

"Exactly."

"Okay, okay," said Richard. "Fine. I still say you can reuse some of the numbers in the other boxes. That won't be suspicious."

"Fine," said Jodie.

Mark went about filling in the other boxes with numbers.

"Done," he finally said.

"Let's go do it."

They took the ticket back to the newsagent

"You sort it out?" she asked.

"I believe so," said Mark. He handed the ticket over.

"That's $2.40."

"Rightey-o," said Mark. He pulled out his wallet and paid. The newsagent put the ticket into an automatic processing machine. She grabbed the receipt and handed it back to Mark.

"Good luck," she said.

"Thank you," said Mark. Luck? Prrffrt. Who needed it?

Rebecca's phone rang. She let it go through to her machine. It was probably Mark and she hadn't worked out what she was going to do about him yet.

"Rebecca Tyler," came Katrina's voice. "Pick up this instant."

God. Enough already, Kat. I'm a big girl. I'm settled in now. I can look after myself.

She picked up. "Hey," she said.

"You *are* there," said Katrina.

Well, duh. "Yeah," she said.

"Have you dumped him yet?"

"I only got up twenty minutes ago."

"You're not going to chicken out on this, are you?"

Rebecca sighed. "No," she said. "But I thought it might be easiest if I just let things slowly drift apart. Why make a scene?"

"I think you need to explicitly break it off," said Katrina. "If you don't, things can just slide back."

How do you know? Have you ever even had a boyfriend? The harshness of her thoughts didn't make her proud. But geez, enough already.

"I just don't see the point," she said instead. "Maybe he's not going to call me again anyway. Why go out of my way to start a difficult conversation?"

"For the closure."

Closure? For god's sake, she'd only been seeing him for a week.

"I'm not sure I need the closure," she said. "I've only been seeing him for a week."

Hey, look at that! The girl said something similar to what she was thinking. It was a miracle.

"Then a phone call shouldn't be that messy, should it?"

"Fine, fine, fine," said Rebecca. "I'll call him. Break it off. Okay?"

"Thank you," said Katrina.

"You're welcome," said Rebecca.

"It's the right thing to do, Bec."

Yeah. Whatever.

Mark, Jodie and Richard sat in a cafe, drinking coffee, planning next steps.

"Now you've just got to get to her place on Monday and leave the message," said Jodie.

"I'll call and make the date as soon as I get home."

"Excellent," said Jodie. "From there, we move into Phase Two."

"Phase Two?" said Richard.

Mark's mobile phone rang. He saw the number and smiled.

"Hey, you," he said, answering it. "I was just thinking about you."

"Really?" said Rebecca.

"Yeah." Mark stood up and moved away from the table. "I was hoping we could get together Monday night. *Twelve Monkeys* is on television. I thought I could come over to your place, cook you up something remarkable and we could watch it together."

"Um—"

"Of course," said Mark. "By 'watch it together', I don't mean watch the remarkable thing I cook together. I mean watch *Twelve Monkeys* together."

"Yeah," said Rebecca.

"I thought I should make that clear."

"Listen, Mark," said Rebecca.

Mark paused in his rambling. Something about her tone didn't sound promising.

"I don't think this is going to work out," she continued. "I'm sorry."

"What?" said Mark.

"I don't think things are going to work out between us."

"Why?" This was not good. This was not good at all. "I thought we'd been having fun."

"We were," said Rebecca. "It's just… I just broke up from a five-year relationship. I wasn't looking to get involved with anybody again so quickly."

Mark had no answer to that.

"I'm sorry," she said again.

"Can't we talk about this?" said Mark. His mind raced. How was he going to fix this? "Maybe I can come over on Monday anyway and we can just talk this through."

"I don't think that's a good idea, Mark."

"But…"

"I'm sorry," she said.

"Yeah," said Mark. "Me too."

He hung up. Returned to where Jodie and Richard sat. Jodie looked up at him.

"What?" she said.

"We have a problem."

Rebecca put down the phone. There. Done it.

She sat down. She felt…

Wrong.

Sad.

This wasn't like when she ended it with Andrew. Then, it had been relief. A pinch of sadness, perhaps, that something that had lasted so long had ended so nastily. But mostly relief that it was finally all over.

She wasn't relieved about breaking up with Mark. She was just sad.

Of course, it wasn't a valid comparison. She'd only known Mark a week.

But ending it still felt wrong.

"She what?"

"She broke up with me," said Mark.

"Why?"

"She didn't really say. Something about just getting out of a long-term relationship and not being ready to start a new one."

"This is bad," said Jodie.

"Why is it so bad?" said Richard.

"Um, because a girl I rather like just dumped me?" said Mark.

"Also, because it means the universe might be destroyed by a time paradox."

"Yeah, sorry, Mark," said Richard. "That was the one I was focusing on." He turned to Jodie. "How does this time paradox work?"

"We don't actually know," said Jodie. "It's not like the time wormhole came with an instruction manual. But we figure it's probably safest not to invoke time paradoxes."

"Lest Terminators destroy mankind and pave the way for the machines to take over the future."

"Exactly," said Jodie. "Or, y'know, the universe implodes in self-contradiction. Either, eye-ther."

"How would a time paradox destroy the universe?" said Richard.

"We don't know," said Jodie again. "Look. We heard the message, right?"

"Right," said Richard.

"Which means Mark left the message."

"Right."

"But, because of the time travel, Mark hasn't left the message, yet. He has to do it on Monday night."

"But if he doesn't leave it, so what?" said Richard. "We've still heard it."

"But where did it come from?" said Jodie. "The universe works according to certain rules. If we've heard the message, Mark must have left it. But if he doesn't leave it, then how did we hear it? That's the time paradox."

"I understand the paradox. I just don't see how it would destroy the universe."

"Have you heard of the grandfather paradox?" said Mark.

Richard sighed. "I suspect I'm about to."

"Imagine I can not just leave messages through time, but also travel through time."

"Okay."

"Now imagine that I went back in time and killed my grandfather as a baby."

"Why would you do that?"

"For the purposes of this example."

Richard snorted. "Okay."

"Good," said Mark. "Now, I've shockingly killed my grandfather as a baby. But, by doing so, I've prevented myself from ever being born. I've cut off my family tree. But if I've never been born, I obviously couldn't have gone back in time and killed my grandfather. Which means he didn't die as a baby. Which means my family tree wasn't wiped out and I am born again. Which means I could go back and kill him. Which means... well, I'm sure you get the picture."

"It's another paradox," said Richard. "I get it."

"Right. But now we've got a universe where if I'm alive, I'm not. And, if I'm not, I am. We have a universe that contradicts itself. It can't make up its mind whether or not I exist. Nor, for that matter, large chunks of my family tree."

"And you can go further," said Jodie. "If he goes back in time and kills the earliest form of life, then you have an even worse paradox. If life on Earth exists, then it doesn't. But if it doesn't, then it does."

"Okay," said Richard. "My head is now officially spinning. Your point is: Time paradoxes are bad."

"Exactly," said Jodie. "You can't have a universe that flip-flops back and forth like that. If we heard the message, Mark must have left it. And if he doesn't leave it, then... we can't have heard it."

"Except we did hear it," said Mark.

"Right."

"Okay," said Richard. "I get it. So we need to make sure he gets back with Rebecca so he can leave this message."

"Right."

"Also," said Mark. "Because I kinda like her."

"Of course," said Jodie. She turned to Richard. "Babe, why don't you call Katrina and see if she's got any inside knowledge on why she broke up with him."

"Sure."

"Marcus?"

"Yep?"

"You and I are going to go over everything we know about her and try to work out what you did."

"Oh," said Mark. "That sounds like fun."

"I did it," said Rebecca.

"I'm proud of you," said Katrina. "You did the right thing."

"It doesn't feel right," said Rebecca. "It feels kinda sucky, to be honest."

"I know," said Katrina. A pair of beeps sounded. "But you can do so much better than Mark. You deserve somebody who thinks you're the most amazing woman on the planet."

"What if nobody thinks that?" said Rebecca.

"There will be a man who thinks that," said Katrina.

Another pair of beeps sounded.

"Really?" said Rebecca.

"Sure," said Katrina. "But until then it's okay to be alone, you know. You don't need a man just for the sake of having a man. Why not be single, so you're ready when the man who sees how amazing you are comes along."

The pair of beeps repeated again.

"Do you have another call?"

"Yeah. It's okay. I'll let them go through to MessageBank."

Another call-waiting pair of beeps.

"You're right," said Rebecca. "I *do* deserve somebody who thinks I'm amazing."

"Damn straight."

Rebecca nodded. There may have been a slight self-serving element in Katrina's advice. But deep down, Rebecca knew she had a point. For all Mark's charms, he hadn't been focused on her. And if he wasn't dazzled by her at the beginning, that didn't bode well for the future. Best to nip it in the bud before anybody got hurt.

"Do you want to go see a movie?" said Katrina.

Rebecca thought about it. "Yeah," she said. "Why not?"

"You know what would have been smart?" said Mark.

"What?" said Jodie.

"If I'd mentioned something about this in the message."

"It might have helped, yeah."

"Not that I can, anyway," said Mark. "Since I didn't."

He snorted. This entire situation was insane.

Richard returned.

"So?" said Mark.

"She wasn't there," said Richard. "I left a message."

SATURDAY AFTERNOON

Rebecca stood outside the cinema, two tickets in hand. Bloody Katrina. Always running late. She checked her watch again. They were past the scheduled start of the film.

Katrina emerged around the corner. "Sorry," she said. "I couldn't find a park."

"Come on," said Rebecca, handing her a ticket. "Let's go. It's already started."

"Oh, they'll still be showing trailers."

"I like the trailers."

"Guess who I got a call from?"

"Mark?"

"No. But close. It was Richard."

"Richard?"

"The one I work with? The birthday party guy?"

"Oh," said Rebecca. "Right. Richard. What did he want?"

"He wanted to know why you'd dumped Mark."

Rebecca felt herself holding her breath. "What did you tell him?"

"Nothing," said Katrina. "I didn't call him back. It's none of his business."

Right.

Mark took a deep breath. The three of them had gone over everything he knew several times. Nothing obvious leapt out as the cause for the breakup. Finally, they decided he just needed to call and ask.

And, of course, apologise.

He didn't know what he was going to be apologising for. But, as Richard had said, that wasn't important. He just had to apologise.

He dialled her number.

Her machine answered.

Shit. Did he apologise to the machine? Or did he just hang up and try later?

"Um, hi," he said. Looked like he was going to be apologising to the machine. "It's Mark. Um. Look. I don't know what the problem is, or why you thought it meant we should end things. But I'd like to talk about it."

The apology, stupid.

"If I've done something wrong, then I apologise," he said. "Um, sorry."

This was idiotic. What kind of universe entrusted its sense of self-consistency to an idiot like him?

"Anyway," he said. "Please call me." He hesitated again. "Bye," he finally added.

He hung up. The universe was doomed.

SUNDAY AFTERNOON

The phone rang. Mark pounced on it.

"Anything?" said Jodie.

"Nothing," said Mark. "Should I call her again?"

"I think you can call her once more," said Jodie. "You don't want to push it much further than that. If she takes out a restraining order on you, then you've got no chance of making the call tomorrow night."

"Did Richard hear back from whatsername?"

"No. Whatsername didn't call back either."

"Maybe I should tell her about the MessageBank."

"Do you think she'll believe you?"

"Sure."

"Really? Richard barely believes me. And I'm his wife."

"I could— No."

"What?"

"I was going to say I could show her the Lotto ticket. But that doesn't prove anything yet, does it?"

"Maybe…" said Jodie. "Maybe you just front up over there tomorrow night. She doesn't hate you. If you show up, she'll let you in. You can make the phone call. *Then* you can explain everything to her."

"Without the whole time paradox, universe in the fate of my hands issue hanging over my head."

"Exactly."

"Sounds like a plan."

"It does?"

"Well, it bears a vague resemblance to one," said Mark. "Maybe I should call her again anyway? See if I can smooth things over before we have to rely on this latest plan."

Jodie paused. "I don't think it's a good idea. If you say the wrong thing, she might get so pissed off at you she mightn't let you in tomorrow night. And you have to get in there tomorrow night."

"Okay," said Mark. "I won't call her again. We'll go with your crazy plan."

THIRTY MINUTES LATER

He *had* to call her again. His head was going round and round in circles, trying to work out what it was he might have done. He wouldn't survive until tomorrow night if he didn't sort this out.

He'd just give her a call. Talk to her rationally and sensibly. Try to work out what was going on. He wasn't going to piss her off.

He picked up the phone and dialled.

Rebecca let the ringing phone go through to the machine. Either it was Katrina, who had promised to leave a message if she called today.

Or it was Mark again.

She couldn't talk to Mark yet. She didn't know what else she could say to him.

The phone hung up.

No message.

It had been Mark. She knew it.

For some reason, she started to cry.

MONDAY MORNING

Richard tapped on the door of Katrina's office.

"Hey," he said.

"Hi," said Katrina. "Before you say anything, I think we should just leave Rebecca and Mark to sort out their own problems."

"Fine," said Richard. "Couldn't agree more. It's none of our business."

"Exactly."

"It's just… he doesn't know why she dumped him."

"I don't want to talk about it."

"Okay."

MONDAY AFTERNOON

Rebecca drove home, Libby's latest advice running through her head. She'd noticed Rebecca's glum mood throughout the day and had taken it on herself to offer some more sixteen year old wisdom.

"What's the matter, Miss Tyler?" she'd said.

Rebecca had explained the situation to her. When Libby had pressed on the exact reasons for breaking up with Mark, all she'd been able to say was that he'd been acting 'weird'.

"Weird?" said Libby.

Rebecca had elaborated a little on the weirdness. How his mind was somewhere else most of the time. How he'd been preoccupied when he'd been with her. How she deserved better.

"That's true, Miss Tyler," said Libby. "And far be it from me to offer relationship advice. But, in my experience, if you dumped guys every time they started behaving 'weird', you'd have one mighty turnover rate." She beamed. "Y'know?"

Rebecca had thanked her for her advice and promised to take it into consideration.

She hadn't meant it at the time, but it kept nagging at her on the drive home.

Breaking up with Mark hadn't felt right. Maybe that was because it hadn't been right. Maybe she'd made too much out of this?

Maybe she'd call him tonight and try to talk it out.

MONDAY NIGHT

Rebecca sat in front of the television. *Twelve Monkeys* was about to start, just as soon as the Lotto draw finished. She still wasn't sure whether she was going to call Mark tonight.

Maybe after the movie.

A microwaved Lean Cuisine meal sat in front of her. She prodded it with a fork. Microwaved fish. She wasn't at all sure why she had bought such a thing.

She ventured a bite.

On the television screen, a nine rolled down to join the three, twenty-seven and twenty-eight that had already appeared.

Hmmm. The fish wasn't bad. Who knew?

She took another bite.

Thirty-three.

There was a knock at the door.

Who could that be? "Who is it?" she said.

"It's Mark."

Mark? What was he doing here? She got up and opened the door.

Behind her, the five rolled down.

"What are you doing here?" she said.

"I just won the Lotto," he said.

"Que pasa?"

"I just won the Lotto." He held up the ticket and pointed to the screen. "Three, five, nine, twenty-seven, twenty-eight and thirty-three."

"Seriously?"

"Seriously."

Rebecca didn't know what to say next. "Well, that's fantastic," she finally said.

"I know I've been weird. I don't know if that's why you broke up with me or not. But I promise I can explain everything. I just have to make a phone call."

He marched over to her phone.

He looked at his watch and started counting down.

"This doesn't help with the 'weird' thing," she said. "Just so you know."

Mark nodded. "I know." He waited a couple more seconds and picked up the phone. He hit the keypad and waited.

"It's 8:41pm and 31, 32, 33," he said. "The winning Lotto numbers are 3, 5, 9. 27. 27 and 33. Good luck." Stupid, stupid, stupid. He should have given himself more information. But how could he with Rebecca looking over his shoulder, waiting for an explanation?

He hung up.

"Who did you just call?"

"I called me," he said. "Three days ago."

Jodie and Richard sat huddled together on the couch. The right numbers had come out during the Lotto draw. Now if the universe just didn't end, everything would work out.

"How are we looking?" said Richard. Jodie was staring at her watch.

"He should have made the call by now."

Richard looked around. "The universe is still here."

"I think he did it."

"So," said Richard. "We just won Lotto."

"We just won Lotto," agreed Jodie. "And the universe survived the experience."

"Can we crack the champagne now?"

"I think we can."

"You sent a message back in time to yourself?" said Rebecca.

This was insane. Boy, Bec, you sure can pick 'em.

"I know how it sounds," said Mark. "But look. I have the winning ticket." He held it up.

"I know. I see that. But… you sent a message back in time to yourself??"

"I was knocking on the door to tell you about the ticket halfway through the draw."

This was true. He was knocking before the draw was over.

Maybe the draw wasn't live? Maybe he got his information from somewhere else?

Mark sighed. "Your predilection for tulips?" he said. "I knew about that, because you'd left a message thanking me for them three days before I got them for you."

"Are you serious?"

"I have never been more serious in my life," said Mark. "There's something strange going on between our telephones."

"And that's why you decided to get involved with me?" said Rebecca. "So you could use our strange phones to make yourself a millionaire?"

"No," said Mark. "No, no, no! I… I got involved with you because you're the sexiest, most spellbinding woman I've ever met." He looked at his shoes. "And, like an idiot, I almost ruined it all by using our strange phones to make us millionaires."

How could she resist that? "Come here," she said. He moved towards her. She kissed him gently on the lips.

"I'm sorry," he said.

"Me too."

THE NEXT MORNING

Mark opened his eyes. Ah, make-up sex. There was nothing like it. Especially, when it was make-up sex after avoiding a potential universe-destroying time paradox.

Rebecca smiled at him.

"Hi millionaire," she said.

"Hi," he replied.

"That wasn't a dream, was it?"

"Nope."

"You won the Lotto."

"Yeah. Yeah I did."

He kissed her. She responded eagerly. Eventually he pulled away.

"Come on," he said. "We've got a brunch date with Jode and Richard."

"We do?"

"Yeah. It's time for Phase Two."

LATER THAT MORNING

"You know what this means?" said Rebecca, as the four of them ate brunch. "We can win Lotto every week."

"No," said Mark, scone crumbs falling out of his mouth. "We don't want to draw any more attention. Right, Jode?"

"Right."

"Jode and I had a head-start on this. We've worked out precisely how best we can use this time-travelling MessageBank to set us up for life." He turned to Jodie.

Richard interrupted. "First, I just want to talk about whether we should be doing this."

"Why on Earth not?" said Rebecca.

"I think Rich is worried about destroying the universe."

Rebecca raised her eyebrows.

"That's *exactly* what I'm worried about," said Richard. "Tell her what happens if you murder your grandfather."

"Why would you murder your grandfather?" said Rebecca.

"I don't even know my grandfather," said Mark.

"Then why do you want to kill him?"

"I don't," said Mark. He explained again about the grandfather paradox and the risk to the universe if they didn't leave a message after they'd already heard it. "But I don't think that's going to be a problem any more," he said, looking at Mark.

"It was almost an enormous problem last time," said Richard.

"There were… communication issues at that point," said Jodie. "We have a plan to cover all that off. May I start from the beginning?"

Richard raised his hands. "Fine. Go ahead."

"Thank you. First things first," said Jodie. She tossed a pair of high-end mobile phones to Mark and Rebecca. "From now on, you two call one another on these mobile phones only. I don't want any phone calls from your home phone to his, unless we're leaving a message."

"Okay," said Rebecca.

"Next," continued Jodie. "Contracts."

Mark reached beneath the table and picked up a pile of contracts. He tossed one to each person. Jodie continued speaking.

"From now on, we're all equal partners in this. We will pay our earnings into a trust that will pay all our necessary expenses as well as provide substantial allowances for us all."

Rebecca and Richard picked up their contracts and flipped through them. Jodie continued.

"Mark and I will work on a computer program that will track shares that have risen the most over the previous three days. We'll send messages back in time, telling us to buy those shares. A few hours a week should be more than enough to keep us rolling in profits."

Rebecca looked around the table. This was insane.

"Our first major investments will be the apartments you two are living in," continued Jodie. "We'll buy your apartments first, and then as soon as we've made enough money from our investments, we'll buy the entire two complexes."

Insane or not, there was no denying Mark and Jodie had a plan. Jodie continued to go through it.

"The connection between these two buildings is critical to everything. We'll do whatever we have to do to keep them under our control. Of course, once we've got all that settled, we can all buy mansions in the mountains or Ferraris or whatever takes our fancy. Hell, Mark might even get a dog. Life is going to be good."

She raised her glass of juice. Everybody else did so too. They clinked.

"To insane wealth," she said.

CHAPTER FIVE

"You're a very witty man who doesn't know what goes into a salad."

"A superhero vegetable?"

"You ever worry about those two?"

"Mark and I are engaged."

EIGHT MONTHS LATER

MARK FLIPPED THROUGH the latest comic books. Chewie, his medium-sized hyena-like terrier, sat patiently at his feet. The comic book store had a policy of not allowing animals inside, of course. But they made an exception for Mark.

And rightly so. After all, he was probably single-handedly keeping the store in business. They shipped in fresh hardcover recompilations of his favourite childhood comic books every week. And every week, Mark bought them all. He supplemented his nostalgia with fresh supplies of the latest comics.

Besides, Chewie was harmless. He didn't eat the comics or pee all over the figurines or anything. He just sat happily at Mark's feet.

"You got the *Legion of Superheroes Archives* yet?" he asked

"Still waiting on Volume Six."

"What happens in Volume Six?"

"Oh, y'know, not much. Just the Fatal Five and Sun Eaters and the Death of Ferro Lad." The shop-owner nodded in unconcealed excitement.

"Should probably wait for that one, then," said Mark. "What else you got?"

"This Captain Carrot statue."

"Captain Carrot? Awesome," said Mark. "Any other Zoo Crew members?"

"No. Just the Captain."

"I'll still take it. But let me know when you get Alley Kat Abra in."

"Will do."

Mark's phone rang. He looked at the number. It was Rebecca.

"Hello, birthday girl," he said.

"Hello."

"How's your day going?"

"Don't ask," said Rebecca. "You still at the nerd shop?"

"Geek shop, babe. I'm off to the nerd shop next to pick up an external hard drive."

"Okay. But don't forget to stop off at the butcher and get those steaks for dinner too."

"Will do."

"You should probably get some beers and stuff too. I'm not sure how much we have."

"Will do that as well."

"Can you be trusted to get salad?"

"Almost certainly not."

"Okay," said Rebecca. "I'll pick up the salad. You just get the alcohol, meat and your nerdgeek stuff and any gifts you may feel like picking up for me."

"Gifts?" said Mark. "What makes you think you're getting gifts?"

"Because you enjoy having sex with me?"

"It's a powerful incentive," said Mark.

"I thought it may be."

"Fear not, fair maiden. I have the gift situation under critically acclaimed control, along with the alcohol, meat, nerd and geek situation."

"Excellent."

"So why shouldn't I ask about your day?" said Mark. "Are they not treating you with birthday respect?"

"Well," said Rebecca. "The staff did chip in and get me a massage voucher."

"Can't complain about that, surely?"

"No," said Rebecca. "But, that aside, it's been the kind of day that makes me wonder why I still do this."

"Ah," said Mark. "Is it that Year Ten class?"

"They're just so stupid," said Rebecca. "I know that's supposed to be part of the joy of teaching. The passing on of knowledge to those who would otherwise struggle to learn. But, I'm beginning to think… y'know, perhaps not so much. My god, they're dim."

"It doesn't sound like any fun to me."

"And don't even get me started on Ratchett."

"What's she done now?"

"I'll fill you in tonight," said Rebecca.

"Look forward to it."

Mark hung up and turned his attention back to the store owner. He'd wrapped the comics and placed them with the oversized statue of a superhero rabbit in a carry bag.

Part of him knew these purchases were crazy. But they had money. And they had a big house. And Rebecca had allowed him an entire room to flaunt his inner comic book geek. He had to exploit that mistake.

"One hundred and eighty-four dollars."

Mark handed over his credit card.

His phone rang again. It was Jodie.

"Hey," he said. "Welcome back."

"Thank you," said Jodie.

"You get it?"

"I've got it," she said.

"And?"

"Marcus, my friend. It is better than you could have imagined."

"Where are you now?" Mark grabbed the bag. He gave the store owner a 'see you next week' half wave-half salute. The store owner returned it. Mark and Chewie left the store.

"We're just going through Customs," said Jodie. "Should be home in a couple of hours."

"Excellent. And still on for tonight?"

"Definitely."

"Good. We'll catch up on everything then."

"Dokey-oke," said Jodie.

"Don't forget to bring it."

"I wouldn't dare."

Rebecca turned to her pile of essays. It was about twenty-eight more essays than she felt like marking. Moments like these were when she regretted continuing work.

She picked up the first one. She read the name. Amy Simon.

God.

Amy was hopeless. Every Amy essay came straight from some tedious essay-producing factory. Rebecca had originally assumed she'd been downloading them from the web. Careful searching had shown this wasn't the case.

Amy *was* the tedious essay-producing factory.

Rebecca read the first sentence. "To answer the question of whether or not Hamlet lives or dies by his own choices, or whether his choices are controlled by forces larger than himself, we must consider three factors."

Rebecca put the essay back down.

She didn't want to read the three factors. There was little doubt in her mind the three factors would bore her to the brink of murder. And you shouldn't murder people on your birthday. It threw off the whole vibe of the day.

The essays could wait.

She needed to get out of here.

She looked at her watch. Thirty-five minutes until her next class.

Plenty of time for a sanity-restoring birthday walk.

She stood up and put the essays in her folder. She grabbed her handbag and headed for the door.

"Miss Tyler?"

Rebecca turned around. "Hi Libby," she said. "What's up?"

Libby burst into tears.

Rebecca recoiled, shocked. Why was Libby, the most together teenager in the world, bawling? Rebecca moved in and hugged her. Hugging was officially against protocol these days. But Rebecca didn't care. What were they going to do? Fire her?

"What's the matter?" she said.

Libby didn't reply. She just buried her head into Rebecca's shoulder and continued to sob.

Rebecca hugged her and let her cry.

When she cried herself out, Rebecca ushered the both of them back into the classroom. Looked like the walk was out.

"What's the matter?" said Rebecca, once they'd both sat down.

"I think I'm… uh… I think I might be… uh…" She started to cry again.

"Pregnant?"

Libby nodded, and surged into a fresh gush of tears. Rebecca handed her a tissue.

"Oh," said Rebecca. "How late are y—"

"Over a week," said Libby. "I told myself I wouldn't worry… but it's…"

Her voice cracked again and she started to cry some more. Rebecca gave her a fresh tissue.

God. How did she deal with this? She was sure there was a policy somewhere, but it had been so long since she'd read the policy manual. And, even then, she'd only skimmed it.

"How did this happen?" said Rebecca. "You weren't using protection?"

"Damon doesn't like condoms," said Libby. "He says he can't feel anything with a condom on."

"Oh Libby," said Rebecca. "They all say that."

Libby broke out a sad smile. "So I told him I'd go on the pill. But I didn't want to go to my family doctor and before I found another one, we went out and…"

Her voice cracked once more. Rebecca gave her another tissue.

"He told me he didn't have any condoms on him. He promised he'd pull out. But he didn't." Her voice was suddenly furious.

"Oh, Libby."

"What am I going to do?"

What was she going to do? Rebecca had no idea.

"The first thing we're going to do is find out whether you have a cause for concern," she eventually said. She looked at her watch.

"I've got fifteen minutes until seventh period begins. That's enough time for me to duck into town and pick up a pregnancy testing kit. You take the test, and we'll go from there."

"Okay," said Libby. "But what if I *am* pregnant?"

"We'll deal with that bridge when we get to it," said Rebecca. "I'll meet you back here after seventh period."

"Okay."

"Try not to worry."

Libby snorted out a laugh.

Rebecca smiled. "Try not to worry excessively."

"Okay."

Libby gave her another illegal hug. "Thanks, Miss Tyler," she said.

"You're welcome," said Rebecca.

You silly girl.

She had to get out of this place.

Mark opened the passenger door. "In you get, Chewie," he said.

Chewie jumped in. Mark closed the door behind him. As he walked around to the driver's side, his phone rang.

"Hey babe," he said.

"Hey," said Rebecca. "Can you do me a favour?"

"Name it." Mark opened the door and got in.

"Can you please pick up the salad for tonight?"

"Oh," said Mark. "I thought you were going to get the salad."

"Something's come up."

"Okay."

"One of my students may have got herself pregnant."

"Got *herself* pregnant?" said Mark. "I'm sure she had some help."

"Most likely," said Rebecca. "If not, then something even more important may have come up."

"It's a sad day when the Second Coming of Our Lord is deemed more important than shopping for salad ingredients."

"Very true. But you can get them for me?"

"What do I need to get?"

"Salad. You know. Tomato, lettuce, cucumber, et cetera."

"No," said Mark. "No 'etcetera'. If we work on the assumption that I know what's in a salad then I'll miss something that you think is essential. Or get something that you believe to be superfluous. Either way, there'll be much ridiculing of me that could be avoided by a simple list of ingredients.

"You really don't know what goes into a salad?"

"Bingo."

"Fine," said Rebecca. "Get tomato, lettuce, cucumber… are you writing this down?"

"I was going to make a list on my phone but then I realised I wouldn't be able to hear you if I did."

"You don't have a pencil?"

"Don't need one. I store all my notes in the phone."

"And yet…"

"I'll remember them long enough to put them in the phone," said Mark. "We've got tomato, lettuce, cucumber…"

"Carrots, cheese, salad dressing."

"Salad dressing?"

"Have you ever eaten a salad?"

"They're a bit, y'know, meatless for my liking."

"You are going to eat the salad tonight, mister," said Rebecca. "So you'd better get it right."

"Where am I going to get these ingredients from?" said Mark.

"The supermarket," said Rebecca. "Where did you think you were going to get them from?"

"Ah."

"What? Do you have a problem with the supermarket?"

"It's just that Chewie's with me."

"And?"

"And they won't let Chewie into the supermarket."

"I'm assuming they won't let him into the butcher or bottle shop either."

"No."

"So how were you planning to buy the meat and alcohol?"

"I was just going to leave Chewie tied up outside."

There was a pause. "I have a suggestion for you," said Rebecca. "It's crazy, but it just might work."

"You want me to tie Chewie up outside the supermarket?"

"Yes."

"I can't tie Chewie up outside the supermarket."

"But you can tie him up outside the butcher and the bottle shop?"

"Sure. He can see me when I'm in there."

"And he can't see you inside the supermarket?"

"Bingo."

"Enough with the bingos."

"No more bingos?" said Mark.

"The bingos stopped being cute about a week ago."

"I only started saying them a week ago."

There was a pause.

"Oh," said Mark.

"Now, what happens if Chewie can't see you?" said Rebecca.

"I'm worried he'll freak out."

"*Does* he freak out?"

"I don't know," said Mark. "I've never left him outside where he couldn't see me."

"So," said Rebecca. "The issue is not whether he can see you, but whether you can see him?"

"Bin—" said Mark. "Possibly."

"Do you think you might be able to try leaving him outside the supermarket?"

"I suppose," said Mark. "What am I getting in there again?"

"Salad."

"I know I'm getting 'salad'. But what were the ingredients again? Lettuce. Tomato. Cucumber. Cheese?"

"Forget it," said Rebecca. "I'll get the salad."

"You sure?"

"I'm sure," said Rebecca. "At least this way I'll know what I'm getting."

"I think that's probably best," said Mark.

"But you're still going to eat it tonight."

"Sure," said Mark. "I'll have a little bit."

"You're going to have a lot more than a little bit, mister," said Rebecca. "Look, I've got to go pick up a pregnancy test. I'll see you when I get home. I might be a little late."

"Good thing you'll have that pregnancy test, then," said Mark.

"Yes, very good," said Rebecca. "You're a very witty man who doesn't know what goes into a salad. Your foster-parents would be proud."

TWO HOURS LATER

Jodie dumped her bags in the hallway. She stumbled to her favourite couch and slumped.

"So glad to be home," she said.

"I hear you," said Richard. "There's no place like home."

"Exactly." Jodie paused. "Although, having said that, it's probably only a matter of time before the Japanese work out a way to perfectly simulate your home while on holiday."

Richard laughed.

"They're always thinking, those Japanese," said Jodie.

"That they are," said Richard. He flopped on the other couch.

"They'd probably use some kind of virtual reality glasses, I'd expect."

"I'd imagine so," said Richard.

"But for now," said Jodie. "Still no place like home."

"What time's dinner tonight?" said Richard.

"Seven-thirty?"

"Time for a snooze, then."

"Yeah."

"Y'know, it might have been nice to have a few days to settle back home before being dragged off to a barbecue."

"I know," said Jodie. "But it's Rebecca's birthday."

"Our lives are run by the clock these days, aren't they?"

"Comes with the time-travel territory, my love."

"I suppose."

"Are you complaining?" She gestured vaguely to their mini-mansion.

"No," he said. "I'm just tired."

"Then go have a nap," she said. "I'll wake you when it's time to get ready."

He stood up and kissed her. "You going to have one, too?"

"I might soldier on," said Jodie. She held up a copy of yet another book on quantum theory. "I'm almost finished."

"Rightey-o, then."

Richard left for the bedroom. Jodie reclined the chair and went back to reading.

Four minutes later, she was asleep.

AN HOUR AND A HALF LATER

The phone rang. Mark picked it up.

"How's it going?" he said.

"She's not pregnant," said Rebecca.

"Good for her."

"I think she's late because she just started on the pill."

"I wouldn't care to speculate on such matters," said Mark. "Completely outside my field of expertise."

"Not your milieu."

Mark smiled. "Precisely."

"Anyway, I'm only just leaving now," said Rebecca. "We had a long talk about safe sex and the pill and condoms. All the stuff that seems, to me at least, to be unrelated to English literature."

"I'm sure there are some books that cover this stuff."

"Not on my syllabus there isn't, mister."

"Anyway," said Rebecca. "I'll pick up the salad on the way home."

"Lettuce, tomato, carrots and so forth," said Mark.

"Precisely."

"Salad dressing."

"Why did I have to pick this up again?" said Rebecca. "You seem to know precisely what goes in a salad."

"I googled it."

"You did not."

"Sure I did."

"No, you didn't," said Rebecca. "Nobody googles 'salad ingredients'."

"Okay," said Mark. "I didn't."

"You have everything else?"

"Yep."

"Alcohol?"

"Yep."

"Meat?"

"Yep."

"Gift?"

"Gift?"

"Remember? For future sexual action?"

"Ah," said Mark. "I've got a Captain Carrot statue."

"A what?"

"A Captain Carrot statue."

"A superhero vegetable?" guessed Rebecca.

Mark snorted. "Superhero rabbit."

"Aha," said Rebecca. "And that's my gift?"

"You don't want the Captain Carrot statue?"

"You don't want sex ever again?"

"Fine," said Mark. "I'll keep the statue."

"That's probably best."

"I'll get you some other gift."

"See that you do," said Rebecca. "Now. The house is clean?"

"It sparkles."

"Really?"

"Really."

"You got Angie to come in, didn't you?"

"I didn't have time to clean it myself," said Mark. "I had important shopping to do."

"Salad-less shopping, I should point out."

"Be that as it may," said Mark. "The house is clean."

"Excellent," said Rebecca. "I'll see you when I get home."

HALF AN HOUR LATER

Rebecca left the supermarket, salad ingredients in tow. She'd also picked up some extra wine. She'd earned herself some wine. It had been a long, stressful day. Far too long and stressful for a birthday.

She thought she could stick with the job until the end of the year. See this year's kids through. But any more days like today and she might just leave them to their own devices.

She was a multimillionaire. She didn't need this.

She looked at her watch.

Maybe the massage place was still open. Maybe she could get a quick one in before she left. If she was a little late home, that was fine. It was her birthday. She could do as she pleased. She pulled the voucher out of her pocket.

The massage place was just the other side of the mall.

She strolled over there. With each step, she became more convinced this was a good idea. A relaxing rubdown would end the day nicely.

She arrived to find a vaguely familiar man locking up.

"Oh," she said. "You're closed?"

"Sorry," said the man.

Where did she know him from? "That's annoying," she said.

"You want to book one in for tomorrow?"

"Tomorrow's probably not going to be great."

"How about next week?" said the man.

"Let me check my timetable and get back to you," said Rebecca.

"Okay," said the man. "Have a good night."

"You too," said Rebecca.

Where did she know him from?

The man watched Rebecca leave. As she disappeared down the mall, he pulled out his mobile phone. He scrolled down the names in his contact list until he found the right one.

He dialled and waited for an answer.

"Dude," he said, when the man on the other end picked up. "You're never going to guess who I just saw."

TWO HOURS LATER

Jodie and Richard pulled up to Mark and Rebecca's mountainside home. Chewie raced out to greet them, barking enthusiastically. Mark followed.

"Welcome back!" he said, as they got out of the Ferrari.

"Good to be back," said Jodie. "How have things been in our absence?"

"As great as always."

"Chewie-dog!" said Richard, reaching down to scratch his head. Jodie's eye-roll was almost invisible.

"When's the next message?" she said.

Mark pulled out the stopwatch. It religiously counted down the seconds.

"Nineteen hours. Forty-odd minutes. Come on in."

Chewie continued to bark.

"Yes. Hello Chewie," said Jodie.

They headed inside.

"Happy birthday, Miss Tyler," said Jodie.

"Thank you."

"You had a good day?"

"An action-packed day," said Rebecca. "Pregnant students who turned out not to be pregnant, dimwitted classes who turned out to still be dimwitted."

"Sounds like a hoot," said Richard.

"Let me put that wine in the fridge," said Rebecca. She took the bottle from Richard. "How was Japan?"

"Fantastic," said Richard. "It's an amazing country."

"But it's good to be home," said Jodie.

"I can imagine," said Rebecca. "Thanks for coming over on your first night back. I know you probably just feel like sleeping."

"Ah, but we couldn't miss your birthday dinner."

"We could have had it on Sunday or something," said Rebecca. "Given you guys some time to recover a little."

"But it's not the same if it's not on the day."

"True," said Rebecca. "Anyway, thanks for coming over." She turned to Mark. "How's that barbecue going?"

"It's going well, thanks for asking."

"Is it clean?"

"It has a certain foul-mouthed quality."

Rebecca simply looked at him.

"Am I to blame if the cleaner for whom we pay perfectly good money ignores the barbecue?" said Mark.

"Did you hire the cleaner?" asked Rebecca.

"I'll go clean it," he said.

"I'll help," said Jodie.

"Beer?" said Rebecca, to Richard, after Jodie and Mark left.

"Sure."

Rebecca grabbed one from the fridge. She handed it to Richard.

"You ever worry about those two?" said Rebecca.

"Worry?"

"Y'know. The whole 'man-woman friends but that's all' thing they've got going."

Richard shrugged. "I used to," he said.

"Really?"

"No offence, but Mark used to drive me mental. He would call all the time. And even though I knew she loved me and nothing was going on between them, I'd still… y'know." He let the thought dangle.

"Yeah, I know."

"They've got that rapid-fire banter thing going. It used to drive me nuts that I wasn't a part of that."

"I know what you mean," said Rebecca.

"You and Mark have the same kind of thing."

"Not like those two do."

There was a pause. "No," said Richard. "I dunno, Bec. If there's one thing I've learnt, it's that that's *their* thing. That's how they relate. That's why they're friends. We don't have to be jealous of it. Their friendship doesn't take anything away from how they feel about us."

"But it *is* a little annoying, isn't it?"

"Yeah," said Rich. "It is."

Outside, Mark cleaned the barbecue.

"You got it?" he said.

Jodie reached into her pocket and pulled out the engagement ring. Mark wiped his hands on his shirt and took it. He stared at it. Mesmerised.

"It's perfect," he said.

"That it is."

"She's going to love this," said Mark. Finding the perfect engagement ring had been an enormous challenge. Rebecca had, in the telling of some anecdote or other, mentioned her childhood love for her great-aunt's diamond ring. Mark had noted and, following some lengthy detective work, had finally traced the ring to one of Rebecca's many second cousins. She wouldn't sell the ring. Some gibberish about sentimentality. But she was willing to let Mark take photos of it from every possible angle. For a small cash incentive, of course.

Mark had also traced the origin of the ring back to Japan, and had commissioned the same family jeweller to make a replica of it.

And here it was.

Perfect.

"When?" said Jodie.

"Tonight."

"You don't muck about."

"I don't have any other birthday present," said Mark.

"You are as romantic as ever."

Mark emitted a weak smile.

"You okay?" said Jodie.

"Sure," said Mark. He reconsidered. "Am I doing the right thing here?"

"You love her, don't you?"

"Yeah," he said. "I mean, I assume it's love."

Jodie laughed and shook her head.

"What?" said Mark.

"You 'assume' it's love?"

"I want to know what love is," said Mark. "I want Foreigner to show me."

"No no no," said Jodie. "You're not getting away with the jokey quip on this occasion. Have you seen yourself with this girl? You're crazy about her. And if there's any doubt about that in your mind, then all that proves to me is that you're thinking too much about this shit."

Mark didn't respond.

"Stop thinking so much," she said. "Trust your feelings."

Mark still didn't respond.

"You don't have to be afraid of your feelings," she said. "Not everyone you love will be taken away from you."

Mark nodded. He didn't know what else to do.

Jodie hugged him.

AN HOUR LATER

Rebecca knew the instant Mark returned that this was it. She hadn't seen that look on his face before. It had to be his proposal face.

Katrina had called out of the blue a week or so earlier and clued her in on his attempt to buy the ring. It had been months since Rebecca had heard from her. And that last conversation had been… uncomfortable.

"Hello," Rebecca had said. Not willing to give her anything.

"Hi."

"What's up?"

"Not much. You?"

And so forth. A good eternity of mindless small talk until Katrina had managed to home in on a point.

"I spoke to Tania the other day," she'd said.

"Tania?"

"Cousin Tania."

"Oh yeah," said Katrina. Not sure what this was about. Tania was not technically a cousin. She was a second (?) cousin. Maybe once removed? Rebecca didn't understand how things worked once it got beyond the children of parents' siblings stage.

But Tania was related. Somehow. 'Cousin Tania' was a reasonable description. "How is she?"

"She's good," said Katrina. "Guess who she saw a couple of weeks ago?"

"The King of Norway?"

Katrina half-snorted. "Mark."

It took Rebecca a moment to process this. "My Mark?"

"Your Mark."

"I didn't even know Tania knew Mark." A sinking feeling swept over her. Mark couldn't be cheating on her, could she? With her… cousinesque relative?

Of course not. That would be insane.

"Apparently he does," said Katrina. "He tried to buy her ring off her."

"Her ring?" What on Earth was Katrina talking about?

"Aunt Beryl's ring?"

"I loved that ring," said Rebecca. Cogs started to fall into place. "Mark tried to buy Aunt Beryl's ring?"

"He seems to think being a Lotto millionaire entitles him to just buy up people's memories and heirlooms."

Rebecca sighed. This kind of editorial input was precisely why Rebecca no longer spoke to Katrina.

"Did Tania sell it?"

"Of course not. Your boyfriend learned that some things aren't for sale."

"So why tell me this?" said Rebecca. "What's your point?"

"He took a whole heap of photos of the ring," said Katrina. "Tania thinks he's going to try to get another one made."

"He took photos of the ring?"

"Tania made him pay for it too."

"I'll bet she did."

Katrina ignored the last comment. "Looks like he's going to pop the question."

"Maybe it's just a birthday present," said Rebecca.

Katrina ignored that comment too. "What will you say?"

"I don't know," said Rebecca.

"Do you love him?" asked Katrina. "Or do you love the money?"

"I don't want to listen to this," said Rebecca.

"If he hadn't won the Lotto, you guys would have broken up months ago."

"Goodbye."

Rebecca hung up.

She had no idea why Katrina had turned into such a bitch. But, turn into a bitch she had.

Rebecca hadn't spent too long worrying about Katrina, however. After a few minutes, she'd turned her concentration to working out whether Mark really was going to propose.

And, if so, what she would say.

That had been a week or so ago.

And now seemed to be the moment of truth, if the look of terror on Mark's face was any indication. Of course, she'd thought she'd hit the moment of truth about forty-nine times over the past week.

But this seemed the most likely candidate so far.

"Rebecca," he said. "Since the day we met, my life has just got better and better and better. I can no longer imagine you not being part of my life. And I don't want to ever have to imagine it."

He went down on one knee. Definitely starting to look like the moment of truth now.

"Rebecca Tyler, will you marry me?"

Wow. He didn't even put a joke in there. He was serious.

She wouldn't torture him.

"Yes," she said.

"Oh, thank god," said Mark. The terror began to drain from his face. He put the ring on Rebecca's finger. Got up off his knees. Kissed her. "Really?" he whispered.

"Nah," she said.

Mark pulled back. Rebecca broke into a grin. "Wow," she said. "This whole proposal thing messes with your sense of humour."

A champagne cork popped behind them. Richard started pouring celebratory glasses.

"Congratulations, guys," said Jodie. She moved in and kissed Mark on the cheek, hugging him tight.

"I did it, Jode," he said.

"That you did, Marcus. That you did." She turned to Rebecca. "*You* might have aimed a little higher though."

"Sometimes you just have to take pity," said Rebecca. She smiled and embraced Jodie. "I assume you helped with the ring?"

"Do you like it?" said Jodie.

"I love it."

"Then, sure, we helped."

Richard finished pouring the drinks. He handed one to Mark and shook his hand. "Congratulations, Mark."

"Thanks, Rich."

Richard turned back to get two more glasses. He gave one to Rebecca. He accompanied it with a kiss. "Congratulations, Bec. I'm glad you liked the ring."

"Is this my great-aunt's ring?" said Rebecca. No harm in playing it a little dumb. He'd gone to a lot of effort. Let him have his moment.

"I tried very hard to get your great-aunt's ring," said Mark. "But your second cousin wouldn't sell it."

"Oh," said Rebecca. "It looks exactly the same."

"It's an exact replica," said Mark. "I got photos of your great-aunt's ring from every angle and then these two went to the original jeweller in Japan to get a copy made."

"Wow," said Rebecca. She looked at the ring closely. It was exactly the same. And it was as beautiful as she remembered it.

"Okay," said Jodie. "Time for a toast." She raised her glass. "To Mark and Rebecca. The first couple in history to be brought together by a time-travelling phone message."

Everybody clinked and drank.

"And don't you get too drunk, Marcus. You've got a message to deliver in eighteen and a half hours."

Mark pulled out the stopwatch. "Eighteen hours, sixteen minutes to be precise."

EIGHTEEN HOURS, TEN MINUTES LATER

Mark walked up the stairs to Rebecca's old apartment building. He was feeling more than a little seedy. But if you weren't going to celebrate an engagement with out-of-control drunkenness, when were you going to do so?

He still hadn't been happy when the alarm went off at midday. They'd gone to bed around four am. Eight hours sleep should have been enough.

But his head assured him, in pounding terms, that it wasn't.

He nodded to Jake, the security guard, as he and Chewie went by.

"Mr Campbell," said Jake. He stooped down to give Chewie a scratch on the head. "Chewie dog."

Chewie's tail thumped happily. "Hi Jake," said Mark. His voice croaked a little.

"Big night last night, sir?" said Jake, straightening up.

"Something like that," said Mark. "I asked Rebecca to marry me."

"And the drinking was because…"

"She said yes."

"Well, all right," said Jake. "Congratulations."

He reached out his hand. Mark shook it.

"Thank you," said Mark. He checked his watch. "Sorry, Jake. Got to get in there."

"Right-o, sir."

Mark headed in. Chewie followed him, grinning back at Jake.

Mark wondered if Jake ever wondered what he did in there. He supposed he must. But, if so, he never said anything.

Mark walked up the stairs to Rebecca's apartment. He unlocked the door. He let the lead go. Chewie ran in and leapt on the couch. He sat down.

Mark pulled out the stopwatch and his phone. He had a minute and a half to wait. He sat the stopwatch on the bench. Found the text of the last message in a note saved on his phone. Read over it a couple of times.

As the stopwatch hit zero, he speed-dialled his number and left the list of shares he'd heard three days ago.

He looked around.

No collapse of the space-time continuum. Perfect.

From a building across the road, Federal Agent Scott Darcy watched Mark with interest. He squinted through the binoculars, trying to get a glimpse of what was going on inside.

He scribbled in his notebook.

1606: Campbell arrives at exterior of building. Talks to security guard

1607: Campbell enters building. Makes his way to apartment 4 (former residence of Tyler)

1609: Campbell watches stopwatch, consults notes, eventually makes a call to—he hesitated before he wrote the next note—*unknown number. Talks briefly, hangs up*

1611: Campbell departs

Darcy picked up his phone. Flipped through the contacts. Dialled Toby.

"Toby Latham."

"Hey, Tobe."

"Hey, Scotto. What's up?"

"Just keeping an eye on that Campbell case."

"How's it going?"

"Thrilling. I sit around here all day, eating chips, listening to the radio. Then I spy on him for five minutes as he makes his phone call. And now? Now I get to sit back and do, uh, nothing for the rest of the day, on the off-chance he returns. Which he won't, because he never does."

"Sounds like one hell of a career you've got going there."

"Doesn't it?"

"I suppose you want me to confirm where he called again?"

"If you could."

"What's the initialising address again?"

Darcy told him. There was a clacking of keyboards for several seconds, before Toby returned.

"You want to take a guess?"

"Same place as every other time?"

"I'll give that an emphatic, off-the-record, yessirree."

"Thanks," said Agent Darcy. "Still no chance of finding out what he's actually saying, I suppose?"

"Sorry, Scotto," said Toby. "Way out of my division."

"No worries. Thanks anyway."

"You paintballing next weekend?"

"Definitely."

"I'll see you then."

Darcy hung up. Put the phone down. He leant back and swigged an energy drink. What on Earth was Mark Campbell up to? If he could work it out himself, then they might promote him off surveillance.

He sighed.

He had no chance of working this out. The man was unfathomable.

He picked up the phone again. He speed-dialled.

"He's back," he said.

Oblivious to Agent Darcy's spying, Mark made his way back to the car. He opened the passenger door for Chewie, who leapt in. As he walked to the driver's side, he called Rebecca.

"Hey, fiancé," she said.

"Hey, fiancée."

"Call made?"

"Aye."

"Space-time continuum intact?"

"Seems so."

"Cool," said Rebecca. "How's Chewie?"

"He's good. He enjoyed the drive."

"How are you?"

"Keen to get home and crawl back to bed."

"You don't have the drinking stamina you used to have," she said.

"When did I ever have drinking stamina?" said Mark. "The night we met, I was drunk off my head by half past nine."

"That's true," said Rebecca. "I just assumed you'd had stamina at one point. And, y'know, now clearly don't. So 'you don't have the drinking stamina you used to have'."

"Oh, I get your point," said Mark.

"It's the kind of thing you say to people who are no longer nineteen."

"Well, I am no longer nineteen."

"Exactly my point."

"You probably wouldn't be marrying me if I was nineteen."

"Well…"

"What?"

"You probably had other kinds of stamina at nineteen too."

"Don't be mean to me," said Mark. "I just made us another few million dollars."

"Okay."

"And avoided destroying the space-time continuum in the process."

"Okay."

"Could a nineteen year old do that?"

"Of course not."

"No," said Mark. "He'd be too busy drinking and shagging all night with his never-ending supply of stamina."

Rebecca hung up from Mark.

She sighed. Time to get this over with. She dialled her parents.

"Hello?" said her mother.

"Hi, Ma," said Rebecca. "It's Bec."

"Hello," repeated her mother. "To what do we owe this honour?"

"I've got some good news."

"Really? We love good news. Let's hear it."

Rebecca took a deep breath. "Mark and I are engaged."

An ever so slight pause. "Engaged to be married?"

"Engaged to be married."

Another ever so slight pause. "Well, that's wonderful, dear. Just wonderful. We're very happy for you."

"Thank you," said Rebecca. But her mother wasn't listening. She was hollering for her father. Rebecca waited patiently.

"I'm just getting your father, dear."

"Okay," said Rebecca.

"Do you have any plans yet?"

"Plans?"

"Wedding plans."

"He only asked me last night," said Rebecca. "I haven't had time to plan anything."

"On your birthday," said her mother. "Isn't that lovely?"

Oh dear god. "He's a lovely man," said Rebecca.

"Uh-huh. Here's your father."

"Hello, Muppet."

"Hi, daddy."

"You're getting married?"

"I am."

"To Mark?" he asked.

Could her parents possibly say anything more stupid in this conversation? "Yes," she said. "To Mark."

"Well, that's… great."

"It is," agreed Rebecca. She ignored the not so ever so slight pause in the middle of the sentence.

"Is he there?"

"No," said Rebecca. "He had some errands to run."

"Well, you pass on my congratulations to him, as well," he said. "Tell him to treat you right."

"Will do, daddy."

"Here's your mother," he said. "I think she wants to discuss plans with you."

Rebecca sighed. She didn't often envy Mark being an orphan. But this was one time she did.

Agent Mills stormed into Agent Benson's office.

"Another phone call," said Mills.

"What?" said Benson. He looked up from his desk. Mills was working himself into a lather again.

"The Campbell case."

"Remind me," said Benson. The vein above Mills' eye was starting to go.

"A little over, uh, eight months ago," said Agent Mills, consulting the file. "Mark Campbell won the Lotto. Since then he's set up a trust with his girlfriend and some married friends."

"Oh, right," said Benson. "This is the one who buys the best-performing short-term shares every single week. Without fail."

"That's the one."

"I still say it's got to be insider trading," said Benson.

"How?" said Mills. "All we've got on him are these weekly visits to his old apartment and his girlfriend's old apartment."

"What's he do in there?"

"We don't know what he does in his old apartment. But whenever he drops into his girlfriend's apartment, he makes one phone call."

"Do we know who he calls?" said Benson. He didn't care about this case. Insider trading was a tedious crime. Hardly worth getting so worked up about. There were plenty of real crimes to solve.

"We've got an off the record source," said Mills.

"And?"

"He calls his old apartment and leaves a message."

"What's he say?" said Benson.

"We don't know."

"Phone tap?"

"Can't find a judge who'll let us."

Benson snorted. "What else have we got?"

"Nothing. That's the infuriating bit. We've followed all four of them for months and his regular visits to his old haunts is the only unusual behaviour from any one of them."

"Who lives in his old apartment?"

"Nobody. Their trust bought out both buildings a few months ago. Both buildings are now vacant and guarded by full-scale security."

"It certainly sounds like something's going on in there," said Benson.

"Oh, something's up," said Mills. "I don't know what yet. But there's something."

Benson sighed. "I don't see what we can do," he said. "There's no evidence he's committed any crime."

"He must be doing something, though," said Mills. "He picks the best shares every single week."

"Maybe he's just lucky."

Mills gave him a look.

"Okay," said Benson. "He's not lucky. He's cheating somehow. But we need to work out how before we can do anything."

"Next time he shows up to his girlfriend's apartment, I think we should do something," said Mills.

"Like?"

"I dunno yet," said Mills. "But I'll think of something."

CHAPTER SIX

One in 3.71 trillion trillion millionety billion.

Who knew such a little dog could be so heavy?

Rebecca cursed the children.

"How did he get behind schedule?"

NEXT TIME

"OKAY, BUDDY," SAID Mark. "Time to go."

Chewie looked up at him, ball in mouth, tail thumping.

"Drop it," said Mark. Chewie ignored him. Mark went for his stern voice. "Drop it."

Chewie continued to ignore him.

"Fine," said Mark. "Don't drop it."

He bent down and started to put Chewie's walking harness back on. They were on Rebecca and Mark's property now, and would remain on the property as they walked back. However, Chewie didn't always respect the notion of legal property boundaries. He would cross fences into neighbouring properties when, well, anything caught his eye. After a couple of diversions into Neighbour Stan's duck pond, Mark had adopted the policy of putting the lead on for the walk home.

He clipped the lead to the harness. Chewie spat the ball out.

Mark looked at his stopwatch.

"Okay," he said. "A couple more throws, then Daddy has to go make his call."

Chewie's eyes never moved from the ball. Mark scooped it up and threw. Chewie took off in pursuit.

Mark saw the flash of white an instant before Chewie did. But only an instant. Chewie abandoned the ball and turned his attention to the rabbit.

"Chewie! No. Leave it alone."

Nothing.

Mark went for his stern voice. "CHEWIE!"

The voice didn't work. The rabbit deviated. Chewie followed it. The rabbit ducked under a fence. Chewie followed it again.

"Chewie!!" This was his terrified voice. Mark hadn't known he'd had one of those. But here it was.

Mark raced after him. He dove, as Chewie burst under the fence after the rabbit. Mark grabbed his lead. Chewie's momentum dragged Mark's shoulder under the fence.

He felt the skin of his arm tear. He gripped the lead tighter. This was going to hurt tomorrow.

Heck, it was going to hurt now.

There was a yelp, as Chewie found himself tumbling off the cliff on the other side of the fence. Mark felt all of Chewie's weight on his shoulder. He looked down. Only his grip on the lead prevented Chewie's certain death.

Chewie started to cry.

"Don't cry, mate."

Mark tried to pull him back up. He couldn't do it. His arm was too far under the fence. It was impossible to get his other arm under to help. Nor could he get the support he needed to hoist Chewie to safety.

"Shit," he said.

"Bobs!"

Rebecca froze. She must have misheard that.

"Bobs!" The voice came again. Louder. Closer. Dear god. What was *he* doing here? This was the last thing she needed after a massage.

She turned around. "Andrew." The voice was devoid of emotion. She was not going to offer him anything.

He didn't notice. He'd never picked up on stuff like this. That had been one reason for their breakup.

Not a major reason, if she was going to be honest about it. But a reason. The breakup had more to do with the emotional immaturity and the total lack of responsibility. And the cheating. Probably ninety-five to ninety-eight percent of it was because of those three reasons. The inability of him to pick up on her vocal clues was probably only half a percent or so.

"Oh my god, Bobs!" he said. "It is you."

The fact he called her 'Bobs' was probably another half a percent. It had started out as his annoying nickname for her. The progression had been 'Big Boobs Becky' to 'Big Bobs Becky' to just plain 'Bobs'. Equating her identity to her breasts? Not the best start he could have made.

At some point, she'd started to find it cute.

She had no idea how she could possibly have thought that way. She must have been mad.

"Yep," said Rebecca. "It's me. I tried being that checkout chick over there for a while, but that didn't work out. So I want back to being me."

Andrew smiled. "It is so good to see you," he said. "What have you been up to? I heard you got engaged."

Rebecca held up her ring finger.

Andrew whistled. "That's one impressive rock," he said. "Your new boy must be pulling in some big bucks."

"We do okay," said Rebecca.

"What's he do?"

"He's an… entrepreneur." A 'collector of Captain Carrot statues' didn't sound all that impressive.

"Cool," said Andrew. "Hey, didn't you guys win the Lotto or something?"

Rebecca offered a thin smile. "Where did you hear that?"

"Oh, you know," said Andrew. "Word gets around."

Seriously, where had he heard that? What was he doing here? Why had he chosen to re-enter her life at this point?

"So, what are you doing up here?" she said.

"Oh, you know," said Andrew. "Just up for a visit."

"Who are you visiting?"

Andrew smiled. "Just some friends," he said. "Nobody you know."

Rebecca nodded. Then it hit her. Trevor Falkner. That was the guy from the massage place the other day. Trevor had gone to school with both Andrew and herself. He must have recognised her and told Andrew.

Time to wrap up this stroll down Bad Memory Lane.

"Well—" she began.

Andrew interrupted her. "Hey," he said. "Can I buy you a coffee?"

"A coffee?"

"Do you have some place to be?"

"Well… not… really," she said. She cursed her slow wits. Any excuse would have done. Hair appointment. Waxing appointment. Hell, skydiving appointment would have done. But no. She went with 'not… really.' She deserved to spend some time with him.

"Great. I'll buy you a cup of coffee. We'll catch up on everything."

"Well…" Rebecca looked at her watch.

"Come on, Bobs," he said. "I'm not going to try and seduce you. I just want to catch up. I figure there's no reason we can't be friends. Right?"

Rebecca could think of many reason they couldn't be friends. The deep-seated contempt, for one. Friends avoided that as much as possible.

She didn't say that.

"Just a quick one," she said.

Jodie and Richard wandered around the markets. Jodie knew he was bored, but he should have thought of that before he'd made her sit through every single episode of the first season of *Blackadder.*

A deal was a deal.

She picked up a basket and turned it over in her hands. "This would go well in the sitting room, wouldn't it?" she said.

"Sure," said Richard.

"Your enthusiasm is overwhelming," she said.

"It is?"

"Yeah."

"Huh," he said.

Jodie put the basket back down. "You loathe this, don't you?" she said.

Richard hesitated. "I don't love it," he admitted.

"Fine," she said. "You can go home."

"No," he said. "A deal's a deal."

"No. I don't want you around while I'm doing this. You suck all the fun out of it."

He smiled a weak smile. "I'll try to have more fun."

"No," she said. "I don't think you can have fun here. And I know you're not a good enough actor to pretend otherwise. So you should just go home."

"You won't be mad?"

"I won't be mad."

"Not even secretly mad, but not willing to admit you're mad?"

"Not even secretly mad, but not willing to admit I'm mad," she confirmed.

"I love you," he said. He moved in and kissed her.

"But," she said. "I want you to remember how ball-numbingly bored you've been for the last ninety minutes. Because that's exactly how I feel about watching *Blackadder*. I have never enjoyed it. I never will enjoy it. Season two may be better than season one. Season four may be better than season three. Season six may be the season where it gets funny. I don't care."

Richard's mouth was half-open.

"I don't care that there wasn't ever a season six," said Jodie. Richard's mouth closed. "I hate everything about it, and find sitting through any given episode a mental torture, much like you at a local market. Comprende?"

"So what you're saying," said Richard. "Is that you don't want me to save season two for you?"

"No," she said. "You go home and watch it, by yourself, right now."

"Got it," he said. "Should I take the car?"

"No. I'm taking the car. You get a cab."

"Got it," he said. "I love you."

"Likewise," she said.

"Definitely not mad?"

"Definitely not mad."

"Not even secretly?"

"Not even secretly."

"Okay. I'll see you later."

Agent Mills looked over his calculations again. 3.71E-41, the spreadsheet told him. He tried to convert that into a real number. Was it one in 3.71 trillion trillion trillion, uh, million? Or one in 3.71 trillion trillion billion billion? Something like that. Whatever the exact value was, he knew it was just about as close as you could get to zero without getting there.

This was the likelihood that Mark Campbell and friends had somehow selected the best shares each week by luck alone.

One in 3.71 trillion trillion millionety billion.

It made their Lotto win seem a formality.

They were clearly cheating. He didn't know how. But the laws of probability didn't lie. These guys were cheats. There were few things in life more certain.

He looked over his notes.

It was three days since Campbell had last been to his old apartment. He was due back at his girlfriend's old apartment today.

Agent Darcy was posted outside the apartment block. Campbell wasn't getting in there until he'd provided an explanation to how he was overcoming the one in 3.71 squidillion odds.

"So," said Rebecca. "What's news with you? You seeing anybody?"

"Nah," said Andrew. "I'm enjoying my freedom."

"You're shagging anything that moves."

Andrew smiled. "Something like that."

"How's work?" said Rebecca. This was torture. She'd just dropped into the mall for her massage on the way home. The last thing she wanted to be doing was having a polite chat with her ex-boyfriend.

"Work never changes," said Andrew. "Roger's still insane."

"Something tells me Roger's never going to sane up."

"You're probably right," said Andrew. "You still teaching?"

"Yeah," said Rebecca.

"No classes this afternoon?"

"No," said Rebecca. "I'm probably going to give it up at the end of the year, anyway."

"Guess there's not much point still doing it," said Andrew. "Now you're a millionaire."

"It's not about the money," said Rebecca. "It was never about the money. I like teaching. I like helping kids."

"Then why are you going to quit?"

Arrrggghhh! Couldn't they discuss the weather or something? Wasn't that the traditional stomping ground for mindless chat? She didn't want to be sharing her growing dissatisfaction with the education system with Andrew, for god's sake.

"You're right," she said. "It is about the money." Anything to get him off her back.

"I knew it," he said. He took a sip of his coffee and beamed that smug beam of his.

What on Earth had she ever seen in this dickwad?

She took a large sip of her coffee. Just finish the coffee and go. She took another large sip.

Chewie continued to cry.

"Don't cry, mate," said Mark. "It's going to be okay."

His arm throbbed. Who knew such a little dog could be so heavy?

He fumbled his free hand into his pocket. Grabbed the stopwatch. He didn't even want to look at that.

One hour and seven minutes.

This was very bad.

He reached into his pocket. Pulled out his mobile phone. He flipped it open and hit the speed dial.

Oh, thank god, thought Rebecca, as the phone rang.

She picked it up. "Excuse me," she said to Andrew. She answered the phone. "Hi babe," she said. "What's up?"

"Where are you?" said Mark.

"Still in the mall," said Rebecca. Her heart raced. She felt guilty. Like she was cheating by having a cup of coffee with Andrew. Which was insane. But there it was. "Just finished the massage."

"You've gotta get back here, babe," said Mark. "As soon as possible. Chewie's had an accident."

Rebecca's head jolted back. Forget the stupid self-absorption. "Is he okay?"

"He went under the fence."

"Oh my Go—"

"It's okay. I caught him. But I need help to pull him back up."

"Okay. I'll be right there."

"Hurry. I've got a call to make in an hour."

Rebecca stood up. "I'm already on my way." She hung up.

"Is everything okay?" said Andrew.

"I have to go," said Rebecca. "My dog's been in an accident."

"Oh. Do you need a lift anywhere or anything?"

"No. I just need to go," she said. She took a deep breath. "Thank you for the coffee. Nice to catch up again." What a liar she was.

Andrew stood up. "It was great to see you again, too, Bobs." He moved in for a hug. Rebecca gave him the briefest possible one she could.

"Sorry," she said. "I just have to go."

"Understood," he said. "Go. Go. I'll give you a call sometime. We'll do this again."

Rebecca didn't turn her head back as she strode to the escalators. "Sure."

Liar!

"What's your number?" said Andrew.

"Don't remember."

And she was gone.

Mark looked at his stopwatch. It clocked down under an hour. This was not good.

This was not good at all.

Chewie whimpered again.

"It's all right," said Mark. "Mummy's on her way."

He looked at the stopwatch again.

"'We will not rupture the space time continuum.'"

Rebecca dropped her keys.

"Shit!"

She reached down and picked them up again. She clicked the unlock button on the car.

It didn't work.

Of course it didn't work. She'd hit the lock button instead.

Deep breaths, Rebecca. Just take a moment.

Chewie doesn't have a moment, her head screamed back at her.

Centring yourself for ten seconds now will earn the time back easily enough.

She took some deep breaths.

Felt the calmness wash over her.

That was better. Now, unlock the do—

"Bobs!"

Oh god. The stress surged back.

She turned around. Andrew was running towards her with her purse held high. "You forgot your purse."

Rebecca took it from him. "Thank you." She performed a gesture towards the car. When she realised how vague it was, she supplied the translation. "Gotta go."

"Of course. Hope everything's okay," he said.

She unlocked the door. Clambered in. "Me too."

She turned the ignition, reversed out and drove.

Agent Mills picked up his phone. He dialled.

"Darcy," came the response.

"Scott," said Mills. "It's Paul Mills."

"Hey," said Darcy.

"Any sign of him yet?"

"Not yet," he said.

"Good," said Mills. "He should be there sometime in the next hour or two."

"Okay. What's the plan when he does show up?"

"I want you to stop him from entering the building."

"Arrest him?"

"Don't think we can arrest him," said Mills. "Not yet, anyway. I'm going to speak to Benson. See if we can come up with something.

"Uh-huh."

"But we've analysed the time difference between his visits to his old apartment and the phone calls he makes at his girlfriend's apartment. The time difference is incredibly consistent."

"Oo-kay," said Darcy. Clearly not getting it.

Agent Mills elaborated. "Whatever he's doing in there, it's time critical," he said. "He's not just wandering in there when he feels like it. He's making trips to that apartment and phone calls from it at very specific times."

"Ah," said Darcy.

"If you can hold him up just long enough to miss whatever appointment he has in there, then that might be enough to give us another clue as to what he's doing. And how they're beating odds of one in 3.71 trillion trillion trillion trillion."

"Okay. Understood."

"I'm going to go clear this with Benson," said Mills. "But I don't think there'll be any problem. Just stop Campbell from entering that apartment."

"Will do."

NINE MINUTES LATER

Mark watched the seconds move from 00 to a fresh 59 as the stopwatch clocked down to forty-four minutes.

Where was she?

"Come on Rebecca," said Mark. "'We will not rupture the space time continuum.'"

He looked down at Chewie. The whimpering had died down. This scared him more than the crying had. If anything happened to him…

He was going to be all right. He was a tough little dog.

Mark tried once again to push his left hand through the hole. It just wouldn't go. Not without him rearranging the right arm. And he couldn't rearrange the right arm without letting go of Chewie.

But if he couldn't get the left arm through, he couldn't pull Chewie up and back through the hole.

Goddammit, Bec.

Where was she??

Rebecca cursed the children.

School was out and they were scattering everywhere. She had to stop every few seconds for another gaggle to make their way over a pedestrian crossing.

She should have taken the long way. It was longer (hence the name), but at three pm on a school-day, it would have been a hell of a lot quicker.

Just as the current flock were about to get off the road, a handful of stragglers stumbled on.

Rebecca narrowed her eyes at them. Fat little bastards. Why weren't they doing some after-school sport and working that blubber off?

They ignored her.

If the space-time continuum did rupture, and the universe did explode, then at least that would be the end of those horrid little hobbits.

Deep breaths, Bec. Deep breaths.

Mark strained with everything he had. He'd managed to squeeze the three main fingers of his left hand through the hole. If he could just lift Chewie up to a height where he could transfer the leash to those fingers, then he might be able to change grips and pull him all the way through.

He pulled up with his right arm.

Nrrrgrrghhh!

He had never hurt so much in his life. His arm screamed at him.

But he was almost there. Just a little bit further and he could try to switch hands.

He let out a primeval grunt as he pulled Chewie up to the level of his left hand.

His right arm shook. He had to switch over quickly. He couldn't hold this position for long.

On the other hand—so to speak—he had to make sure of the switch. If he didn't hook the leash properly on his left fingers, it would slip off. And take Chewie with him.

He moved the hands together. His right arm was shaking out of control.

God, maybe time travel *did* give you Parkinson's.

Tasteless, tasteless, tasteless.

He could feel the leash touching his left fingers. He tried to push them closer. Tried to hook them in the loop.

They wouldn't reach.

Damn it!

He had to put his right arm back down. He couldn't hold it up any longer.

He lowered it. Every muscle thanked him.

He dropped his head, exhausted.

Come on, Bec.

Andrew sat in his car. He pulled out his street maps and looked up the address. He couldn't believe his luck when she'd left her purse behind. How could he be expected to resist having a quick peek before he returned it? Hell, she'd probably left it behind on purpose so he could do so. Maybe not consciously. But on some level.

She'd looked fucking awesome. God, she'd looked good. She'd lost some weight, so her butt wasn't as big as it had been over the last year or so they'd been together. Which was typical. Chicks always let themselves go once they'd been in a relationship for a while. Her new dipshit boyfriend had that to look forward to.

But despite the weight she'd lost, her tits were still great. Still as full and round and large as ever. God, how he'd missed those tits.

Her hair was longer too, and, damn, if that didn't suit her.

He'd been surprised when Trev called him a week or so ago. He hadn't spoken to Trev in ages. But there he was, calling him up with the scoop on Bobs. Trev was a good guy. Still hard to believe he was queer.

And as soon as he'd started talking about her, Andrew knew he had to go see her. Things hadn't been the same since she'd left town. Sure, they'd slipped into a comfort zone in their relationship. And sure, he'd strayed a little. But for her to pack up and leave town? Clearly an overreaction.

There was still obvious chemistry between the two of them. And he'd seen a photo of Captain Dipshit in her purse. Hard to imagine anybody having any chemistry with him.

She probably hadn't had a decent fuck since the two of them broke up. God knows, things had died down in the sack between them over time. Another example of chicks in relationships coasting along. That's why he'd had to look elsewhere for some relief now and then.

But when they *had* fucked, it had still been to an Olympic standard. She was a wildcat in the sack. Even with that extra weight on.

God. Imagine what she'd be like now. Skinnier butt. Same awesome tits. That longer hair, hanging down. And those lips. God, those lips.

His dick was about to burst through his jeans.

He checked his watch.

Fuck it. He'd head back to the mall toilets, have a quick wank and then go check out where she lived.

Agent Mills approached Agent Benson.

"The Campbell case," said Mills.

"What about it?"

"He's due at his girlfriend's apartment today."

"Due?"

Mills refused to sigh. He explained again. "The three day gap between his visits to his apartment and his girlfriend's."

"Oh," said Benson. "Right."

"So he's due."

"Okay," said Benson. "What are you proposing?"

"I want Darcy to intercept him."

"Intercept?"

"There's something time-critical in that apartment. Here, look." Mills pushed the spreadsheet into Benson's hand. He pointed at the column of time differences. "Look at the standard deviation on this."

"It's small," said Benson.

"He's got a very specific time frame he's working in."

"Apparently so."

"I think if we stop him from making the call, we might get a clue to what he was trying to achieve by doing it."

"That's it?" said Benson.

Mills shrugged. "We don't have any other leads," he said. "I'm working with what we've got."

"Okay," said Benson. "Here's what worries me. If you intercept Campbell before he makes today's phone call, it's a one-shot deal."

"What do you mean?"

"You're intercepting him in the hope it'll give you evidence on what he's been doing, right?"

"Right."

"If it doesn't give you a clue, then that's it. He's now fully aware we're on to him. And, if he's as smart as his actions so far suggest, that's it."

"He'll stop?"

"Wouldn't you?" said Benson. "He doesn't need any more money. He could stop right now and live very comfortably indeed."

Mills nodded. "True," he said. "But let's flip it around. Worst case scenario: we've put the cheating bastard out of commission and made the share market a fairer place for the rest of the punters."

Benson sighed and nodded slowly. He pointed to another number on the spreadsheet printout. "What's this number?" he said.

"That's the probability they've been picking the right stocks by chance."

Benson snorted. "Okay," he said. "Give Darcy the go-ahead. Stop Campbell from making his call."

NINE MINUTES LATER

Mark opened his eyes. Lifted his head off the ground. He looked at the stopwatch and saw it reach thirty-one minutes. Even if Rebecca showed up now, there was no way he could get back to the apartment in half an hour.

"Mark!"

He turned his head. Rebecca was, indeed, running over.

Maybe he *could* make it.

"Oh babe," said Rebecca, as she arrived. She slid down. Looked over the fence to see Chewie dangling. "Oh Chewie…"

"Come on," said Mark. "I'm not going to make this phone call in time."

Rebecca pulled back, trying to work out what to do.

"Lift the fence," said Mark. "I need to get my other arm down there."

Rebecca put her hands under the rim of the fence. She lifted. Mark swung his other arm underneath. Both arms now held the leash. He lifted.

Chewie began to wheeze.

"You're hurting him."

"It's just for a second."

Mark pulled him up a little further. He slipped his arms underneath Chewie's front legs. "It's all right, Chewie."

Rebecca pulled the fence up even further.

Mark heaved Chewie through it.

Rebecca grabbed for Chewie. She cuddled him. Mark collapsed, exhausted.

"Oh baby. Are you okay?"

"Yeah," said Mark, eyes closed.

Rebecca turned her attention from Chewie. She reached out to Mark and touched his leg. "That's good."

Mark pushed himself up. He looked at the stopwatch. Twenty-seven minutes.

"I have to go," he said. He turned and sprinted off.

"How long have you got?"

"Twenty-seven minutes," he shouted back. His head did not even turn.

"You won't make it," Rebecca shouted after him.

"I have to." His voice surged to a roar. "We will not rupture the space-time continuum."

Andrew returned to his car. That was better. Now he could concentrate on the job at hand.

Huh.

Now he'd had the hand job he could concentrate on the job at hand.

That was pretty good.

Couldn't share the joke with anybody, but it was still good.

Maybe he'd share it with Trev. He'd like it. Trev might be a queer, but he'd appreciate something witty like that.

He looked at the address again. It was an apartment. Why was Mr Dipshit Lotto Winner still making her live in an apartment?

You'd think with that much money he could buy her a decent fucking house to live in.

Hell, if he'd won the Lotto, he'd have bought himself a goddamn mansion. And if Rebecca was still his girlfriend, he'd have dedicated one room just for fucking. The fuckroom. And he'd have maids to change the sheets every day. Keep the room clean.

Maybe he'd even fuck some of the maids in the fuckroom while they were cleaning it. Why the fuck not?

But not Captain Dipshit. He made her live in an apartment. What on Earth did she see in this dweeb?

He picked up his street directory. Found the address.

Time to get a closer look of what he was up against.

He turned the ignition, released the handbrake and started to drive off.

Now he'd had the hand job he could release the handbrake and concentrate on the job at hand.

No. Keep it simple.

He'd had the hand job so he could concentrate on the job at hand.

Brilliant.

Agent Darcy flipped open his phone. His stare never wavered from Rebecca's old apartment building.

"Darcy," he said.

"Scott," said Mills. "It's Paul Mills again. He shown up yet?"

"Not yet."

"Okay, good. He's due there within the hour."

"Okay."

"I've got the go-ahead from Benson to intercept him."

"How much force can I use?"

"As little as possible," said Mills. "We don't have anything on him yet. We might be able to argue in a court that we've accrued enough statistical evidence to warrant questioning. So if he resists, you're within your rights to try to restrain him. But you can only get more physical than that if he throws the first punch."

"Got it," said Darcy. "Consider him intercepted."

TEN MINUTES LATER

Rebecca plugged the hands-free into the phone.

"It's all right, Chewie," she said. "We're going to take you to the nice vet and she'll make sure you're all okay."

Chewie, curled in a ball in the front passenger seat, thumped his tail.

"And, if we're lucky," she said. "Daddy will make his phone call on time and the universe won't be destroyed."

Chewie thumped once more at this notion.

"Now," she said. "Mummy's going to call Aunt Jodie and fill her in on what's going on."

She flipped the phone and speed-dialled.

Jodie put down the rug and reached for the ringing phone.

She flipped it open. "Hey, Bec."

"I've got some bad news," said Rebecca.

Jodie frowned and turned away from the noise of the markets. "What kind of bad news?"

"Mark might, um, might not make it to the phone call in time."

"What?"

"He's running late."

"Shit," said Jodie. "How is he late? The phone calls are the only time-critical things in his life."

"Chewie had an accident," said Rebecca. "He almost fell over the cliff. Mark had to hold him until I could get back there and help rescue him."

Jodie exhaled. Damn it. There was no arguing with an excuse like that. "Is Chewie okay?"

"I think so," said Rebecca. "I'm taking him to the vet now to make sure."

"When's Mark due at the apartment?"

"I'm not sure," said Rebecca. "Maybe twenty minutes?"

"How long ago did he leave?"

"Ten minutes ago."

"He's trying to get from your place to the apartment in half an hour?"

"Yeah."

Jodie dropped her head. They were screwed. They *were* going to rupture the space-time continuum.

"I hope he took the Ferrari," she said.

EIGHT MINUTES LATER

The stopwatch sat on the Ferrari's dashboard. It flipped over to nine minutes. Mark changed gears and accelerated past a struggling Mazda. He was driving well over the speed-limit. The Mazda woman shook her head at him in disapproval.

"'We will not rupture the space-time continuum'," said Mark

His phone rang. He glanced at the number. Hit the button.

"Jode," he said.

"Rebecca called and said there was a problem. What's going on?"

"We had a mishap with Chewie."

"Yeah. Rebecca said she was on her way to the vet's. Is he okay?"

"He's fine," said Mark. "At least, I think he's fine."

"Where are you?"

"I'm about fifteen minutes away."

"When are you due?"

"Less time than that."

"How much less?"

Mark looked at the stopwatch. It clocked over to eight minutes.

"Seven minutes less."

"Shit."

"Yes."

"This is very bad."

"My foot is to the floor."

"This is very, very bad."

"My pedal is to the metal."

Jodie didn't speak for a few seconds. "It's very bad, Marcus," she eventually said.

"I wasn't going to drop my dog off a cliff."

"I know, I know," said Jodie. "But, y'know. The whole space-time continuum thing."

"I know. 'We will not rupture the space-time continuum'."

"Let's hope not."

"What do you think happens if we do?"

"I don't know. I don't want to think about it. You're just going to have to make it."

Mark looked at the stopwatch again.

"Sure," he said.

ONE MINUTE LATER

Jake's phone rang. He turned off his radio and answered it.

"Mr Campbell," he said.

"Unlock the front door. Clear my path. I'm in a huge hurry."

Jake's brow furrowed. "Of course, sir," he said.

He walked up the steps. Fished the keys out of his pocket. Unlocked the front door.

That was odd, he thought.

In fact, it was quite the day for the odd events. If he wasn't mistaken, there was a man with a yellow tie just down the road, watching him. He'd just been standing around for the past hour or so, trying not to look suspicious.

This, of course, was an incredibly suspicious thing to do.

Jake wasn't sure what the man with the yellow tie was doing, but he didn't like the look of him. *Or* his tie.

He wondered whether the man with the yellow tie had anything to do with Mr Campbell running late.

Perhaps not. But he would still keep an eye on him.

He sat back down and turned the radio on.

Twenty metres up the road, Agent Darcy watched this with interest. He looked at his watch.

What was going on here? Why would the security guard be unlocking the door?

Mills might know. He picked up the phone.

No.

Come on, Scott. They're never going to promote you if you keep running to your superiors every time you have a question. Time to do a little deducing for yourself.

Now, why would the security guard unlock the door?

Because Campbell's forgotten his keys?

No. Because there would be no need to do it now. He could unlock the door when Campbell arrived.

Why would the security guard unlock the door before Campbell arrived?

Because… he wouldn't be able to unlock it later?

Why wouldn't he be able to unlock it later? Maybe the security guard had to leave?

He looked over at the guard. He didn't seem in any hurry to leave. He looked well settled in, listening to the radio.

No.

The guard wasn't in a hurry.

Campbell was in a hurry.

Campbell was running late.

This was perfect. The later he was running, the shorter the time period he needed to detain him.

Excellent.

If he did this right, he might just get himself a promotion.

Andrew saw the Ferrari flying up behind him. One second it was a speck in his rear view mirror. The next, it was right on his tail. It flashed its lights at him, urging him to get out of the overtaking lane.

Wanker.

Andrew looked at his speedometer. He was doing twenty kilometres over the speed-limit as he overtook this Volkswagen. Ferrari wanker must have been doing sixty to seventy kilometres over.

He flashed his lights at him again.

What a dickhead. Andrew eased his foot off the accelerator. The closer you get, the slower I go.

The speedometer inched down toward the speed-limit. He was still overtaking the Volkswagen, which was struggling up the hill. But he was overtaking him within the speed-limit.

Because he was a law-abiding driver.

And Ferrari wanker could just hold his horses for a bit.

Or not.

There was a sudden roar as the Ferrari pulled out into an emergency lane. A squeal as he changed gears. And then he was gone, disappearing into the distance.

What a total wanker. Overtaking in the emergency lane. Where were the cops when you needed them? They'd pulled him over a couple of months back for doing eighty in a sixty zone. It had been perfectly safe. No other cars on the road. And he'd been running late for work. He wasn't just speeding for the hell of it.

But he'd still got himself a ticket and a couple of demerit points.

But here was Ferrari wanker. Trying to break a land speed record. Driving like a maniac.

And not a cop in sight.

With a bit of luck he'd get himself killed.

Jodie looked around the markets. Everybody was oblivious to what was happening. Not surprising, really. They rarely announced the collapse of the space-time continuum over the emergency broadcast system.

She looked at her watch.

Probably another six minutes.

She'd called Richard, who hadn't answered. He'd still be in the car and didn't have his hands-free. She'd left a message, but if he didn't get it soon it might not matter.

A salesperson thrust a kaftan at her. She waved it away. This was no time for kaftans.

She didn't want to call Mark again. He probably had enough on his mind without her distracting chatter.

There was nothing to do.

That was the worst bit.

All she could do was wait for everything to come tumbling down.

The second hand completed another circuit.

Five more minutes.

FIVE MINUTES LATER

Mark's phone rang again. He hit the button.

"Not going to make it," he said.

"How much time?" said Jodie.

Mark glanced at the stopwatch. "Twenty-seven seconds."

"Where are you?"

"Not close enough," he said. "We need to brace ourselves. We *are* going to disrupt the space-time continuum."

"Maybe you should pull over."

"Really?"

"I dunno. But if reality alters around us, you may not want to be in a car doing one hundred and twenty kilometres per hour."

"More like one hundred and sixty," said Mark. "But I see your point."

He braked. Pulled over to the side of the road.

"Maybe it won't be that bad," tried Jodie.

Mark smiled. "We'll find out in six, five, four, three, two, one—"

And the space-time continuum ruptured.

TIME

It felt like somebody was trying to tear his head in two.
The stress came in. The stress went out.
"Nobody lives in that building any more."
"Your friend is in big trouble."

IN MARK'S CAR

MARK CLUTCHED HIS head, screaming.

It felt like somebody was trying to tear his head in two. Brain cell by brain cell.

Jodie's voice came through the phone. "Are you okay?"

The question echoed around his head. Smashing into the newly cleaved brain cells as it did so. Each collision seemed to cause a fresh tear in his skull.

Mark continued to scream.

"Marcus!" yelled Jodie.

Her scream pierced every remaining synapse. Mark stopped screaming. He collapsed, his head smashing into the steering wheel.

There was a pause.

"Marcus?"

IN THE APARTMENT

Several seconds earlier, the universe had protected itself from inconsistency. Three days earlier, Mark Campbell's MessageBank had received a call. The wormhole that connected that MessageBank to Rebecca Tyler's telephone required Mark to be making the call now.

If Mark could not make the call, the universe would supply a version of him that could.

There was a cosmic shudder. It emanated from the phone, dispersing within metres. Nearby quantum particles danced in unlikely formations. Reality flipped one million coins. They all came up heads.

And a different version of Mark appeared, talking into the phone, leaving the message that was received three days ago.

The wormhole was consistent once more.

The universe could relax.

The Other Mark finished his phone call. "—and the share price of Manilla Folder Enterprises will treble. That's it."

Now what?

AT THE MARKETS

Jodie ran to her car. The universe seemed okay. But she was less confident about Mark. That had not been a healthy sounding scream.

She unlocked the door and threw the bags of shopping into the back seat.

Just get on the highway, she told herself. Trace the route he would most likely have taken. He would have been looking for the quickest possible way there.

She turned the ignition and pulled out.

What had he said? He'd been fifteen minutes away eight minutes before he'd been due. That meant he would have been about seven minutes away when he'd pulled over. How fast had he said he'd been driving?

One sixty?

One sixty kilometres per hour was about… um…

One twenty was two kilometres per minute.

One sixty was a third more than that. So, what? Two and two-third kilometres per minute.

Eight kilometres every three minutes.

Sixteen kilometres in six minutes.

Plus another two and two-thirds kilometres for the seventh minute.

He must have pulled over about eighteen to nineteen kilometres short of the apartment.

Which put him where, exactly?

She needed to see the map. She'd pull out the map at the next set of traffic lights.

Until then, she'd redo the arithmetic.

To make sure.

Concentrate on the arithmetic, Jode.

Don't think about that scream.

Let's see.

He'd been fifteen minutes away eight minutes before the time ran out…

ON THE ROAD

Well, well, thought Andrew. Look at that.

There was Ferrari wanker, pulled over on the side of the road. And it looked like he was crying.

He motored past.

That's what happened when you drive like a lunatic. You blow your car up and end up crying into your steering wheel.

And the people who you overtook with your maniac driving eventually get wherever they're going faster anyway.

Andrew beamed as he drove on. He took a final look back at the Ferrari and the dickhead slumped into the steering wheel.

Beautiful.

Sometimes the universe was just a wonderful, magical place.

AT THE APARTMENT

The Other Mark closed and locked the door behind him.

He strolled down the internal set of stairs. Another successful call made, no thanks to his idiot doppelganger. He felt like he should celebrate, but he had a lot to think about. For one thing, how was this universe going to work with two Mark Campbells running around in it?

He opened the external door.

Jake turned, startled, as The Other Mark came through the door. "Sir?"

"Jake," nodded The Other Mark. He couldn't help but grin a little. This was going to freak poor old Jake out.

"How did you…?" He looked up at the door. "Uh, how did, uh… I didn't see you go in," he finally said.

"Not a great thing for a security guard to be admitting," said The Other Mark.

He continued to grin. There was one advantage to this doppelganger thing. It had the opportunity to provide a few laughs. Maybe the two of them could get together and start a magic show or something.

Of course, his doppelganger's unreliability would probably ruin any illusion they attempted. So, that wouldn't work.

"I'm sorry, sir. I don't know what—" He continued to turn and look at the door.

The Other Mark patted him on the shoulder. "Don't sweat it."

ON THE ROAD

Jodie pulled out the map. She used the legend to measure out a five-kilometre increment with her index finger and thumb. She then walked four finger steps from the apartment down the route Mark would have been taking.

He would be just a little further along than her thumb.

Which put him around about, say, Winston Hills.

Assuming she was remembering his speed right.

Assuming he'd more or less kept that speed.

Assuming he'd taken the route she was assuming he'd taken.

The light turned green.

Only one way to find out. She drove on.

TWENTY METRES FROM THE APARTMENT

Shit, shit, shittedy shit.

Agent Darcy couldn't believe what he was seeing.

How had Campbell got past him? There wasn't a back entrance to the building. Or a garage entrance.

And he had not taken his eyes off the front entrance for a second.

Campbell could not have possibly got past him.

And yet, here he was, standing out the front door he'd just exited. Chatting merrily to his security guard.

He must have been on to him somehow. Darcy didn't know how. Or how he got past him even if he was on to him, but the evidence seemed clear-cut.

Mills was going to have his balls for this. And without balls, a promotion seemed less likely than ever.

Shit, shit, shittedy shit.

Maybe he could somehow fix this shambles.

He strode towards Campbell and the guard.

It was time to get some answers.

AT THE VET

Rebecca sat amid the noise. Chewie sat on her lap. More quiet than she'd ever seen him.

She closed her eyes. Took a deep breath. A yoga instructor had once explained to her the importance of breathing.

The importance of breathing? It had seemed pretty self-evident to her. But apparently it could be more than just a way of getting much needed oxygen molecules into one's bloodstream.

A pair of dogs barked at each other.

Rebecca exhaled. She took another breath, deep in her stomach. She visualised breathing in the stress of the day—Chewie's accident, Mark's dash to the apartment, coffee with Andrew.

Breathe out the stress. It's a red cloud leaving your body.

A cat hissed as one of the barking dogs backed up too close to her cage.

Rebecca breathed in again.

The stress came in.

She breathed out. The stress went out.

Chewie seemed okay. Maybe a little shocked. But he was okay.

The stress came in. The stress went out.

Andrew was gone. She'd survived the coffee with the ex-boyfriend. And now he was gone.

The stress came in. The stress went out.

And the space-time continuum hadn't collapsed around them, as far as she could tell. Which meant Mark had made it.

There was no more stress.

Everything was okay.

OUTSIDE THE APARTMENT

The Other Mark saw Agent Darcy approach.

What the fuck was he doing here? He wasn't allowed to bug them any more. And he certainly couldn't hang around the apartments.

He chose to ignore him. There'd be time to deal with this breach later. Right now he needed to bunker down and work out what he was going to do next.

"I'll see you next time, Jake," he said.

"Yes sir," said Jake. He was also keeping one eye on Agent Darcy.

The Other Mark started to walk off. Agent Darcy broke into a trot and intercepted him

"Mark Campbell?" he said.

"What the fuck are you doing?" said The Other Mark. "You know you're not allowed to approach me."

"Sorry?" said Agent Darcy.

And The Other Mark saw it. His idiot doppelganger hadn't even noticed yet that he was under investigation. He was just going blindly about his business, oblivious. He hadn't got the court order. Hadn't secured his legal position. Shit, no wonder he couldn't get to the phone call on time either. He was a joke.

"Just leave me alone," he said. He turned and started to walk away.

Agent Darcy grabbed his shoulder. "Mr Campbell. I have some questions to ask you about your share trans—"

"Get off!" shouted The Other Mark. Who did this guy think he was? Grabbing him like that? He turned and pushed Agent Darcy away. He fell to the ground, landing awkwardly on his elbow.

The Other Mark walked over to him. He bent down and grabbed him by the tie. He leant into his face. "I have not done anything wrong."

He tightened Agent Darcy's tie, pulling it up to choking point. Agent Darcy kicked back, hitting The Other Mark in the groin. He recoiled, wincing.

Jake ran over. "Mr Campbell," he said. "Are you okay?"

Agent Darcy had regained his feet. He loosened his tie and started to walk over.

The Other Mark, stooped over, tried to regain his breath. Bastard, bastard, bastard. He felt in his pocket. He pulled out the gun and pointed it at Agent Darcy, whose eyes widened. He stopped in his tracks.

The Other Mark smiled. "Yeah. Didn't expect me to have a gun, did you?" he said.

Agent Darcy held up his hands. "Whoa," he said. "Stay cool, Mr Campbell."

"You stay cool too," said The Other Mark. He wanted to tell him that he was no longer dealing with the joke version of Mark Campbell. But of course he couldn't begin to explain that. "Just leave me alone," he said instead. "I've done nothing wrong."

He took a deep breath. The sickening nausea of the groin blow swept over him.

He bent over slightly.

Agent Darcy—the idiot—lunged at him, going for the gun.

And, before he knew it, The Other Mark had shot Darcy in the throat. Blood began to flow from the wound. Darcy's eyes widened in horror.

The Other Mark closed them with two more bullets. Darcy slumped to the ground.

There was an infinitely long pause.

The Other Mark looked at his gun. What had he just done?

Until today, this had been the easiest, most boring job of Jake's life. Mr Campbell paid him a lot of money just to stand in front of a building all day.

Nobody ever tried to break in.

So Jake stood. Listening to the radio. For forty-two hours a week.

The shifts sometimes varied, if one of the other guards needed to switch for some reason.

But that was the extent of variation in the job.

Once every week or so, Mr Campbell entered the apartment block for a quarter of an hour. Jake didn't know what he did in there. He didn't need to know. When you get paid as well as he did for doing nothing all day, you're happy to give up being curious.

Boring, easy job.

Until today.

Today had been different. Today had not been boring at all.

First, there had been the yellow tie guy, standing around, watching him. It might have been a coincidence. Might have had nothing to do with anything. But it was the first time he'd ever thought there might actually be a need for a security guard in front of the building. So, that was a little interesting.

The second mildly interesting thing had been Mr Campbell's urgent phone call, demanding the doors be unlocked. Not that interesting, sure. But a variation on the usual routine.

Those two items by themselves would have made today's shift the most interesting shift he'd ever done on this job. Which was fine. A security guard doesn't want an interesting shift.

He especially doesn't want interest in the form of the most recent events.

Mr Campbell's emergence from the building was very troubling. Jake had not seen him go in. There was no back entrance. How could he have possibly got past him?

In the few short moments since Mr Campbell had emerged from the building, Jake had wracked his brains.

He didn't believe he'd been asleep on the job. Or that he'd been distracted in a way that had allowed Mr Campbell to sneak past.

It was possible, of course. Anything was possible. But, if so, it meant his memory was playing large tricks on him. And once you start allowing for that possibility, you have to allow for, well, anything.

Which meant Mr Campbell *hadn't* got past him. He'd been in there all along. Since before Jake's shift. Jake had just begun to wonder why that would have been so when the most interesting, and most troubling, surprise of the day began.

It was a cliché to say these things happen in slow motion. But that was what it was like.

Yellow Tie had approached Mr Campbell. There had been a few words exchanged, then a scuffle. Just as Jake had decided to step forward and help Mr Campbell, time had slowed.

In the first hour or so, Mr Campbell had reached into his jacket and pulled out a gun. At first, Jake hadn't seen what it was, but around the forty-five minute mark, he'd identified it.

Yellow Tie had also recognised it and taken half a step back. As the clock ticked over to the hour mark, he started to raise his hands.

During the second hour, Mr Campbell raised the gun to a shooting height. Yellow Tie started to lift his hands higher. Whatever he'd asked Mr Campbell had gone down poorly. Jake couldn't imagine what kind of question warranted this response, but it was time for him to intervene. He spent the rest of the second hour unclipping his holster. There was no need for him to take his gun out at this stage, but best to have access to it if things got serious.

Jake planned to spend the third hour talking to both parties. Calm it down. Get Yellow Tie out of here. Mr Campbell would have given him a good scare. He'd know not to come back. Then, maybe in the fourth or fifth hour, talk to Mr Campbell. Find out what was going on. Progress from there.

About five minutes into the third hour, he abandoned this plan. Yellow Tie had lunged at Mr Campbell. He, in turn, had begun to squeeze the trigger.

Serious shit was about to go down.

Half an hour later he finished squeezing. The bullet came out and hit Yellow Tie in the throat. He went down.

An hour or so later, Mr Campbell was shooting him twice more and Jake had his own gun out.

Time returned to its regular speed.

The Other Mark stooped down. He rolled Darcy over. The roll made Darcy twitch a little. Just excess reflex nerves. He wasn't coming back from this.

From behind him came Jake's voice. "Sir! Drop your weapon immediately."

The Other Mark didn't respond. How was he going to get out of this? He hadn't meant to kill the idiot. Why on Earth had he lunged at him like that?

This was not going to be a good day.

Jake's voice came again. "Sir! Drop your weapon immediately."

The Other Mark turned his head slowly. He looked at Jake, who had his gun out. He wasn't even shaking. Impressive.

Things were not going to plan. Unless he fixed this mess quickly, he was looking at a lifetime in prison.

But how? It was difficult to undo a dead Federal Agent.

"Sir!!"

Got it. The Other Mark let a slow smile spread over his face. "Jake," he said. "Remember who employs you."

"Sir. Drop your gun." His voice didn't waver either.

They'd hired well. Jake was cool in a crisis.

"Fine, fine," said The Other Mark. He dropped his gun. Jake stepped slowly over. He picked up The Other Mark's gun and stepped back.

"Now stand up. Slowly," he said.

The Other Mark didn't do so.

"I said 'stand up!'" repeated Jake.

The Other Mark continued not to do so. Instead he grabbed Darcy's gun. He turned and shot Jake in the shoulder. Jake reeled back. He let off a shot. It missed by a long way. The Other Mark steadied himself and shot Jake in the left eye. Jake fell down. The Other Mark made sure of it again with two more bullets.

"And I said, 'remember who employs you'," said The Other Mark.

He shot Jake once more.

This was a mess. He scanned the area. There were no obvious witnesses. But that didn't mean there wouldn't be. A couple of dead bodies in the street would soon attract a crowd.

Still, he'd had no choice. When you're sitting on a goldmine like this phone, you had to be ruthless in protecting it. Sure, this was a mess.

But he could clean it up. Jake was now gone, so nobody need trace him to Yellow Tie's murder. A little bit more work and he might just get out of this cleanly.

He put Agent Darcy's gun back in his hand. He moved over to Jake, where he picked up the two guns Jake had been holding. He also fished through Jake's pockets for keys.

Looking from side to side, he quickly wiped the fingerprints off his own gun. He put it back in Jake's dead hand. He then put Jake's gun in his own pocket and strode down the alley to where Jake always parked his four wheel drive.

He didn't notice the old woman looking out the window as he left.

ON THE ROAD

Andrew took another glance at the map. Not the next left, but the one after that. Then a right, and he was there.

He looked back up. There was a four-wheel drive coming the other way. Andrew locked eyes with the driver for a second.

Something nagged at him. The driver looked familiar. Where did he know him from? Andrew frowned, trying to work it out.

As the cars passed, the four wheel drive driver bugged his eyes out in a 'quit staring at me' face. He made sure the message was clear by mouthing an additional 'fuck off'.

Andrew looked away and drove on.

So many dickheads on the road today.

ALSO ON THE ROAD

Jodie drove down the road. He had to be somewhere around here. She looked from side to side. One positive—the whole disrupting the space-time continuum didn't seem as bad as everybody always made out. Everybody else was going about their business happily. Now, if she could just make sure Mark was okay, they might get out of this unsca—

There he was. She braked and pulled over behind where Mark was slumped over his car wheel.

She got out and ran over to him. She opened the door.

"Marcus?"

No response. She shook him. Still no response.

She leant over and undid his seatbelt.

What to do now?

It was times like these when she wished she had some first aid knowledge.

And, of course, just wishing it made it so. No time to wallow in bad choices. She just had to do her best with the knowledge she had.

She shook him again.

Still no response.

OUTSIDE THE APARTMENT

Andrew pulled the car to a halt. What on Earth was going on here? A small crowd had gathered on the footpath outside the apartment block. People were screaming and crying.

One man was vomiting in a garbage bin.

He looked at the address he had written down again. This was the right place.

He parked the car and clambered out.

Walked over to where the crowd had gathered. He pushed his way through.

"What's going o—"

The question didn't get a chance to finish. It was obvious what was going on. A couple of men were lying on the footpath. Dead.

Blood was everywhere.

Andrew looked away. This was fucked up. And just outside Rebecca's apartment, too. What was going on here? What kind of neighbourhood was she living in?

He looked back at the body of what seemed to be a security guard.

Blood trickled out of his eye.

That was enough for him. He ran to a nearby bush and threw up his doughnuts.

ON THE ROAD

Jodie opened Mark's car door.

She needed to drag him to her car so she could get him to the hospital.

The fact that he was twenty-five kilograms heavier than her was going to make this a challenge. It would have been a lot easier if *she* was the one passed out.

And, once more, wishing made it so.

She hooked her arms under his armpits, took a deep breath and hauled him out of the car.

He hit the ground with a thud. Maybe it would wake him up?

Nope.

She dragged him over to her car. God. He was heavier then he looked.

She opened her passenger door. Raced around to the driver's side where she crawled over the driver's seat to the passenger seat. With one final grunt, she lifted him into the passenger seat.

She exited via the driver's side and made her way back round to the passenger's side. She lifted his feet into the car, seatbelted him in and closed her door.

Did it.

As she raced around to the driver's side, a four-wheel drive roared past. Jodie jerked her head around. There was something… She couldn't place her finger on it.

She climbed in and took off.

Jodie!

That had been Jodie back at that car.

And that was his—or his doppelganger's—Ferrari.

He looked in the rear view mirror. Jodie's head had followed him as he went past. He didn't think she'd recognised him, but she'd definitely sensed him somehow.

Having both he and the doppelganger in the same universe at the same time was a problem. A problem he needed to fix.

Still, plenty of time for that later.

It was strange. He knew he was the interloper in the universe. He didn't know how he knew that. But he knew it. He had his own past, his own reality in which he'd also used the time-travelling MessageBank to make his millions.

The difference was that he never missed a phone call.

Did he still exist in that reality? Or had he been pulled out of there, into this reality to fix his idiot doppelganger's fuckup?

Who the hell knew? He was in this reality now. He was going to have to make the most of it.

But the continuing existence of his doppelganger could well be the key to sorting out the problem of Jake and the dead Federal Agent.

ALSO ON THE ROAD

As Jodie drove to the nearest hospital, she hit a speed dial button on her phone.

Rebecca answered. "Did he make it in time?" she said.

"No."

"Really?" said Rebecca. "I thought that if he didn't make it, the universe would blow up or something."

"I guess not."

"So did anything bad happen?"

"To the universe? No."

There was a pause. "To Mark?"

Jodie took a breath. "I don't know. He's in the car with me right now."

"Is he okay?"

"I think so," said Jodie. "He's had some kind of seizure."

"Seizure?!"

"It's okay. Don't panic. I'm taking him to the hospital now. He's— He's unconscious. That's all I know."

Rebecca paused. Gave Chewie an extra hug. "Okay," she said.

"How soon can you get here?"

"Um, I think Chewie's next. I don't think it will take long. Say, an hour?" she said. "Do you need me there sooner?"

"No, it should be okay. I'll keep you updated."

Jodie hung up. Police cars flew past the other way. Something was up. She looked down at Mark.

"I've got a bad feeling about this, Marcus."

OUTSIDE THE APARTMENT

Andrew went to open the door of the apartment block. Locked.

"Nobody lives there," came an old woman's voice.

"What?" said Andrew.

"Nobody lives in that building any more."

"My friend lives in that building."

"Afraid not," said the woman. "Nobody lives there any more."

"The entire building is empty?"

"I'm afraid so," said the woman. "They booted everybody out… oh, must be six months or so ago now."

Of course. Rebecca didn't live here any more. Rebecca used to live here. Before she met Captain Dipshit. She just hadn't updated her driver's licence since then. Shit. This had been a waste of time.

The old lady was still talking. As old ladies tended to do. "Refunded everybody a year's worth of rent to end their leases."

"What?" Andrew hadn't been listening to the old bat.

"I say, when the young lass and her beau bought out the place, they gave everybody a year's worth of rent to encourage them to end their lease."

Young lass? "That's very… generous," said Andrew.

"They'd won the Lotto a while earlier."

Of course they had. How did this all tie together? Why on Earth had Captain Dipshit used his Lotto winnings to buy out Rebecca's apartment? Was he some kind of control freak? And why would he evict all the tenants? That didn't make much business sense. You invest in property to rent the thing out. You don't invest it to kick everybody who lives there out.

"Do you know where they live now?" said Andrew. "The girl and her, uh, beau?"

"They did say," said the woman. "Where was it now? He comes back now and then you know."

"Comes back?"

"Just for a half-hour visit."

Andrew peered at her. "Why?"

"Hmmm?"

"Why would he come back to an empty block of apartments?"

"Couldn't rightly tell you," said the old woman. "But he does." She scratched her chin hair in thought.

"Muriel will remember where they moved to," said the woman. "I'll just go ask."

"Thank you." Andrew sighed. What was going on here? This guy was a nut job. Oh, Rebecca, what had you got yourself into?

Maybe Rebecca had a beef with somebody in the apartment and kicking them out was payback? And Dipshit came back to, what? Make sure they hadn't moved back in?

That didn't make any sense at all. She'd moved away. Why did she care who lived there after she was gone?

Andrew looked over at the dead security guard.

What had he been guarding? He looked around. There was nothing on this street that needed a security guard.

He looked back at the locked door on the apartment building.

Why had they moved everybody out of the building?

Why did Captain Dipshit return here regularly?

Why did they have a security guard guarding the building?

Why had a man in a yellow tie killed the security guard?

What, in short, was going on here?

AT THE HOSPITAL

Jodie pulled up at the hospital. She leapt out of the car. Ran to the Emergency entrance. A nurse looked up at her.

"My friend. He needs help," said Jodie.

"What's the problem?" said the nurse.

"He's had some kind of seizure. He's in the car. Hurry."

The nurse did not hurry. She shuffled out from behind her counter.

"O'Donnell!" she yelled.

No response.

"O'Donnell!" she yelled again.

A stout nurse emerged.

"Help this woman," ordered the original nurse.

"It's my friend. He needs help," said Jodie. "This way."

She ran back to the car. O'Donnell ambled after her.

O'Donnell looked in at Mark, sprawled unconscious in the passenger seat. She opened the door. Called Jodie around to help.

The pair of them dragged Mark into the hospital.

After several long minutes of heated debate with the original nurse, O'Donnell eventually secured a bed. She and Jodie pulled Mark on to it and O'Donnell gave him a quick examination.

"I'll be back in a second," she said.

"We'll be here."

OUTSIDE THE APARTMENT

Where had the old biddy gone? Andrew peered through the crowd. Police were everywhere now, questioning everybody. They probably wouldn't let him leave, making today a total write-off.

But if he found the old woman and her friend he might at least be able to get some clue to where Rebecca had moved.

He looked at the door of the building again. His curiosity was killing him. What was inside this building that made it so special? If it weren't for all the police, he'd be tempted to break a window and sneak in.

Maybe some other time. Perhaps when there were fewer corpses around. He looked around again for the old woman.

There. There she was. Over on the far side, behind a set of news reporters setting up cameras.

He strolled over to her. She was talking to another old woman. No doubt the one who knew where Rebecca had moved to. The other old woman was pale.

"Hello," he said.

The original old woman looked up. "Oh, sorry, love. I was going to get back to you, wasn't I?"

Yes you were, you silly senile old bat. "Yes," he said instead. "Is everything okay here?" He beamed.

"Not really," said the original old woman. "Muriel's had a bit of a shock."

Andrew looked around. "I think we've all had a bit of a shock. This is hardly an everyday event."

"No, it's not that," said the original old woman. "Muriel saw the shooting take place. She saw it all from her kitchen window."

Andrew's eyes widened. "Really?" he said. "We need to get you talking to the police. Did you see who did it?"

"That's the thing, dear," said the original old woman. "It was your friend."

"Rebecca?" said Andrew. His stomach dropped.

"No," said Muriel. "Mark."

His stomach dropped even further.

"Let's get you over to the police."

AT THE HOSPITAL

Significantly more than a second later, O'Donnell returned. Jodie could not resist glancing at her watch.

"How is he?" said O'Donnell.

"Aren't you supposed to tell me that?"

O'Donnell did not find this amusing. "So no change?" she said.

"No."

"Okay. Fill these in," she said. She handed Jodie some paperwork. "The doctor will be with you shortly."

"I'm sure."

O'Donnell left. Jodie peered down at the paperwork and sighed.

AT THE VET

Rebecca and Chewie were having more luck. They had made their way in to see the vet. She was examining the scratches on Chewie's stomach.

Rebecca's phone rang. She picked it up and saw the display read 'Mark'.

"Babe?" she said.

In Jake's four-wheel drive, The Other Mark responded. "Hi babe," he said. "Where are you?"

"I'm still at the vet's. Where are you?"

"I'm on my way to pick you up."

Rebecca hesitated. "Really?" she said. "I thought Jodie was taking you to the hospital."

The Other Mark paused. "She was," he said. "I got better."

"Really?" said Rebecca. She didn't know what to make of that news. Half an hour or so ago he was unconscious, having a seizure on the way to the hospital. And now he was on his way to pick her up? That was some recovery.

"Sure. Can't keep a good man down."

"Are you sure you're okay?" said Rebecca. "Jodie was worried about you. She said you needed to see a doctor."

"Nah," said The Other Mark. "Jodie was just being a worrywart. And you know how I can't abide warts that worry. Any kind of fretting skin blemishes really."

He *sounded* like his usual self. "Okay. Well, that's… great," said Rebecca. "It looks like Chewie's going to be okay, too. So—"

"Chewie's okay?" Rebecca could hear the delight in his voice.

"Sure. He's had a bit of a scare and he's got some cuts and bruises. But he'll be fine."

"That's fucking brilliant news. I'll pick you up in fifteen, twenty minutes."

The 'fucking' took Rebecca aback slightly. Not that Mark was averse to swearing—he just tended not to drop it so casually into a sentence. He must have been more worried about Chewie than he'd let on. "I can just meet you at home if you like."

"Nah," said The Other Mark. "I'll pick you up."

"Okay. See you soon."

AT JODIE AND RICHARD'S HOUSE
Ahhhh… brilliant.

Richard sat back. How could Jodie possibly hate *Blackadder*? The show was pure, unmitigated brilliance.

He ejected the DVD and switched the input back to television. He tried not to be annoyed by the fact he needed three remote controls to do this.

Now what? How much longer was his humourless wife going to be? What on Earth could she still be doing at the markets? There wasn't that much to see there. Was there? Surely it was all just table after table of pointless crap you'd sit on a bookshelf for three years before throwing out?

How looking through that was more attractive than watching the genius of Atkinson, Fry, Laurie, and the rest was beyond him.

He could call her.

Engh. Why bother? Let her browse her bric-a-brac in peace.

Besides, this was a perfect opportunity for him to conquer the world.

He pulled out his laptop and fired up his game.

As always, he asked the computer to select a nation randomly.

It chose the Bantu.

Bantu? How was he supposed to conquer the world as the Bantu?

Better knuckle down to it.

"—Mark Campbell—"

Richard lifted his head. He turned it to the television. On his laptop, the marauding Mayans butchered several of his peasants. Damn it. He paused the game.

There was a news report on the television. Reporters. Police. Onlookers.

They'd said something about Mark. Which was strange. Mark was not a newsworthy individual.

Probably a different one. It wasn't the least common name in the world.

On the other hand… He peered at the background of the news report. Was that Rebecca's old apartment building? It looked like it.

What was going on here? The reporter had been prattling about 'senseless tragedies' and 'police cordoning off the area' but hadn't yet mentioned what had happened. Or, if she had done so, he'd been too busy rallying the Bantu to have noticed.

"Just repeating, a security guard and a federal police officer have been shot dead on a leafy suburban street—"

Richard turned the laptop off and the television sound up.

AT THE HOSPITAL

Back at the hospital, Jodie completed the final form. She picked it up and scanned through each box. Didn't want to miss anything and have the idiot hospital bureaucracy make her start again or something.

Maybe they charged by the minute. Maybe all the paperwork was just a scam to keep them trapped here as long as possible.

Her phone rang. It was Richard.

"Hi babe," she said.

"Hi," he said. "Sorry. I only just got your message. Where are you?"

"I'm in the hospital with Mark. We're planning to spend eternity in here, waiting for doctors and filling in paperwork."

"Is there a television in there?"

"No." She paused. "Why?"

"You should find one and turn it on," said Richard. "Your friend is in big trouble."

CHAPTER EIGHT

"This is Muriel Moore. The witness."

"Who is this really?"

"Forgot to turn mine off."

"My head is killing me."

AT THE HOSPITAL

"WHAT DO YOU mean?" said Jodie.

"Do you have a television set there?" asked Richard.

"I'm sure I can find one."

"Turn it to Channel Nine."

"Can't you just tell me what's on there?" said Jodie.

"There's been a shooting outside the apartments. The police want to speak to Mark about it."

Jodie recoiled from the phone a little. "What?"

"I think somebody shot Jake. And I think the police think Mark did it."

"But that's crazy. He's in hospital here with me."

"I know. But, are you sure—"

"He didn't even make it to the apartments," said Jodie.

"Okay."

"He passed out fifteen kilometres away."

"Okay," said Richard again. "I'm just giving you a heads up. Turn on the television. See for yourself. The police are looking for him. It may be simplest if you just called them and told them what you just told me."

"I'll get a doctor to look at him, first. That should occur in about a year and a half. Then I'll talk to the police."

"Okay," said Richard. "Just… be careful."

"Of what?" said Jodie. "It's Marcus! He didn't shoot anybody."

"I know," said Richard. "Just humour me and be careful anyway, okay?"

"Fine. I'll be careful."

ON THE ROAD

Agent Mills stared out the window. The two of them had been driving in silence for what seemed like half an hour. And every minute of silence made it that much harder to break the next minute.

But eventually he could stand it no more.

"Do you think it was Campbell?" asked Mills.

"We'll soon find out," said Benson.

Agent Mills exhaled. "Well, obviously," he said. "But do you think it was him?"

Agent Benson turned his head slowly to look at Agent Mills, who glanced quickly off the road to meet his eye. "Yeah," said Benson. "It was him. Who else would it be?"

Agent Mills sighed and took the next left. "I sent Scott to his death," he said.

"No. You sent Agent Darcy to question a man suspected of share market manipulation." Agent Benson stared out the window. "Mark Campbell sent Scott to his death."

Agent Mills nodded. "You're right."

"And Mark Campbell is going to pay for it."

Agent Mills nodded again, as he turned the corner on to the street. Almost there now. "You're right," he said. "He is going to pay for it."

OUTSIDE THE APARTMENT

Andrew leant against the pole, frustrated. He didn't want to be here any longer. He knew everything he needed to know.

Well, almost everything.

He knew Rebecca—the one woman he'd ever loved—was involved with a murderer.

He knew that he had to save her from him.

What he didn't know, of course, was where to find her.

And the two old bags who did have that information were being badgered by a couple of badges.

Huh. Good one.

Badgered by badges.

Another one for Trev.

Even if he'd known where to find her, the police weren't letting him leave until they questioned him as well. Which was stupid. He'd arrived long after the shootings had taken place. He had zero information to offer them.

He looked around again at the locked door of the apartment building. The locked door of the empty apartment building.

So, okay. He didn't quite have zero information to offer the police. He knew about the Lotto win. And the fact they'd bought this apartment block. And that they'd evicted all the tenants. And that Captain Dipshit—sorry, Captain Murderous Dipshit—visited the place once a week for reasons unknown.

So he didn't have zero information.

He just had zero useful information.

He looked over at the police talking to the old bats. They were still badgering away.

The badges weren't budging on their badgering.

Heh.

Another good one.

Unfortunately, his brilliant puns weren't going to rescue Rebecca from the man responsible for all of… this.

He sighed.

Rebecca, where are you?

AT THE VET

The Other Mark pulled up. He leapt out of Jake's four wheel drive and ran to the door. He opened it, which rang the bell attached to it.

Rebecca was at the counter paying the bill. She heard the door open and turned. When she saw him, she abandoned the desk and the bill-paying, ran over to him and hugged him. She kissed him hard on the lips.

The Other Mark kissed back. God, her lips. Her mouth. It felt so good to taste her. Smell her. Feel her. He rubbed one hand through her hair before the kiss broke off.

"You're all right!" she said.

"Never been better." He smiled. This was true. He felt fantastic, alive. There was something about this version of his life that felt so much better, so much more *right*, than his reality.

Which was weird, right? Y'know, for what one usually expected when jumping from one version of reality to another.

It had to be Rebecca. He ran his eyes over her again, smiling. She was just stunning. Bright in every sense of the word. Not just with her intelligence. But also in the way she radiated pure sunniness and joy.

Any reality that contained Rebecca in his life was a good reality to be in.

"I was so worried," said Rebecca. "I wasn't sure whether you'd make it."

"I made it," he said.

"You must have driven like a maniac."

The Other Mark smiled some more. "Yeah."

He kissed her again. Then kissed harder. Chewie, leashed back at the desk, growled at them.

"Somebody's jealous," said the vet's assistant.

The Other Mark looked up. "I'm sure you'll find somebody some day," he said. "Have you tried internet dating?"

The vet's assistant stared at him, a puzzled expression across her face. Rebecca shot him a look.

"Ignore him," said Rebecca, returning to the desk. "It's the only way to deal with the more inane of his remarks."

"I meant Chewie," said the assistant, in case clarification was still necessary.

"Of course," said The Other Mark. He was now just a step away from Chewie, who continued to growl. "Chewie? What's the matter, buddy?"

He went to scratch Chewie's head.

He growled again.

"Chewie. No," said Rebecca. She signed the Visa receipt and turned back to The Other Mark.

Chewie was still growling. The Other Mark had his hand's raised in a 'what's all this, then?' gesture.

"He's probably still in shock," said the vet's assistant. "He's had a scary day."

"I know how he feels," said The Other Mark.

Rebecca walked over to Chewie. He thumped his tail hard. She picked up his leash.

"Oh, sure," said The Other Mark. "He doesn't growl at *you*."

"I am the one who initiated the rescue. You just dangled him from a cliff for an hour."

The Other Mark grunted.

"I'm kidding," said Rebecca. "It's a joke." She turned to the assistant. "Mark saved Chewie from going over the cliff. He held on to him until I showed up."

"I heard," said the assistant. "You're quite the hero."

"Tell that to him," said The Other Mark.

"He may just be associating you with the fall," said the assistant. "If you were the only one there, he may be projecting all the fear on to you."

"Well, that's not very bright," said The Other Mark.

"Chewie's never been the brightest dog," said Rebecca. "Fast, sure. Good at catching? You bet. Kissy? Right up there on the all-time smoocher list. But there are smarter dogs out there."

The Other Mark looked hard at Chewie. He couldn't possibly know. He was identical to this world's Mark Campbell. More identical than an identical twin. He was, in effect, the same person. Just a little more reliable when it came to phone calls, that's all.

He didn't care how finely tuned a dog's senses were, there was no possible way he could detect a difference between this world's Mark and him. The vet's assistant must be right. It must be something to do with bad associations from the fall. Chewie would be behaving the same way with his doppelganger.

That was the only explanation that made sense. It didn't make sense for Chewie to have some kind of—what?—inter-universal ability to detect which owner was his owner, and which was a perfect replica from another reality.

And, of course, it made even less sense for Chewie to somehow know how he was here. To know that, in The Other Mark's reality, he'd made the phone call only because, faced with Chewie, the cliff and time running out, he'd made the tough decision.

He'd chosen to let go of Chewie.

OUTSIDE THE APARTMENT

Mills and Benson did their best to ignore the news crews. It wasn't easy. They were multiplying by the minute.

They saw Agent Darcy's body and the security guard's cordoned off.

"Oh, Scott," said Agent Mills. "How did this happen?"

Agent Benson stood silently, staring at the corpses.

A police officer approached them, with an old woman.

"Agent Mills? Agent Benson?" said the police officer.

They turned. "Yes," said Mills.

"This is Muriel Moore. The witness."

"Hello," said Agent Benson, standing up. "I'm Agent Benson from the Federal Police. How are you, Mrs Moore?"

"Miss."

"My apologies."

She nodded. "I'm… I'm a bit shaken up, to be honest, Agent Benson," she said.

Agent Mills had now stood up as well. "I can understand that, Miss Moore," he said. "This is an awful turn of events. I'm Agent Mills."

She nodded again. "Hello. Yes, it's heartbreaking," she said. "As I was saying to Officer King here, it's like a bad dream. I keep hoping I wake up from it soon, but somehow I don't think I will, will I?"

"I'm afraid not," said Agent Mills.

"I used to see Jake all the time. Sometimes I'd bring him muffins."

Agent Mills looked at Agent Benson. Jake?

"Jake was the other victim?" said Agent Benson.

Muriel started to nod, then started to quiver, before starting to sob.

This was going to take some time.

AT THE VET

"Give him time," said the assistant. "He'll soon be back to the old Chewie."

Chewie continued to growl at The Other Mark. Come on, Chewie. No need to hold a grudge. You weren't even dropped in this reality. All's well that ends well.

"Let's hope so," said Rebecca.

"Are we done here?" said The Other Mark.

"Sure," said Rebecca. She put her copy of the receipt in her purse.

"Then let's go."

The pair of them left the vet and headed for the car park. Chewie continued to eye The Other Mark. Rebecca made her way to her car. The Other Mark grabbed her arm and pulled her over to Jake's four wheel drive.

"My car's just here," said Rebecca.

"No," said Mark. "It's not safe."

"Safe?"

"Not safe."

"Like 'dangerous'?"

"Exactly."

"Are you really okay?"

"One hundred percent."

"Really? Jode said something about a seizure."

"Engh," said Mark. "Seizures are overrated."

"Always suspected as much," she said. "So why isn't my car 'safe'? And where, for that matter, is your car?"

"It's a long story," said The Other Mark. "I'll explain as we go."

He unlocked the door of the four wheel drive.

"Whose car is this?"

"I'll explain that too. But let's go." He leant over to pick up Chewie, who began to bark.

"Chewie!!" yelled Rebecca. "No!"

"Bad boy!" said Mark.

"Don't yell at him," said Rebecca. "He's still in shock. I'll get him." She bent down and picked Chewie up.

Her phone rang.

"I've got it babe," said The Other Mark. He reached a hand into her bag. Chewie continued to growl. The Other Mark glared at him. Quit it!

He fished out the ringing phone and noted the number. "Jode!" he said.

"Who's this?" said Jodie.

"It's me," said The Other Mark. "Marcus."

AT THE HOSPITAL

Back at the hospital, Jodie took her eyes from the communal television set and poked her head back around the corner. Mark was still asleep on the bed.

"Who is this really?" she said. This was not the time for pranks, even if he did sound exactly like him.

"You're right," said The Other Mark. "I'm going to get Rebecca to safety and then we'll give you a call once we're there."

What? What was he babbling about? Who was this guy? What was Rebecca doing with him?

"Where's Rebecca?" said Jodie. "What's going on?"

"You too. Speak soon."

He hung up. Jodie looked at the phone.

This was incredibly odd.

She looked back up at the television. Reporters continued to speculate on the incident.

OUTSIDE THE APARTMENT

"So I understand you saw the incident?" said Agent Mills.

"Every terrible second of it," said Muriel. "It happened so fast… but also so slowly." She gave a hollow laugh. "That doesn't make sense, does it?"

"It makes perfect sense," said Agent Mills. He put a hand on her shoulder. "That's just how our minds process terrible moments like this."

Benson pulled out a series of photos of Mark taken in front of the building. He showed them to her. "Was this the man who shot Agent Darcy and, uh, Jake?"

Muriel looked it over. She nodded and started to cry again. "Yes," she said. "It was Mark." The tears became stronger. "I don't understand why he'd do such a thing. He's always been such a pleasant young man."

"We're going to find out why he did it," said Agent Mills. "And then we're going to lock him away so he can never do it again."

"Thank you," came a gruff voice. "That's all we need."

Mills and Benson turned to the voice. It came from a large, suited man, with flecks of grey in his hair. He put a finger up to silence Mills' and Benson's questions, before putting the finger in his ear.

"We have eyewitness confirmation on Campbell," he said. "Yes. Thank you." His gaze returned to Mills and Benson.

"Can we help you?" said Agent Mills

"Agent Benson?" said the man.

"I'm Mills."

"Fine," he said. "I'm Federal Agent Innes. I'm taking over this investigation."

"What?" said Agent Benson. "This is our case. We've been tracking this guy for months."

"This is no longer a share market scam," explained Innes. "It's a double homicide. One of whom is a Federal Police Officer. You two can go home. It's time for the big boys to take over."

"I'm not going home," said Agent Mills.

But Innes had already lost interest. He put his finger to his ear again as he walked away. "Innes," he said.

Watching all this with ever-growing interest was Andrew.

AT THE VET

Rebecca finished strapping Chewie into the back of the car and made her way to the passenger door. She opened it and climbed in.

"Was that Jodie?" she said.

"Yeah," said The Other Mark. "We should probably keep the phones off for a while now." He turned it off and gave it back to Rebecca.

Rebecca put it in her purse. "What is going on, Mark?"

"Once we're driving," he replied.

"You're enjoying being Mister Mysterious, aren't you?"

The Other Mark grinned. "It has its moments."

"Fine. Be mysterious. I'm just going to admire the beautiful scenery of this wonderful country." She emphatically stared out the window.

The Other Mark smiled some more. He turned the key, put the four wheel drive in gear and pulled out.

AT THE HOSPITAL

Jodie quickly grew tired of watching the reporters speculate the same things over and over. She ran the phone call to Rebecca over in her mind, trying to make sense of who could possibly have answered.

Was Rebecca having an affair? It didn't seem possible. She was clearly besotted with Mark. After all, somebody had to be. And, anyway, why would some fling guy be answering her phone and pretending to be Mark? That wasn't the way to avoid getting caught.

Maybe they didn't care about being caught. Maybe it was all over and she was leaving Mark? But that was crazy, wasn't it? Just a few weeks after getting engaged, she moves on to somebody else? That wasn't the way the world worked.

But if she wasn't having an affair, who was the guy who answered? And why would he pretend to be Mark?

Maybe it was somebody at the vet's? And, by coincidence, his name was also Mark?

Which didn't explain the familiarity with which he spoke with Jodie, nor his gibberish about 'getting Rebecca to safety'.

Something very curious was going on.

But it was pointless to speculate on it. She had nowhere near enough information to unravel this. She'd just call Rebecca back and ask her.

She speed-dialled her.

"Hi, you've found Rebecca. I'm getting married! Leave a message."

Jodie hung up. "Shit," she said. She'd turned her phone off.

But that message wasn't the message of a woman unhappy with her engagement. Quite the opposite.

It was safe to rule out an affair.

But, in that case, who was that man?

Jodie sighed and looked up at the television set again. The reporter there was repeating the grim story.

"Authorities are searching for the owner of the building, who they hope might be able to help them with their enquiries. Just repeating, an undercover Federal Police Officer and a local security guard have been brutally slain—"

Jodie turned away. She went back to Mark's room.

This was very bad.

OUTSIDE THE APARTMENT

Andrew finished talking to the police. He'd been forthcoming, but hadn't told them anything of any real use. He'd told them his name, but not how he was related to Rebecca (and, hence, how he was related to Captain Murderous Dipshit). And not what he knew about the building.

Nothing.

It wasn't going to help them. It was just going to confuse matters and raise a whole heap of questions about why he was here.

As far as they knew, he was just a passer-by. A passer-by who hadn't passed by, but had, instead, stopped. A stopper-by.

Besides, they'd learn all about the empty apartment block whenever they talked to the old bats. Heck, they may have already known. No need for him to drag the glare of the spotlight on to himself by telling them weird stuff they already knew.

He was just a stopper-by.

Once they'd finished with him, he headed back to his car.

There wasn't much else to do. After speaking again with the old bat, he now knew where Captain Murderous Dipshit and Rebecca lived, but then, so did the police. He had nothing more to offer.

He passed the three detectives who'd shown up on the scene. Two of them were scowling in the background, muttering to each other. The older one, standing in front of them, dialling a phone, had clearly usurped them. Andrew got the impression they weren't happy about it.

Maybe this was a way in.

ON THE ROAD

The Other Mark's phone rang. He turned to Rebecca and flashed a sheepish grin. "Forgot to turn mine off," he said.

He fished it out of his pocket. Without even looking at who was calling, he turned it off.

Now they could drive in peace.

AT THE HOSPITAL

Jodie leant over and grabbed Mark's ringing phone. The number was not one she recognised.

"Hello?" she said. "Mark Campbell's phone."

"Who is this?" said Agent Innes.

"Who are you?" replied Jodie.

"I'm Federal Agent Innes. I'm looking for Mister Campbell."

Jodie glanced at Mark, unconscious in the bed. "Mark's not available right now," she said. "Can I help?"

"Can you tell me where he is?"

"Why do you want to know?"

She already knew why he wanted to know.

"Mr Campbell is wanted for questioning over the double homicide that took place in front of one of his blocks of apartments an hour or so ago. If you know his whereabouts then it is a—"

But Jodie had already hung up. Yep. That was why he wanted to know all right.

Shit, shit, shit. She heard Richard's voice in her head, urging her to co-operate with the police, but she was beginning to get an inkling of what was going on. And co-operating with the police could well end with her friend spending the rest of his life in prison.

Of course, fleeing from the police wasn't exactly a sure-fire method for retaining freedom, but until she got her head around what was going on, she was going to make sure she laid low.

She ran down the hospital hall.

Her thoughts on what was going on were insane. Impossible.

But no more so than an answering machine that sent phone messages back in time.

And once you allowed an answering machine that sent phone messages back in time into your world view, you had to allow other insane and impossible possibilities in there as well.

It's just these other possibilities seemed a lot less profitable.

There. A wheelchair. Exactly what she was looking for. She stopped and peered around. Nobody was using the wheelchair. Nobody was here to see her take it. So it was hers.

She grabbed it and wheeled it briskly back to Mark's room.

"Time to go," she said.

She pushed the wheelchair over to the side of the bed. She scooped her arms under Mark's armpits and dragged him toward the chair.

He was so heavy. Just a total lump of dead weight.

She was starting to develop a new sense of respect for nurses.

Not the ones in this hospital, of course. They didn't seem able to even find one doctor in an entire hospital. But, boy, they made up for their lack of tracking skills with sheer physical strength.

She crashed him into the chair. One leg was draped over the armrest. His head was askew and lolling aimlessly. But his butt was in the seat. And that was good enough for her.

She took a deep breath and straightened him out.

She pushed him down the hall and out of the hospital. Nobody paid her any attention.

ON THE ROAD

"So?" said Rebecca. She'd waited long enough for an explanation about what was going on. It was time for her fiancé to stop acting weird and start filling her in.

Of course, expecting Mark to stop being weird was asking too much. But there was a certain weirdness she adored. And then there was this slight undercurrent of unwelcome weirdness that was currently hanging around.

She didn't know where this extra layer of unwelcome weirdness had come from. But it was time for it to go.

"So what?" said The Other Mark.

"We're driving."

"Ah," said The Other Mark. "This is true. Kinda explains the trees whizzing by."

Dumb jokes. Normal weirdness.

"So what's going on?"

There was a long pause. The Other Mark changed gears with extra force.

Hesitation and unwillingness to talk. Unwelcome new weirdness.

"I'm… not sure," he finally said. "I didn't make the call on time."

"Which is officially 'bad', right?"

"Right. I'm hazy on the details, because I had a bit of a—"

"Seizure?"

And what was with this seizure business? Is that where the extra weirdness came from? Had he bumped his head or something? She was sure it wasn't safe for him to be driving so soon after collapsing. But he seemed adamant about it all.

Weird. Unwelcome weird.

"I suppose so," said The Other Mark. "There was a seizure-like situation when the time ran out."

"Probably something to do with that rupturing space-time continuum."

"Probably. Anyway, it caused some trouble at the apartment."

"Trouble?" said Rebecca. "What kind of trouble?"

"I… I don't know," said The Other Mark. "It's all hazy. I just know it's not good. The police are involved."

Police? "Rupturing the space-time continuum is against the law?" she said.

"It seems so. Let's just get to safety, then reassess from there."

"Sounds like a plan."

There was a pause, while the two of them tried to work out what to say next.

OUTSIDE THE APARTMENT

"I can't believe this," said Mills.

"We had to expect it," said Benson.

"But we're off the case."

"We're off the murder investigation," said Benson. "We're still on the share market manipulation."

Agent Mills snorted. "That's hardly a consolation."

"We need to focus on the things we can control. And the thing we can control is our investigation of Campbell's share market activities."

"Fine," said Mills. He sighed. "Well, I guess it's safe for us to assume now that he is up to no good."

"Probably safe, yeah," said Benson. "You worked out how yet?"

Agent Mills shook his head.

"Terrible business, huh?" came a voice behind them. Both turned to see Andrew, gesturing at the bodies.

The agents straightened ever so slightly, adopting a 'dealing with the public' stance. A virtual wall dropped between them and Andrew.

"Yes," said Benson. "It's a senseless tragedy."

"Worst part of the job," said Mills. He'd never actually been to a scene like this before, but the civilian didn't know that.

"I can imagine," said Andrew. "Sorry, I didn't mean to eavesdrop, but I couldn't help overhear. Did you say this was something to do with a share market scam?"

"We can't discuss investigations in progress," said Benson. They'd now fully established the wall between them and Andrew.

"Of course, of course," said Andrew. "Didn't mean to pry. But if it was just because of a share market scam, then that would be… well, that would be sick, wouldn't it?"

"If it was, it would be," agreed Benson.

"No amount of money could possibly justify… this."

Agent Mills gave a wry smile. "I don't think you're going to find any arguments here," he said. "Agent Darcy—Scott—was our friend." He turned his head away.

"Of course," said Andrew. "I'm sorry. How terrible."

"Did you have any information that might help the investigation, sir?" asked Benson.

Andrew paused.

AT KATRINA'S HOUSE

Katrina sat in front of the television set. Her head slowly shook from one side to the other.

"I knew it," she eventually said. "I fucking knew it."

"What's that?" said Janine, her room-mate. She looked up from the kitchen table where she'd spread various glues, photos and cutting tools.

"I fucking knew it," she repeated. She stood up and ran to her mobile phone. Janine's gaze followed her, before giving up. She wandered over to the television set, looked at it for a moment and then returned to her scrapbooking.

Katrina continued to pay her no attention. She held the phone to her ear. Come on, come on, come on.

"Hi, you've found Rebecca. I'm getting married! Leave a message."

Shit.

Katrina hung up. Looked at the phone. What to do. What to do.

She couldn't believe it. She'd known there was something wrong with Mark from the beginning. But this? She looked back over at the television set. This was beyond her worst nightmares.

Andrew had been bad, but somehow Rebecca had found herself a worse'un. The girl had a gift.

She tried Rebecca's home number. No answer. Just Mark's slimy MessageBank message.

She hung up.

She may have had a gift for finding the worst possible boyfriend material in any given room. But the girl did not have a gift for answering the phone.

Shit. Shit. Shit.

Oh, Bec. What have you got yourself into, girl?

ON THE ROAD

"Where's 'safety'?" said Rebecca, eventually.

"My foster-parents' farmhouse."

"Your foster-parents have a farmhouse?" said Rebecca.

"They did," said The Other Mark. "It's been abandoned since they died. It's a good place to lie low and reassess what's going on. Make plans on what to do next."

He'd already started making plans. He didn't particularly like them. But he didn't see much of an alternative. Agent Darcy had forced his hand and got himself killed. Maybe he could have handled that differently, but it was too late to fix that now. What was done was done. The agent was dead and somebody was going to have to pay for that.

Now, if he was incredibly lucky, the police might believe that Jake and Agent Darcy had shot each other and that would be that.

But, in his experience, one was never that lucky. Still, once they got to the farmhouse he could check that out.

Depending on how lucky he was, he then had to make a plan to deal with his doppelganger. It wasn't seemly to have two versions of him running around. And, since he was the one who'd saved the universe from paradox, he wasn't going to be the one to go. No, it was time for the original Mark to leave. How he left would depend on what the police knew.

He stole another glance at Rebecca. God, he'd forgotten how stunning she was. How had that lucky bastard managed to trick her into agreeing to marry him? He hadn't seen his Rebecca in months, not since that insane fight they'd had. Stupid, stupid fight.

He wasn't going to let her slip away in this version of reality.

His counterpart had to go.

Rebecca saw his look and smiled at him. His heart pounded.

And so, for some reason, did his head. God, where had that thumping come from. He clutched his head with one hand. He grimaced.

"Are you all right?" said Rebecca.

"Headache."

"Bad?"

"I'll live."

ALSO ON THE ROAD

Mark regained consciousness with a similar headache. He groaned. Jodie looked down at him.

"Welcome back," she said. "You okay?"

"My head is killing me." He looked around. They were in Jodie's car, driving in a suburb he did not recognise. "What's going on?"

"I'd tell you," said Jodie. "But I don't think it would help your head any."

"Then forget it." He put both hands to his head. Maybe he could suck the pain straight out. When this didn't work, he pulled one hand away and flipped open the glove box. His head was pounding. He'd never felt anything like it before in his life.

The last thing he remembered was watching the stopwatch count down to zero. And then pain. Not like the current POUND POUND POUND in his head. More a sharp, burning branding of his synapses.

And now this relentless bass drum in his noggin.

Mess with the space-time continuum and you clearly get a variety of headaches to choose from. He was certain Mr Hawking hadn't mentioned that in any of his impenetrable books. Or not before page 22 anyway.

The drummer inside his skull double-kicked.

This POUND-POUND was POUND-POUND ridiculous. POUND-POUND.

Jodie's glove box contained nothing but a street directory and an endless supply of Flake wrappers.

"You got any aspirin?" he said.

"I don't think so."

"Can we stop and get some?"

"We'll get some when we get to the hotel."

"Hotel?"

"Yeah," said Jodie. "I decided it was time we took our relationship to the next level."

"Whatever," said Mark. "Just hurry. This is the worst pain in history."

ON THE ROAD

The Other Mark lifted one hand off the wheel and put it to his head.

"Are you sure you're okay?" said Rebecca.

"I'll be fine."

"I can drive if you like."

"Thanks," said The Other Mark. "But it's fine. Just a headache."

Rebecca gave him a worried smile. "Maybe I *should* drive," she said. "If you had some kind of seizure, it's probably not safe to have you behind the wheel."

"Well, in my experience, it's even less safe trying to drive when you're not behind the wheel," said The Other Mark. "Messes up your pedal-work like nobody's business."

Rebecca gave a half-laugh. The Other Mark watched her laugh. He held his gaze on her a little longer. "I adore you," he said.

She beamed back at him. "I adore you, too, Mr Campbell," she said. "Now, eyes on the road, mister."

"Aye-aye."

"And let me know if that headache gets any worse. I don't want you collapsing while driving."

"But if I move to the passenger's seat, I can collapse away?"

"You can pass out all you like in the passenger's seat," said Rebecca. "That is, after all, what it's there for."

"I'll keep that in mind.

"See that you do."

The Other Mark smiled. "Don't worry," he said. "Having me over this side is perfectly safe."

AT KATRINA'S HOUSE

Katrina walked around in circles.

What should she do? Should she call Uncle Rog? Tell him what was happening (if he didn't already know)?

Maybe she should call her own father. Get him to call Uncle Rog. That might be a better way of doing it.

But she didn't want to call and worry everybody over nothing. Especially if they weren't able to do anything about it. She needed to find out where Rebecca was, and if she was safe.

Then she'd call Uncle Rog or her dad.

That was the correct order to do things in.

Aha.

What if…

Katrina grabbed her mobile phone. She scrolled through the names, down to the R's. Rachel. Rebecca. Renee. Renee (hairdresser). Rich.

She pressed 'dial'.

She hadn't spoken to Rich in ages. Not since things had blown up between her and Rebecca. She kinda understood why he'd cooled the friendship off. His wife's best friend was the reason she and Rebecca were fighting. That can't be an easy thing to be in the middle of.

But, still, she missed him. She still saw him at work, of course, and everything was civil.

But it wasn't how it used to be.

Which was a shame.

Mark had fucked all kinds of things up.

"Hello?" came Richard's voice.

"Rich? It's Katrina."

There was a pause.

"Tyler," she added. "Katrina Tyler."

"Hi Kat," said Richard. "Sorry. I thought you might have been Jodie."

"No. Sorry."

There was another pause.

"I assume you've seen the news," said Katrina.

"Yeah."

"Do you know where she is?" said Katrina. "Where Rebecca is?"

"No."

"She's not answering her phone." said Katrina.

"Maybe she's getting a massage. Or a manicure. Or something."

"Maybe."

Another pause.

"But you know where Mark is?"

"Uhhh, yeah," said Richard. "Sort of."

"Have you called the police?"

"Jodie's looking after it," said Richard.

"Jodie's with him?" said Katrina. "And you're okay with that?"

"It's Mark," said Richard. "I know you don't like him much. But he's not dangerous."

"A couple of dead people on my television screen would probably argue otherwise."

"That can't have been Mark," said Richard.

"Rich," said Katrina. "When the police say they're looking for a particular person to help them with their enquiries, that usually means they're pretty certain he did it."

"But it's Mark," said Richard. "He's harmless."

"Is he?" said Katrina. "You know his family history."

Richard didn't say anything to that.

Fine. What happened to Mark's parents was supposed to be a big secret. Whatever. Katrina continued.

"All I know is that I wouldn't trust my wife in the company of a man responsible for the murder of two people," said Katrina.

There was one last pause.

"Not 'my' wife, obviously," said Katrina. "You know what I mean."

CHAPTER NINE

Maybe he didn't know Mark as well as he thought he did.

"I said 'fuck me'."

"You don't have an all-day goddamn massage."

"I am soooo marrying you."

AT RICHARD AND JODIE'S HOUSE

RICHARD HUNG UP from speaking with Katrina.

It was not clear what he should do. On the one hand, he could see her point. Just sitting back and allowing one's wife to run around with a man suspected of killing two people? Not the behaviour of a good husband.

On the other hand, it was Mark. He'd known him for years. Jodie had known him even longer. He wasn't going to hurt her.

However, it was only a matter of time before Katrina decided that, even if she couldn't turn in Mark and Jodie, she could turn him in. He'd admitted to knowing where they were. The police probably wouldn't take kindly to him withholding that information.

Having said that, there was no way on Earth the police were going to believe what was going on here. Heck, he barely believed it and it had made him a millionaire many times over.

He unmuted the television.

"—have released this picture of Mark Campbell, the man wanted for questioning over the double homicide here earlier today. He is considered 'extremely dangerous' and members of the public are cautioned—"

He muted it again.

Had Mark killed Jake and the other man? What reason could he possibly have for doing that? He knew Mark had been running late to leave the message. Had Jake and the other man tried to slow him down somehow? Why would they do that? And why would Mark respond by shooting them? And since when did Mark have a gun anyway?

Maybe he didn't know Mark as well as he thought he did.

Maybe Jodie didn't know him that well either.

He knew about his childhood. How his mother had shot his father, then killed herself. He never spoke about it. Or the time he'd spent in various foster homes.

But that would have to mess you up a little.

Hell, it would have to mess you up a *lot*.

Mark was aloof, detached, disconnected. He covered it with an amiable, joking surface. But nobody really got close to him. Nobody knew what was bubbling below.

Jodie knew him best. But maybe she didn't know him as well as she thought.

He still didn't think he'd hurt Jodie on purpose.

But what if she got caught in the cross-fire? Either metaphorically or, god forbid, literally.

Katrina was right. He wouldn't be much of a husband if he didn't get his wife out of harm's way. If she got hurt aiding Mark's escape from the authorities, he'd never forgive himself.

He grabbed the phone and pressed a speed dial button.

AT THE HOTEL

Jodie and Mark closed the door of their hotel room. Mark had three aspirin in his hand. He made a beeline for the glass on the sink.

He picked up the glass. Filthy. He ran it under the tap and scrubbed it into something closer to clean.

"Beautiful ambience," said Jodie, looking around the room.

Mark swallowed the aspirin. Washed it down with the glass of water. Made his way to the bed where he collapsed.

Jodie's phone rang. She looked closely at the number.

"Hi," she said.

"Where are you?" said Richard.

"Fine, thank you. Lovely to hear your voice also."

Richard sighed. "Sorry," he said. "I'm just a bit… frazzled by the day's events."

"You're not the only one," said Jodie. "It's been a frazzley day."

"Down in Frazzle Rock," said Mark, from the bed.

"So where are you now?"

"Tell him to dance his cares away," said Mark.

Jodie took her ear away from the phone and shushed him.

"Sorry, Boober," he said.

Jodie returned to the phone. Her head shook slightly.

"Sorry about that," she said. "Mark has decided that now is a suitable time to invoke childhood memories of Muppets."

Richard ignored that. "So where did you say you are?" he said.

"We've just checked into a hotel in the city."

"Which one?" said Richard.

"I'm not sure it is a hotel," said Mark.

"The, uh, Merriman?" said Jodie.

"It's more like the interior of a giant vacuum cleaner bag."

"And Mark's obviously with you," said Richard.

"Except not as clean," continued Mark.

"Um, yeah," said Jodie. Obviously.

There was a pause. Jodie didn't like the sound of the pause.

Or, to be more precise, given the that pause made no sound at all, she didn't like the implications of the soundlessness of the pause.

Richard was about to say something stupid.

"Babe, I need you to get as far away from him as possible," he said.

And there it was. "Rich," she said. This was ridiculous.

"Jode."

"Don't be stupid," said Jodie. "You know he didn't do it."

"The police think otherwise."

"They don't know the full story though, do they?" said Jodie.

"Two people are dead," said Richard. "It's time to end this."

Okay. She could see this was a conversation that wasn't going to end well. All she could do was end it quickly. "We'll discuss it later," she said.

"We'll discuss it now."

"Later," whispered Jodie.

There was silence at the other end.

What was he thinking? He knew Mark. He knew Mark would never kill anybody. This overbearing protective husband thing was sweet. But misguided beyond all measure.

"Everything will be okay," said Jodie. "Trust me."

No reply.

Stubborn stupid man.

"I love you," she said.

Still no reply.

Well, screw you buddy.

She hung up.

AT RICHARD AND JODIE'S HOUSE

Richard looked at his phone.

That hadn't gone well. He didn't know what he'd expected. Jodie was not going to see sense on the Mark front. She was more concerned with helping him than with looking after herself.

Which was noble and loyal, of course.

But he had his own course of nobility and loyalty. She may have taken it on herself to look after Mark. But he'd made a vow a few years back to look after *her*.

Now was the time to live up to it.

It would piss her off but he didn't see how he had any other choice. This nonsense with Mark had to end before anybody else got hurt.

He dialled a new number.

"Yes," he said, when the voice at the other end answered. "I have information on the whereabouts of Mark Campbell."

AT THE HOTEL

"What didn't I do?" said Mark, from the bed.

"Hmm?" said Jodie.

"You said 'Don't be stupid. You know he didn't do it' to Rich," said Mark. "What didn't I do?"

"What's the last thing you remember before you passed out?" said Jodie. She dropped her phone on the dresser.

"Pulling the car over," said Mark. "In retrospect, a fine suggestion."

"You didn't make it to the apartment, did you?"

"Not that I recall. Why? What happened?"

"Well," said Jodie. "It seems as though there *was* a rupture in the space-time continuum."

"Oh," said Mark. "I thought we might have escaped without one. I mean, the universe looks kinda solid to me." He tapped the wall behind him. "Not this wall so much. But the rest of it."

"The rest of it seems fine, yes," said Jodie.

"So if there was a rupture, what did it do?"

"I'm not… I'm not sure." She paused. "We know the phone call was made. Because you heard the message three days ago."

"Right."

"And yet we also know you didn't arrive in time to leave the message today."

Mark sighed. "Right."

"I think…" said Jodie. She shook her head. "It's too crazy to even say."

"Now you know how I felt the night I first told you about the MessageBank."

"But you at least had alcohol."

"True," said Mark. "Go on. Tell me. My mind is open."

"Okay," said Jodie. "Here goes. The phone call was made. That's undeniable. You didn't make it in time to make the phone call. That's also undeniable. So… how does the universe get around this inconsistency?"

"I give up," said Mark. He shrugged.

"I think the universe had to create a version of you to make the phone call and leave the message."

"What do you mean, a 'version' of me?"

"Another you."

"I've never heard of time travel working like this," said Mark. "They never mentioned this in any of the *Back to the Future* movies."

"No. Stephen Hawking didn't mention it either," said Jodie. "But it makes sense, doesn't it?"

"Because I couldn't make the phone call, another copy of me who *could* make the phone call just popped into existence?"

"Yeah."

"Yeah, that makes loads of sense, Jode."

"Look," said Jodie. "What would have had to have happened for you to have made that phone call in time?"

"A faster car?" said Mark. "My personal helicopter?"

"Perhaps," said Jodie. She rubbed the back of her neck. "You could have also let go of Chewie."

"Never an option."

"Not for you, perhaps. But a more ruthless version of you might have done so."

"No. Never."

"You're missing my point. *You* would never have sacrificed Chewie. The other version of you—the one who made the phone call—he's the kind of person who wouldn't hesitate."

"How do you know?"

"For one thing, it's the definition of his existence. He was able to make the phone call precisely because he's the kind of person who would sacrifice a dog to do so."

"Oh," said Mark. "Brilliant. An evil doppelganger. Not at all clichéd."

"Hey," said Jodie. "I just relate the clichés. It's the universe that makes them."

"And you're serious?" said Mark. "You believe the universe created a dog-murdering version of me to make the phone call?"

"I do."

Mark let out a half-laugh. "I have an evil doppelganger," he said. "Brilliant."

There was another pause. "That's not all," said Jodie.

"It's not?"

"I'm afraid not," said Jodie. "The evil doppelganger also… He also killed Jake and some government agent."

Mark lifted his head from the bed. "What?"

"Yeah."

"He what?"

OUTSIDE THE APARTMENT

The conversation between Andrew and Agents Mills and Benson remained stilted. Andrew had decided not to let them know about how he fit into the picture. In return, the two agents had kept their defensive shields up.

They'd ended up talking about football.

"I just think they have to select Harrison," said Andrew.

"He's too young," said Mills. "They'll kill him."

"He'll be fine," said Andrew. "They'll never catch him. He'll run rings around them."

"He's just a kid. Give him another year or two. Then he'll be ready." Agent Mills turned to Agent Benson. "What do you think?"

"If he's good enough, he's old enough," said Benson.

"Exactly," said Andrew.

"Sorry to interrupt this intellectual think-tank," said Agent Innes, appearing from nowhere. "But we've got a murderer to catch. And I need you two to help me follow up on some leads."

"Yes, sir," said Benson.

"Or would you rather discuss the football?"

"No, sir."

"Good. Come with me."

AT THE FARMHOUSE

The Other Mark unlocked the door to the farmhouse. He gestured for Rebecca to enter. She did so, pulling a growling Chewie along with her. The Other Mark followed, closing and locking the door behind him.

"We should be safe here for a while," he said.

Rebecca reached for her phone. "Should we call Jodie or somebody? Let her know where we are?"

"No," said The Other Mark.

Rebecca looked up at him. "Why not?"

He grinned. "Because I have a better idea."

He moved in and kissed her. God, he'd waited too long for this. Those lips. That face. That body. He needed her. And he needed her now.

She kissed back. Her hands ran up through his hair.

The Other Mark grabbed her butt. He squeezed. He had missed her so much. How had he ever let a woman this incredible go?

He wasn't going to make that mistake again. With one motion, he picked her up and carried her to the bed.

He threw her on to it.

Her eyes widened in surprise. She let out a little moan of satisfaction.

The Other Mark grabbed for her blouse. He tore it open. Rebecca moaned again.

He grabbed her hands, pinned her beneath him and kissed her again.

She returned the kiss with even more passion. He felt her hips grind beneath him. He moved to her neck, kissing her in that spot she loved. She threw her head back, moaning.

"Jesus, Marcus."

He kissed her behind her ear.

"Ooooh, fuck," she said. She moaned again. He moved back to her mouth and kissed her. Hard.

He broke away from the kiss slowly. As he lifted his head from hers, she followed. Her eyes were half-closed.

"Fuck me," she said. "Please fuck me."

"Not yet," he said.

The Other Mark released her right arm. He reached beneath her and, in one deft motion, undid her bra. It fell away, revealing her breasts.

My god. They were still the best set of tits he'd ever seen. Just perfect. He pinned her right arm down again and bent down to savour them.

Her nipples were hard and erect. He took the left one in his mouth and ran his tongue around it.

Rebecca moaned some more.

He moved her right arm over beside her left and pinned them both down with one hand. He continued to kiss her left breast, as he moved his free hand down to her jeans.

Rebecca continued to grind her hips beneath him. He undid the fly on the jeans and reached his hand inside.

A fresh moan, louder than the previous ones.

Her hip motions became more extreme. Hungrier.

As The Other Mark moved on to the other nipple, she broke her arms free of his grip. She grabbed for his shirt and tugged it up. The

Other Mark broke away from her breast and lifted his arms so she could pull it off.

She sat up and kissed his chest. Then a small bite. She continued to straighten up, working her way up his chest and neck to his mouth.

She kissed him again. She pressed hard against him, pushing him back. Eventually he fell back to the bed and she sat atop him. While she continued to kiss him, her hands worked away at his pants, undoing the belt.

He ran his hands up the side of her face and back through her hair.

He pushed back with another kiss. This time, Rebecca broke away and pulled his pants off.

As she threw them to the floor, The Other Mark sat up and crawled across the bed to her. He grabbed the bottom of her jeans and pulled them off.

Rebecca reached inside his boxers. The Other Mark's head threw back. He groaned happily.

Rebecca straightened up and kissed him. Hard. As they kissed, the last remaining underwear was discarded.

Rebecca broke the kiss. They were kneeling in front of each other, naked.

"I said 'fuck me'," said Rebecca.

The Other Mark shoved her back on to the bed.

Happy to oblige.

AT THE HOTEL

"What?" repeated Mark. He was now sitting up on the bed. The pounding headache momentarily forgotten.

"He's with Rebecca," said Jodie.

"How do you know?"

"I spoke with him," she said. "You didn't think I'd *deduced* that space-time rupturing evil doppelganger theory, did you?"

Mark rolled over. He fumbled for his phone. "We have to get her away from him."

"First, we have to make sure you don't get captured in the process."

Mark wasn't listening. "Shit," he said.

"Yes. They turned their phones off."

"So what do we do?"

"First things first," said Jodie. "Like I said, you mustn't get captured. The police are looking for you and if they find you, they're going to stop looking for *him*."

"Okay," said Mark. "That makes sense. How?"

"We stay here for the night. Lie low."

"No."

"Marcus."

"I said 'no'. I'm not letting her spend a night with him. The guy's a murderer."

"The police know we were at the hospital. They are actively looking for us. It's much safer to lie low. If they're going to find one of you, let it be him."

"But what if…" said Mark.

"What?"

"What if they… well, you know…"

"Have sex?"

Mark exhaled. "Yes. Have sex," he said. "What if they have sex?"

Jodie shrugged. "If they do, they do," she said. "We can't do anything about that."

"This is my girlfriend—"

"Fiancée."

"Thank you. This is my fiancée we're talking about here. I can't just sit back and let her have sex with another man."

"Technically it's *not* another man."

Mark looked at her, eyebrows raised.

"It's, well, you," she said.

"It's not me," he said. "Trust me. I know."

"I know," sighed Jodie. "Look on the bright side. Maybe they'll be too stressed out for sex."

AT THE FARMHOUSE

Rebecca lay back. She throbbed with exhilaration. "My god, Mr Campbell," she said. "Being a fugitive brings out a somewhat wild side of you."

The Other Mark grinned. His fingers traced her thigh. "You like?"

"Oh," said Rebecca. "I like."

"Excellent," said The Other Mark. He grabbed her, rolled her over and began to ravage her some more.

AT THE HOTEL

"Do you know where they are?" asked Mark.

"No."

"Perfect."

"Our best chance is to wait it out. Let the police find him and bring him in," said Jodie. "That's what they're trained to do."

Mark dropped his head back on the bed. "What if he hurts her?" he said.

"He's not going to hurt her."

"How do you know?"

"Would you hurt her?"

"He's not me."

"No," said Jodie. "But I think it's safe to assume he'll have similar feelings for her. If you wouldn't hurt her, he's not going to hurt her."

"He dropped Chewie off a cliff."

Jodie sighed. "I was hoping you'd forgotten that."

Mark gave her a wry smile.

"Look," said Jodie. "We can't do anything anyway. We don't know where they are. We'll keep checking in with Rebecca. If we get through to her or she calls us—"

Jodie's phone rang. She looked at the number.

"Just Rich," she said. She answered the phone and spoke to him. "I'm not abandoning him."

"That's fine," said Richard. "But you should know the police are on their way."

"What?"

"Don't… don't do anything stupid. Just surrender and turn Mark in."

"Rich, you stupid—"

"I'm sorry, babe. I can't leave you alone with him. It's not safe."

She hung up on him. "Shit."

She ran to the balcony. Police cars were pulling in on the street below.

"Oh shit, shit, shit," she said.

"What?" said Mark from the bed.

"My husband is a moron," she said. "Shit, shit, shit."

Mark got up off the bed and stumbled to the balcony. "Oh shit," he said. "Do you think the concierge will tell them what room we're in?"

Jodie snorted. "Yeah. Somehow I don't think the awesome power of concierge-client privilege is going to save us this time."

"What do we do now?"

OUTSIDE THE HOTEL

Andrew pulled up outside the hotel. The older cop had interrupted his conversation with the other two. He'd sent them off to some hospital where they'd reported Mark Campbell being checked in.

Andrew wasn't stupid.

He knew the older cop was the top dog here. He wasn't going to send the other two off to the hospital if he thought there was any real chance of Captain Dipshit being there.

So he'd gone back to his car, sat and waited.

Shortly after the first two cops left for the hospital, the older cop led another group away, sirens blaring.

Andrew followed them.

If he was right, they were off to arrest Captain Dipshit.

With Captain Dipshit taken away for murder, Rebecca was going to be clearly distraught. She was going to need a shoulder to cry on.

Andrew had two shoulders, either of which could be used for crying.

He would loiter in the background, wait for them to take Captain Dipshit away and then swoop back into Rebecca's life.

Perfect. Fiancé out of the picture and him back into the picture as the sympathetic boyfriend. All with minimal work on his part. Sometimes life was just too easy.

AT RICHARD AND JODIE'S HOUSE

Richard stared at the phone.

What was done was done. She was pissed now, but she'd eventually see it from his point of view.

Running from the police was insane. Better to turn yourself in and explain everything. Richard wasn't sure what Mark's explanation was, but if he was innocent, then he could explain that to the police and they'd sort everything out.

And if it meant spilling the beans about the time-travelling telephones, then so be it. They'd had a good run with it, made more money than they could possibly have imagined.

The police wouldn't believe them, of course, but a few demonstrations would clear the matter up.

Who knows? Maybe they'd become famous for discovering some kind of scientific breakthrough as well.

And his wife wouldn't be running around like a fugitive any more.

It was a small price to pay for her temporary fury.

He called Katrina back.

"Rich," she said.

"Hey Kat."

"How'd you go?"

"I called them, tried to convince them to turn themselves in."

"And?"

"No luck," he said. There was a pause. "So I called the police, told them where they were."

Katrina sighed. "And Rebecca's all right?"

"Hmm?" said Richard.

"Rebecca's all right?"

"I don't think Rebecca was with them."

"What?" said Katrina. "Who were you talking to?"

"Jodie," he said. "And Mark."

"And Rebecca's not with them?"

"I don't think so."

"Then where is she?" asked Katrina. "And don't try and tell me she's having a massage. You don't have an all-day goddamn massage."

"I'm sure she's all right," said Richard. "She's probably just got her phone turned off."

"Why would she turn her phone off?" asked Katrina.

"I don't know," said Richard. "But it doesn't really matter, does it?"

"What?"

"Look, if you were worried about Mark doing something to her, then… there's no problem. Mark's with Jodie. The police are on their way. Even if—for whatever reason—Mark was going to hurt her somehow, he's not going to be able to."

"I suppose."

"Don't sweat it, Kat," said Richard. "She'll turn up."

AT THE HOSPITAL

Agent Mills and Agent Benson waited for Nurse O'Donnell to return.

"This is ridiculous," said Benson.

"What?" said Mills.

"He's not here."

"What do you mean?"

"Campbell's not here," he said. He elaborated. "Innes isn't going to send us where the action is. He's going to make us follow the dead leads."

Agent Mills snorted. "You're probably right."

Nurse O'Donnell scurried past. She didn't notice either of them. Agent Benson grabbed her by the sleeve.

"Hmmm?" she said. "Oh. We're just trying to track him down now."

She scurried off again.

"Sure," said Benson. "Look at this." He gestured to the roomful of people.

"We're low priority," said Agent Mills.

"To be fair," said Agent Benson. "I think everybody's low priority. When you have a zillion people trying to get your attention and a limited number of staff to deal with them, then that brings the average priority way down."

"We could be here for hours," said Agent Mills.

"We could be, yes," said Agent Benson. "Or we could leave and get on with our investigation."

"But—"

Nurse O'Donnell returned. "We're just struggling to find him at the minute," she said. "Nobody seems quite sure what room he's in."

"Is it possible he left?" said Agent Mills.

She consulted some paperwork. "He was unconscious when he was brought in."

Agents Mills and Benson peered around to look at the paperwork. "Maybe he regained consciousness," suggested Mills.

"Maybe the person who admitted him, unadmitted him," said Benson. He pointed at Jodie's name.

"Flannery," said Mills.

"I don't know," said Nurse O'Donnell. "I've got somebody trying to track them down. I'll let you know as soon as they find anything." She lifted Mark's paperwork over and looked at the next piece of paper on her clipboard.

She turned back to the rest of the room.

"Mr Hoxton," she said.

A man with a bloodstained shirt stood up.

"This is ridiculous," said Agent Benson again. "Come on, we're getting back to our investigation."

"What about Innes?"

"Screw Innes."

IN THE FOYER

Agent Innes and several other police officers strode through the door of the hotel. The concierge, having heard the sirens, met them as they came through.

"Can I help you?" he said. Sweat rolled down his forehead.

"I sincerely hope so," said Agent Innes. He simultaneously flipped open his badge and held up the photo of Mark. "Have you seen this man?

"Um, sure," said the concierge. "He checked in twenty minutes or so ago with some woman."

Agent Innes smiled. "Would you mind telling me what room?"

"Of course," said the concierge. He trotted back to his desk. He picked up the incomplete Sudoku and put it beneath the counter. He replaced it with the guest book. "What's he done?"

"We need to ask him a few questions," said Agent Innes. He stared at the concierge, as if daring him to ask for further details.

The concierge dredged up some fresh sweat particles. He reached below the desk again, and handed over a set of keys.

"Room 442," he said.

Agent Innes took the key. "Thank you," he said. He turned to the other police but was interrupted by the concierge.

"You're not going to, uh…"

Agent Innes turned his head back. "Sorry?" he said.

"You're not going to disturb the other guests are you?" he said.

Agent Innes forced a smile. "We shall do our best." He turned back to the police officers. "Let's go. Seal all exits." He pointed out a pair of officers. "You two cover the stairs." He pointed at two others. "You two cover the elevator. The rest of you, come with me."

As they ran for the stairs, the elevator dinged.

Agent Innes froze. So did his officers. The two covering the elevator had their holsters unclipped and hands on their guns.

The door opened. Jodie came out.

"Thank god you're here," she said.

Agent Innes's eyes narrowed. He tapped his fingers together three times, before pointing at Jodie. "Mrs Flannery?" he said.

"Yes," said Jodie.

"Where's Mr Campbell?"

"You've just missed him, I'm afraid," she said. "He left about ten minutes ago. He said something about taking the money and running."

"Did he say where he was going?" asked Agent Innes.

"No. He just drove off."

"In his car?"

"Of course."

Agent Innes turned back to the concierge. "Did you see him leave?"

The concierge looked up, eyes wide. "Sorry?" he said.

"Did you see him leave?"

"I wasn't really watching—"

"That's not what I asked," said Agent Innes. "Did you see him leave?"

The concierge hesitated, as if considering whether this was a trick question. "No," he eventually said.

Agent Innes tossed the keys to one of his officers. "Check the room."

"You're letting him get away," said Jodie.

"Check the room," repeated Agent Innes.

OUTSIDE ROOM 442

Two minutes later, the two policemen arrived at Room 442. One of them rapped on the door.

"Mr Campbell," he said. "Would you open up, please. It's the police."

There was no response.

The knocking policeman glanced over at the other one, who shrugged.

The knocking policeman tried again. Three taps on the door.

"Mr Campbell. Please open this door," he said. "If you don't open this door in three seconds, we will be forced to, uh, force our way in."

The second policeman made a face at this awkward sentence. This time, the knocking policeman shrugged.

"One," he said.

No response.

"Two."

Nothing.

"Three."

On three, the non-knocking policeman slid the key in and out of the door lock and pushed the door open.

They stepped back, away from the door entrance.

Nothing.

The knocking policeman intercepted the self-closing door with his foot.

"Do you think he's here?" said the non-knocking policeman.

"Let's assume he is," said the other one. "Probably safer that way."

They had their guns out of their holsters. The knocking policeman silently counted to three with his fingers and the pair of them burst through the door, gun held out in front of them.

The hallway was clear.

The door closed behind them, giving them both a start.

Knocking policeman pointed to the bathroom to their right. Non-knocking policeman stepped in. He checked behind the door. Nothing.

The shower cubicle was also empty.

Bathroom was clear.

He stepped out, closing the door behind him.

Now he stood guard in the hallway while knocking policeman opened the closet to their left. Nobody could possibly fit in there.

And nobody had.

The closet was empty.

He closed the closet door again.

The pair of them walked slowly down the hall.

There was only the bedroom and the balcony left. The hall opened into the bedroom. Knocking policeman scanned to the left. Non-knocking policeman to the right.

Nothing. And nothing.

Non-knocking policeman dropped to his knees and looked under the bed.

The bed didn't even have an under for anybody to use for hiding. The base went all the way to the floor. He stood back up.

Knocking policeman circled to the other side of the bed. Nobody was hiding down that side.

The bedroom was clear. That just left the balcony,

Knocking policeman went to the side of the balcony door and, with one motion, pulled the blinds open.

The balcony was empty.

Non-knocking policeman had made his way around the bed and now opened the door to the balcony. He stepped out on to it. Looked over the edge.

Nothing.

There was nobody here.

"She's telling the truth," said the non-knocking policeman. "He's gone."

The knocking policeman swore slightly. He picked up his walkie-talkie.

"He's not here," he said.

IN THE FOYER

Agent Innes swore. "Damn," he said. "Get back down here."

"I tell you, he's not in the hotel," said Jodie.

Agent Innes spoke to his other officers. "Okay. Keep this place sealed. We'll conduct a room-to-room search when more officers arrive."

"Is this necessary?" said the concierge. "It seems the man you're looking for has already left the building. Do you need to disturb the rest of my guests?"

Agent Innes turned to him. "I'm sorry, sir," he said. "I understand your situation. But we need to be one hundred percent sure he's not in the building before we leave."

"He's not in the building," said Jodie.

"The lady seems rather certain he's not here," said the concierge.

Agent Innes smiled. "The lady is a friend of the man we're looking for," he said. "I think we should take her claims with a grain of salt."

"Well," said Jodie. "I've never been so insulted in my life." She looked Agent Innes in the eye. "I promise you. Mark Campbell is not in this building."

The concierge gestured to Jodie, as if to say 'See? We can trust her.'

Agent Innes was less easily convinced. He turned back to his officers. "We're keeping this place sealed for now," he said.

The concierge sighed and raised his hands to the sky, exasperated.

Agent Innes turned back to Jodie. "Mrs Flannery," he said. "Would you mind accompanying Detective Jackson to the station. Maybe you can shed some light on Mr Campbell's actions."

"I'll do my best," she said.

AT KATRINA'S HOUSE

Katrina was mad now.

She couldn't believe Rebecca's rudeness. Okay, Rebecca was mad at her because she didn't like her boyfriend—sorry, fiancé, blurgh, vomit—and any other day, she'd have no problem with Rebecca ignoring her phone calls.

That's what happened when you tried to point out people's poor romantic choices and help them make better ones.

Fine. Whatever.

But when your boyfriend-fiancé-blurgh-vomit makes the news for murdering a couple of people, then, it's probably time to take a deep swallow, admit that you were wrong and answer your damn phone.

Because, theoretically, she was still worried about her.

And a phone call confirming she was okay would be nice.

She picked up her phone again. Found Uncle Roger's number. Dialled.

It was Aunt Sue that answered.

"Hi Aunt Sue," said Katrina. "It's Kat."

There was a brief, uncomfortable pause, before Aunt Sue answered. "Hello, Kat," she said. "How are you?"

"I'm fine," she said. They chit-chatted with further awkwardness for another minute or so before Katrina finally got to the point. "Have you spoken to Rebecca today?"

"Today?" said Aunt Sue. "No, dear. Not today. Spoke to her a week or so ago. You heard that she and Mark are—" She half-stopped herself, as if realising she'd raised a forbidden topic, before seemingly shrugging and powering on regardless. "Getting married," she concluded.

"I did hear that," said Katrina. "You must be very excited."

"Very."

"But you haven't heard from her today?" said Katrina. "And Uncle Rog hasn't either?"

"No, dear," she said. "Your Uncle Roger's out golfing today. Getting ready for the tournament next week."

"And you haven't heard the news?" said Katrina. Shit, shit, shit.

"What news, dear?" Her voice had a colder edge to it suddenly.

Shit, shit, shit. This was why she'd held off calling. She didn't want to be the one to break this to them.

Didn't they have any friends who had a television on? Who might have told them about this by now? Sure, they were country folk, but they still got emergency news bulletins, didn't they?

Shit, shit, shit.

Katrina took a deep breath and prepared to fill her Aunt Sue in on the story so far.

And, still lumbering around her subconscious was one thought.

Rebecca, where are you?

OUTSIDE THE HOTEL

Andrew squinted. He was a fair distance from the hotel. Because, hell, didn't want to get too close, have the old cop notice him and get him tangled up in this mess. No. Better to keep a distance until they brought Rebecca out, safe. Then he could step in to be the comforting guy.

The police had stormed the hotel about fifteen to twenty minutes ago.

Well, 'storm' was too strong. They'd 'drizzled' it.

It was difficult to tell what was going on in there. There hadn't been any shooting yet, which was a good sign. A couple of cops had wandered in and out of the building.

But no sign of Captain Dipshit or Rebecca yet.

Wait.

There she was. With some dude too important to wear a uniform.

Time to go.

He started to open his door, but then looked again.

That wasn't Rebecca. Looked a bit like her from a distance, except older. Chunkier around the lower half. Generally not as hot.

He squinted further.

Tits weren't as good either.

On closer inspection, the woman didn't look much like Rebecca at all.

False alarm.

The uniform-less cop marched her to his police car. Whoever she was, it looked like she was in trouble.

Maybe she was Captain Dipshit's accomplice.

Maybe Captain Dipshit was having an affair with her.

Andrew smiled. That would be perfect. Hell, there was always a chance that Rebecca, overcome with stupid love for Captain Dipshit, would still pine for him despite his murderous ways. Chicks could be stupid like that.

But if he'd cheated on her…

Well, that changed everything.

AT THE FARMHOUSE

It was the fourth one that almost blew her brains out. Her eyes rolled back into her head.

"Dear god, man," she said, between open-mouthed pants. "Have you been taking lessons?"

The Other Mark lifted his head and smiled up at her. "You like?"

Rebecca gave a glazed nod. "Don't stop."

He smiled and resumed. Rebecca found religion.

"Sweet Jesus," she said. "I am soooo marrying you."

IN THE HOTEL

Mark scrambled up the stairs. He took another look back down to make sure nobody was following.

All clear. Jodie had bought him enough time.

He reached for the door handle. Please don't be locked. Please don't be locked.

It wasn't. He opened the door and climbed the remaining three stairs to the roof of the hotel. He ducked around the corner and sat down, panting.

For now, he was safe. Still, unless Jodie could convince the police he'd already gone, it was only a matter of time until their search for him made its way up here.

Shit, shit, shit. Richard, you big dick.

CHAPTER TEN

Avuncular was the word she wanted to use

Movement at the station.

Katrina's madness was getting to her.

"It's a space-time continuum fuckup thing."

ON THE ROOF

MARK PEERED OVER the edge of the roof.

Yep. Police cars everywhere. This was ridiculous. He was sitting up here, hiding from the police, while the real killer was out there with his fiancée.

He returned to the centre of the roof, outside any possible line of sight.

How had they got themselves into such a mess?

It was just a simple matter of leaving some phone messages to the past and making themselves multimillionaires. A perfectly simple process, assuming one had the correct equipment. Which they did.

It was certainly not a process that should have led to them being pursued, a la The A Team, for crimes they did not commit.

The four of them weren't the A Team. Hell, they were barely the C Team.

Although, Jodie did do a mean Mr T impression.

Mark sure hoped she was pitying those fool police officers right about now.

He sat down with a grunt.

He was going insane.

Which would probably make him H M 'Howling Mad' Murdoch, the certifiably crazy helicopter pilot from the A Team.

He looked around.

A helicopter pilot would come in handy right about now. Especially if he had the foresight to bring with him a helicopter.

He couldn't see any other way he was going to get off this roof.

Which, of course, was all kinds of bad. He needed to get off the roof, so he could save Rebecca. While he was stuck up here, he couldn't do anything.

Or could he?

He took a deep breath. If he just stopped and thought for a second, there was probably a lot he could do to help Rebecca, even while stuck up here.

He tried the obvious one first.

He pulled his phone out of his pocket and called her.

"Hi, you've found Rebecca. I'm getting married! Leave a message."

He hung up. There was no message he could sensibly leave that would expand on Jodie's previous messages. Plus, the fact that she'd received a phone message from the person in the car seat beside her might confuse the hell out of her.

And if he was going to confuse the hell out of her with doppelganger talk, he was going to do it in a live call.

Leaving phone messages was precisely how they got into this mess in the first place.

Or, to be more precise, failing to leave phone messages was how they got into this mess in the first place.

Okay. No need to panic. Her phone was still off. That was okay. He could still do stuff up here.

For example, he could try to work out where his doppelganger might have taken her. If they were slightly modified versions of each other, they must think alike.

Where would *he* take Rebecca if he was trying to get her away from the police and the rest of the outside world?

He had no idea.

He rubbed his chin. People deep in thought often rubbed their chins. Maybe the cause and effect were the opposite of what he normally assumed. Maybe rubbing one's chin was enough to put one deep into thought.

It wasn't.

It had just put him into shallow thoughts about chin-rubbers.

He stopped rubbing his chin.

Where on Earth could he have taken her? If he could come up with a halfway convincing idea, he'd be able to call the police and send them there anonymously. Get the right version of him arrested. Leave him free to go back to his life.

That was what it was all about now. Which one of them would the police catch first. Because that version of Mark Campbell was going to jail for a long time.

The other version got to live out their life with Rebecca and the millions of dollars they'd earned.

Of course, the police were a couple of floors below him and, presumably, working their way up.

So he didn't like his chances of them catching The Other Mark first.

Shit.

How had they got themselves into such a mess?

IN THE POLICE CAR

Jodie sat in the back seat of the police car, frowning.

That hadn't worked as well as hoped. All she'd managed to do was split them up. The police weren't abandoning the hotel at all. Well, apart from the two sitting in the front of the car, taking her away from the scene.

Definitely not how she'd planned it.

Of course, there hadn't been much time for planning, but still, even on an ad hoc basis, you'd hope to do better than this.

She reached in her bag and pulled out her phone.

"Can I call my husband?" she asked the plain-clothes officer in the front passenger seat. What had the other one called him? Detective Jackson?

He turned and smiled. Avuncular was the word she wanted to use to describe him, but she was never sure that was the correct one. She sort of knew what it meant. Or, at least, the context in which it was often used. But she was never bold enough to apply it herself, in case she used it in an embarrassingly wrong manner.

"Let's just wait until we get to the station," he said. It was a suggestion rather than an order.

Jodie hesitated. "Am I under arrest?" she said.

"Of course not," said Detective Jackson.

"So I *can* call my husband."

"No," said Detective Jackson. "You can wait until we get to the station." This time it was an order. He didn't appear so avuncular any more either. Or perhaps he did. Stupid adjective. She should really look up its meaning one day.

Her lips tightened.

How had they got themselves into such a mess?

IN THE FOYER

The concierge interrupted Agent Innes yet again.

"How much longer do you think this will take?" he asked. "It's just that I have several guests who need to leave the building."

"Sorry," said Agent Innes. "What did you say?"

"I was just wondering when you might—"

But Agent Innes was shaking his hand at him. "Not you," he mouthed, pointing to his ear.

The concierge fixed Agent Innes with a stare. Agent Innes responded by turning his back on him.

"You're sure?" he said to the person in his earpiece. "You've double-checked it?"

A short pause.

"Okay, that's great. And where exactly?"

Another pause. Agent Innes scrawled details in his notebook.

"Great," he said. "Thank you."

He turned back around to face the concierge, who hadn't moved. Or blinked.

"Excuse me, sir," he said. "I'll be with you in just a moment."

Still no blink. Or movement.

"And I'll have good news," added Agent Innes.

"I look forward to it," said the concierge. He turned and walked back to a small crowd of guests.

Agent Innes walked over to his officers.

"Okay, men," he said. "Prepare to move out. We've found Campbell's car."

Walkie-talkies sprung into action.

OUTSIDE THE HOTEL

Hello, thought Andrew. Movement at the station. Police were running out to their cars. Three sped off, sirens blaring.

Still no sign of Rebecca, however. Or Captain Dipshit. Or, for that matter, the cop in charge. Andrew wasn't budging until he saw at least one of those three.

Another pair of officers burst out of the hotel and into their car. Something was definitely up.

The fact they were all speeding off with their sirens blaring probably meant they hadn't found Captain Dipshit yet. But there was still a chance they'd found Rebecca.

Wait.

Here was the head cop now. He was walking out, talking to a couple of remaining officers. Telling them about something. They nodded and made their way back into the building.

The older cop and his personal chauffeur headed to their car.

But no sign of Rebecca.

Looked like this party was moving on.

ON THE ROOF

Mark had heard the sirens also. He made his way to the edge of the building and peered over. The police were leaving.

Three cars disappeared down the street.

You had to hand it to Jode. Mark didn't know how she'd done it, but she'd got the cops to move on. He might actually get away from here.

Another pair of cops ran out of the building. They scrambled into their car and disappeared down the street, sirens blaring.

How had she managed it?

It didn't matter. All that mattered was that they were going. And that meant he had a chance to save Rebecca.

He made his way back to the door. Time to go.

AT THE POLICE STATION

Detective Jackson led Jodie into a small office at the back of the police station. It didn't look as if it was an office that belonged to anybody. The desk was bare, free of any personal touches. No photos of loved ones. No joke gifts. Nothing.

Just a note pad, a pen and a phone.

"Can I call my husband now?" asked Jodie

"Sure," said Detective Jackson. He picked up the desk phone and handed it to her.

Jodie looked at it warily.

"I'll just use my mobile," she said.

"I'm afraid these offices don't get good reception," said Detective Jackson. "Not sure why—we've discussed it with all kinds of boffins. But nobody can explain it. So I'm afraid it's our phone or nothing."

Jodie glared at him. No reception. Sure. "Fine," she said. She picked up the receiver and dialled.

Detective Jackson walked over to the window and looked out of it. As if by simply turning his back on her that gave her some privacy. As far as Jodie knew, soundwaves didn't work that way.

On the other hand, he wasn't going to go away. So she was best to ignore him.

"Hello?" said Richard.

"It's me."

"Are you okay? Where are you?"

"I'm fine. I'm at the police station."

"Did they get Mark?"

Jodie hesitated. "He got away," she said.

"Which station are you at? I'll come and get you."

"They want to question me."

"What?" said Richard. "What for?"

"About Marcus."

"Okay," said Richard. "I'll still come and get you."

"No. I don't know how long I'll be," said Jodie. "Just stay there."

"I'll—"

"Just stay there," repeated Jodie. "I'll call you when I'm done." She hung up.

OUTSIDE THE HOTEL

Andrew had just turned the engine over to follow the last of the police cars leaving when something caught his eye.

There. At the back exit of the hotel car park. Was that somebody sneaking out?

One of the myriad of officers had previously locked off the area. But now, with all but two having left, it was a clear way out of the building.

Andrew peered harder.

It could easily be Captain Dipshit.

He put the car into gear and moved slowly towards the exiting man. He looked suspicious enough. He was peering back over his shoulder with every other step.

Andrew cast a glance down the road to the last cop car. He had about three seconds to decide. If he didn't turn now and start following that police car, he'd have no way of knowing which way to go. And no chance of being on the spot when they captured

Captain Dipshit and Rebecca needed a strong man's arms to collapse into.

On the other hand, if this *was* Captain Dipshit sneaking out of the building, he could be a hero.

He sped up slightly.

The exiting man turned his head and saw him. His eyes widened.

Andrew got a good look at his face. Oh, that was Captain Dipshit all right.

He accelerated towards him.

Time to be a hero.

AT RICHARD AND JODIE'S HOUSE

Richard sighed and stared at the phone. Oh, she was pissed all right. Not surprising. From her perspective, he was betraying one of her oldest and best friends.

Eventually she'd see it from his point of view. See that he was keeping her safe from a dangerous mess.

Of course, the phone call from the police station was just one of her passive-aggressive ways of making a point. See what you've done now, Rich. You've got me arrested and interrogated.

Which he felt bad about. But not as bad as he felt about having her running from the police.

People who ran from the police sometimes ended up being shot to death.

People who turned themselves into the police? Much more likely to avoid being shot to death.

So he'd let her have her 'I'm-over-at-the-police-station-and-am-so-mad-at-you-I'll-not-even-tell-you-which-station-I'm-at' tantrum, and he'd pick her up on the other side.

The anger would pass. He just had to lie low until it did.

He looked around the house.

A quick tidy-up wouldn't go astray either.

OUTSIDE THE HOTEL

Mark watched the car pull to a halt in front of him. Wasn't this the car that had deliberately slowed down to prevent him from getting to the apartment in time?

Surely not.

The window wound down. A man poked his head out.

"Oi," he said. "Captain Dipshit. Stop right there."

It *was* the same car. What was this? Some kind of delayed road rage incident? "What?" he said.

"I know who you are," said the man.

"How wonderful for you," said Mark. He turned to walk away. The car jerked forward and gave him a nudge. "Hey!" said Mark, turning around. He hit the bonnet of the car. "Watch it."

"You're the guy who shot the cops," said the man.

Mark turned and glared at him. How could this guy possibly know that? He can't have gained that much notoriety in such a short time. Could he? God, if members of the public were going to recognise him and make citizen's arrests, he had no chance of saving Rebecca.

"I think you've mistaken me for somebody else," said Mark.

"Oh, I don't," said the jerk in the car. He gave him another nudge. "Where's Rebecca?"

Mark was too stunned to even hit the bonnet of the car this time.

AT THE FARMHOUSE

Rebecca climbed out of bed. The Other Mark was snoring softly.

He'd certainly earned himself some rest. My god, the man had been insatiable. She didn't know where such passion had come from but, by god, she'd liked it.

She made her way to the bathroom. Oh, she was going to be sore tomorrow. She stepped over The Other Mark's jacket. Like most of the clothes, they'd discarded it in a lust-driven frenzy. She noticed her phone hanging out of her jacket pocket.

She looked back at The Other Mark. He dozed on. She leant over and picked up her phone.

She stood back up and went into the bathroom, closing the door behind her. She sat down and turned her phone back on.

Messages.

Nine of them.

Nine of them?

This is what happened when you turned your phone off for even a short period of time. Sure, you could have undisturbed crazy animal sex with your soul mate for a few hours. But you missed phone calls.

She dialled MessageBank. As she listened to the messages, her eyes widened in disbelief and confusion.

OUTSIDE THE HOTEL

"Who are you?" asked Mark.

"I'm a concerned citizen who is going to put you away, you dip-shit murdering creep," said the man. He pulled his head back inside the window. He reached into his pocket for his mobile phone, then poked his head back out again. "Now, tell me where Rebecca is before I call the cops."

Mark frowned. This was insane.

But if this crazy man thought he was a murderer, then that might be his way out of it. He put his hand in his jacket pocket and pointed a hidden finger at the crazy man.

"Drop the phone," he said.

The man hesitated. "You don't have a gun," he said. But he'd pulled his head back in the window slightly.

"No?" said Mark. "I've already shot two people today. Difficult to do that without a gun."

The crazy man hesitated again. "Show it to me," he said.

"What?"

"You heard me," he said. "Show me the gun."

"Why should I?"

"If I don't see it, how am I supposed to know you have it?"

"Buddy," said Mark. "I don't care if you know I have it or not. Your belief in the existence of my gun is irrelevant. The fact that a bullet will enter your head if you don't do what I say? That's relevant."

More hesitation. The man shook his head. "It's just your finger."

Mark shrugged. "Okay," he said. "If you believe that, go ahead and call the cops." He smiled as creepy a smile as he could muster. "You've got more balls than I do."

The crazy man didn't do anything. "It's clearly a finger," he said.

"You one hundred percent sure?" said Mark. "Because, y'know, you're gambling your life here."

The man stared at the pocket. "It's your finger," he said.

"Fine," said Mark. "Call the cops."

"Definitely your finger." He pulled the phone back up, ready to dial.

Mark raised his hand in the pocket slightly higher, pointing his imaginary gun at the man. "Sorry, mate," he said. He smiled and winced in imaginary preparation for the gunshot.

The crazy man bought it.

"No, no, no," he said. He lowered the phone again.

"Drop it now," said Mark. "Or I will shoot you."

"It is *so* not a gun," said the man. But he dropped the phone.

OFF THE HIGHWAY

Agent Innes screeched to a halt beside Mark's abandoned car. The other police officers had already started to divert traffic and seal the area around the car.

Agent Innes leapt out of his car. An eager officer ran over to him.

"We've confirmed the numberplate," said the officer. "It's Campbell's car, all right."

"We need to seal this area," said Agent Innes.

"Already on it."

"Excellent. We also need to do a door-to-door. Find out how long the car's been here and if anybody saw where Campbell went next." He raised his voice to pass the message on to all the officers. "Witnesses, people! We need witnesses. Comb the area."

He dropped his voice again and spoke to Officer Eager. "Forensics?"

"On their way."

"Excellent."

OUTSIDE THE HOTEL

It was so not a gun. Andrew knew it. Captain Dipshit knew it. All he had to do was charge the guy, tackle him to the ground and call the cops. He'd be a goddamn, bona fide hero.

And he could take him. Now that he'd had a good look at him, Captain Dipshit was clearly a wimp. What Rebecca saw in him was a total mystery.

The dipshit had moved around to the passenger side of the car now. He tapped his spare hand on the passenger window.

Andrew wound it down. Captain Dipshit took a step back and pointed his imaginary gun at him.

"Turn the engine off," he said.

Don't turn the engine off, his brain screamed at him. With the engine still on, you can accelerate away, call the cops and get out of here.

Captain Dipshit raised his pocketed hand. "I said, turn it off."

It is not a gun. He knew it wasn't a gun.

"You've got to the count of three," said Captain Dipshit. "And don't even think about driving off. You will be dead before you reach second gear."

Bluff, bluff, bluff. It was so obviously a bluff.

So drive, goddammit.

"One," said Captain Dipshit.

"It's not a gun," said Andrew.

"We've already gone through this," said Captain Dipshit. "Two."

Andrew turned the engine off. "Fine."

Bastard, bastard, bastard. He hated being so obviously bluffed like this. But what if he *did* have a gun?

"Throw me the keys."

"The keys?"

"Yeah," said Captain Dipshit. "The things in your hand right there. Toss them to me."

Andrew had an idea. He pulled the keys out of the ignition and tossed them to Captain Dipshit's pocketed hand. Instinctively, he pulled the hand out to catch them. Andrew peered closely at the jacket pocket. It was empty. There was no gun in there.

It had been a finger all along. He knew it.

He opened his door and climbed out. No phone. No car. No gun. It was now just the two of them.

Mano a mano.

Let's get ready to rumble.

AT THE FARMHOUSE

Rebecca tried to make sense of the phone messages she'd just heard. Some of them were easy enough to understand—Jodie's urging to 'get away from Mark now', for example, was short and to the point.

Katrina's rambling was less so. She'd left several messages, each more rambling than the last. However, the essence of her messages seemed to be the same as Jodie's.

There was also some rambling elaboration about why she might want to get away from Mark.

Something about shooting a police officer?

But that didn't make sense. Why would he do that? Even if he was desperate to make the phone call, she just couldn't see Mark shooting anybody about it. Especially not a cop.

And, heck, even if he did get that desperate, he didn't have a gun.

So that put paid to that particular theory.

On the other hand, while she could rely on Katrina to go completely mental and over the top on matters Mark, the same could not be said about Jodie. So why on Earth was she telling him to get away?

Only one way to find out. She pressed Speed Dial 5 on her phone.

OUTSIDE THE HOTEL

Before Mark had dropped the keys, he knew he'd made a mistake. All he'd had going for him was the gun bluff. And now that was gone.

The crazy man wasn't messing about either. He was out of the car. Charging at him.

Dear god. He was going to be in a fight. This was stupid. He hadn't been in a fight since he was a kid. He hoped he remembered how to do it.

Mark stood up. Just in time to have crazy man tackle him back down. He hit the ground with a thud. The crazy man raised himself to his knees. He went to punch him. Mark blocked the punch with his forearm.

He still remembered how to not get hit. That was a goodish starting point. At some point, however, it might be sensible to retaliate. Bit difficult from a pinned position, however. If only he'd gone through with the wrestling classes Principal Fine had recommended.

No time for regrets. He'd just have to improvise. He blocked another crazy man punch. Then brought his knees up into crazy man's backside.

Crazy man lost his balance for a second. Mark took the chance to push him to one side. As he did, he twisted and rolled the other way. Free of the crazy man, Mark climbed to his feet. He ran around towards the front of the car.

Crazy man chased. Straight into the car door Mark opened behind him. He reeled back, stunned.

First rule of fight club. When your opponent is stunned, finish him off.

Okay, so maybe that wasn't the proper first rule of fight club. But, hell, the real first rule was ridiculously self-referential.

While crazy man reeled, Mark stepped forward. He threw one punch at crazy man's head. When he brought his hands up to protect himself, Mark threw the follow-up. Stomach punch.

Stomach punches were far smarter than head punches. Much easier on the knuckles, too. It was fine for movie action heroes to go around punching people in the head. But in real life, it hurt one's fists like nobody's business.

Crazy man doubled over. Mark made a double-fist and hit him on the shoulders. He fell to the ground.

A kick in the head to make sure of it. And that was that.

Like riding a bicycle.

AT THE POLICE STATION

Detective Jackson leant in to Jodie. "So you were unaware of Mr Campbell's actions from earlier in the day when we called you?" he said.

Jodie put her most innocent face on. "Of course," she said. "If I knew he'd done that, I never would have—"

Her phone rang. So much for the 'no reception' claim. Of course, it had been an obvious lie, but, still, a little embarrassing to catch Detective Wacko Jacko in the middle of it.

Detective Wacko didn't seem at all embarrassed. He picked the phone up off the table before Jodie could get to it. He looked at the name on the screen.

"Rebecca?" he said. "Mr Campbell's girlfriend?"

"Fiancée."

Detective Wacko answered the phone.

"Hello?"

There was muffled talk from Rebecca.

"Detective Dan Jackson," he said. He smiled at Jodie.

Another brief pause while Rebecca talked at the other end.

Detective Wacko smiled some more. "My name is Detective Dan Jackson," he repeated. "I'm part of the team trying to track down your"—he smiled again at Jodie—"fiancé. Do you know where he is?"

He pulled the phone from his ear. Looked at it. Then looked back at Jodie.

"She hung up," he said. "I think that means she knows where he is."

He got up and left, taking Jodie's phone with him.

Jodie remained in her chair and stewed.

OUTSIDE THE HOTEL

Mark closed the boot. It was too dangerous to leave the crazy man unconscious outside the hotel. Who knew when he'd regain consciousness and tell the cops what he knew? Far safer to dump him in the boot. If he'd had rope and time he'd have tied him up as well.

But he had neither of these things. He had to get going. He climbed into the car, turned the ignition and pulled out.

He still didn't know where Rebecca was, but he was going to find her. However, he couldn't do so alone. And, unfortunately, the only person left who knew about the phones was Richard.

He didn't want to rely on the Big Dick for help. But he couldn't do this alone.

AT THE FARMHOUSE

Rebecca looked at her phone. That was weird. Why had a detective answered Jodie's phone? What in blazes was going on here? Mark couldn't be wanted by the police.

Although, he *had* mentioned something about the police when she'd got into the car. But he couldn't have killed anybody.

Could he?

She listened to the messages again. She'd deleted the first few, but had saved some of Katrina's more frantic later ones. She skipped to one of the last ones.

"Bec," it said. "Where are you? Please, please call me the instant you get this. And stay away from your boyfriend. He's—" her voice choked— "shot and killed two people. Don't let him get—" starting to sob now— "Don't let him hurt you too."

Then some more sobbing to end the message.

It was madness, of course. Because, let's not forget, Mark didn't even have a gun. That made shooting people all kinds of difficult.

Nonetheless, Katrina seemed rather insistent.

No.

Katrina had taken some crazy pills and got the wrong end of some random news article. Mark Campbell was a commonish name. Maybe there'd been some reports of some other Mark Campbell shooting people.

That made sense. In fact, that explained everything. Somebody had been killed and the police were looking for a different Mark Campbell. That—

Something nagged at her.

When they'd first walked into the farmhouse, Mark had gone over to the bedside table. Pulled something out of his pocket and put it in the drawer.

She hadn't noticed what it was. And he'd jumped her soon after, so it had slipped her mind.

But it couldn't be—

She opened the door a crack and peered through. He was still dozing.

She watched his chest rise up and down. Smiled at his faint snore. Peered over at the bedside table. What had he put in there?

No.

Mark was not a killer. Katrina's madness was getting to her. He'd probably just put his keys and wallet in the drawer.

Except, there were his keys on the floor, beside his jacket.

And there was his wallet, underneath her bra.

Goddamn it, Katrina. You and your goddamn craziness.

AT RICHARD AND JODIE'S HOUSE

Mark pulled the car over in front of Jodie and Richard's house. He got out and looked around. There was no sign of any police.

Not yet, anyway. Surely it was only a matter of time before they arrived here.

He opened the boot. Crazy man was still unconscious. Good. Richard would have some rope. They'd tie him up, leave him somewhere he couldn't cause any trouble, then put their heads together and try to find Rebecca.

292

He closed the boot. Went over to the door of the house. He knocked.

"Rich," he said. "It's me."

Nothing.

He knocked again. Louder this time.

He looked around nervously. Where could he have gone? They didn't ask much of the Big Dick. The least he could do was be around when he needed him to help tie up the crazy owner of the car he'd stolen and help him find his fiancée, who his evil doppelganger had kidnapped.

If he couldn't do that, what was he good for?

Screw it. Mark unlocked the door with his spare key and made his way in.

"Rich?" he said. "You home?"

He tiptoed around a corner, where Richard confronted him, holding a golf club above his head.

"What are you doing here?" said Richard.

Mark took a step back. He held his hands in the air. "Rich, I need your help."

"Are you insane?"

"That wasn't me who killed those people," said Mark.

Richard raised his golf club higher.

"You know me," said Mark. "I'm not a killer."

Richard did not respond.

"It was…" Mark sighed. He couldn't believe he was about to say this. "It was an evil doppelganger."

"What?" said Richard.

"I know how it sounds," said Mark. "But I swear it's true. It's a space-time continuum thing. The universe created an evil version of me."

"Oh come on," said Richard. But the golf club dropped a little.

"He's the one who killed those people. He's the one who has Rebecca now."

"You're serious?"

"You've got to trust me," said Mark. "You're the only one left who knows about the phones. I can't do this alone."

"This is insane."

AT THE FARMHOUSE

Rebecca tiptoed along the side of the bed. Mark continued to snore slightly.

This was insane. There was no gun in this bedside drawer. To even consider it was crazy.

And yet, here she was, slinking along the bed, trying not to wake him up, going to check on the non-existence of the gun.

She could try to convince herself that she was trying to be quiet so as not to disturb Mark's sleep. But she was quite sure she was incapable of that level of self-delusion.

Bloody Katrina. Even when she was mostly out of her life, she was still capable of messing things up with Mark.

She made it to the drawer. Mark snorted and rolled over. Rebecca held her breath.

The snoring resumed.

Rebecca opened the drawer. Slowly. Quietly.

And there it was. A gun.

Mark had a gun.

Why did Mark have a gun?

Her heart pounded. Okay. Maybe he had…

He could have needed a gun to…

She couldn't think of one good reason for this gun being in this drawer.

One thing was for sure. She wasn't going to leave it there. Not that she thought Mark was dangerous. Of course not. But, y'know, if there was going to be a gun in the house, she wanted it with her.

She picked it up. Closed the drawer. Quiet, quiet.

Mark didn't move.

She turned and tiptoed back to the bathroom.

Grabbed her phone. Who could she call? Some cop had commandeered Jodie's phone. Katrina was a babbling idiot.

Richard.

She called him.

AT RICHARD AND JODIE'S HOUSE

Richard's phone rang. "Don't move," he said to Mark.

Mark rolled his eyes. "Wouldn't think of it."

Richard smiled. With one eye still on Mark, he picked up the phone. Looked at the number.

"It's Rebecca," he said.

"Rebecca." Mark took a step toward the phone. Richard pulled the golf club back, ready to swing.

Mark stopped. Richard answered the phone. "Rebecca. Where are you?"

"Rich. What's going on?" came Rebecca's voice. She was whispering. "I just called Jode and some detective answered her phone."

"Where is she?" said Mark.

Richard nodded to him. "Where are you?" he said.

"I'm with Mark," she said. "We're safe. What's going on? The messages on my phone were a tad… disturbing."

"You're with Mark?" said Richard.

"Yes," said Rebecca. "Why? What's going on?"

"*I'm* with Mark. He's right here beside me. He wants to talk to you."

"What do you mean he's right there beside you?" said Rebecca. "Where are you?"

"We're at our house," said Richard.

"What?" said Rebecca.

"Look, I'll let him explain."

AT THE FARMHOUSE

Rebecca frowned in fresh confusion.

People everywhere were going crazy. Katrina babbling away. Mark with an inexplicable gun. Now Richard talking out and out nonsense. This was a strange day.

"Babe," came the voice of Mark through her phone. "It's me. You're in great danger. You have to get out of there. Tell us where you are and we'll come and get you."

"Mark?" said Rebecca. She opened the bathroom door and saw the sleeping Other Mark. She closed the door again so as not to disturb him.

Okay. Maybe it wasn't everybody else going crazy. Maybe it was her.

She didn't feel crazy. But then, crazy people never did, right? That was one of the things that made them crazy.

"Who is this?" she hissed into the phone.

"It's me, babe. Look, I don't have time to explain. It's a… It's a space-time continuum fuckup thing."

This was weirding her out. It couldn't possibly be Mark. But, by god, it was a perfect impression.

"Put Rich back on," she said.

"Babe, you have to trust me. The Mark that's with you is a murderer. An… an evil doppelganger."

Oh, come on. "Put Rich back on," she said.

There was a sigh at the other end. "Babe…"

"Put Rich back on."

The phone clunked. "Rebecca?" came the voice of Richard.

"What's going on, Rich?" she asked. If she wasn't crazy—and it seemed the only sensible course of action was to assume she wasn't—then Richard was the only person speaking any sense.

He was the only person she could trust at this point.

"It's true," said Richard. "The rupture in the space-time continuum apparently created another version of Mark. A bad version. He's already killed two people. You have to get out of there."

Okay. There went *that* theory. Richard was crazy too.

An evil doppelganger? Created by a rupture in the space-time continuum? Crazy, crazy, crazy.

Except, of course, that it explained everything. The gun. Katrina's claims that Mark had killed two people. The fact she could talk to Mark on the phone at Rich's house while he also slept in the bed in the next room.

And this Mark's previously hidden sexual aggression.

Oh, god. "This isn't the real Mark?" she said.

"It seems not," said Richard.

"I'm gonna be—" She put the phone on the sink, then turned and vomited into the toilet.

"Are you all right?" said Richard.

Rebecca reached up for the phone. She spat the last remains of vomit into the toilet and put the phone back to her ear. "I'm all right," she said. "God, I slept with him."

"You bitch!" came the voice from the doorway. "What have you done?"

Rebecca whirled around. The Other Mark was awake. He pushed the door open and advanced on her. She screamed.

CHAPTER ELEVEN

"This maniac has Rebecca and I can't do anything about it."

"I'm racing off to confront a murderous evil doppelganger."

Your butt is not that big.

"Please don't kill me."

AT THE FARMHOUSE

REBECCA REACHED FOR the gun. She was too slow. Way too slow. The Other Mark was on her before she knew anything. He grabbed her wrist and pushed it back. She felt something snap and the gun fell to the ground.

The pain shot up through her wrist. She blinked a long, swimming blink before snapping her eyes open again.

Don't you dare faint, girl.

"You stupid, stupid bitch," she said. "Why did you have to poke your nose into it?"

"Help me," she gasped into the phone.

"Where are you?" came Richard's voice.

Before she could answer, The Other Mark had grabbed the phone from her. He smashed it against the wall. "What are you doing?" he roared.

Rebecca didn't say anything. The pain from her wrist was immense. She looked down at it and immediately wished she hadn't. Was that bone?

Her head spun. Oh my god. Don't faint. Don't faint. Don't faint. She looked up at The Other Mark. Why was he so angry?

"You've fucked everything up," said The Other Mark. He punched her hard in the face. She fell against the wall.

This was crazy. This was crazy. She was trapped with this murderous madman. What was she going to do?

He punched her again. She held up an arm to stop him. It didn't help. He landed another blow in her stomach.

All the air left her.

"You silly, silly bitch!" he yelled again.

Rebecca fell to the ground beside the toilet. The smell of vomit and blood filled her nostrils. This had become a very bad situation.

"Please don't hurt me," she said.

"Shut up," said The Other Mark. He picked up the gun from the floor. "Just stay there. Don't move. I need to work out how I'm going to fix this mess."

He opened the door and turned back to her.

"If you open this bathroom door," he said. "I will kill you."

Rebecca whimpered.

"Don't make me do that."

He left, closing the door behind him.

Rebecca curled up in a ball on the floor.

Please, Mark. Please come save me.

AT RICHARD AND JODIE'S HOUSE

"What's going on?" said Mark.

Richard looked at his phone. "The Other Mark got her."

"'Got her'?" said Mark. "What do you mean 'got her'?"

"She started screaming. He'd walked in on her talking to us," said Richard. "And he didn't sound happy about it."

"No, no, no, no, no," said Mark. "This isn't happening. Did she say where she was?"

"No," said Richard. "The phon—"

"Call her back."

Richard nodded. He pressed a button on his phone. Held it up to his ear. There was a pause.

"Well?" said Mark.

"There's no connection."

"Try again."

Richard did so. "Still nothing."

Mark threw his head back. "Oh, this is not happening," he said. "This maniac has Rebecca and I can't do anything about it." He looked up at Richard. "You believe me now?"

Richard put the golf club on the bench and nodded. "Yeah," he said. "Yeah I do."

"You've got to help me fix this. Please."

"We'll work it out," said Richard.

"I don't know what I'd do without her."

AT THE FARMHOUSE

The Other Mark prowled around the bedroom. How was he going to fix this? It didn't seem possible. His whole plan, such as it was, revolved around key people—Jodie, Rich, Rebecca—accepting him as *their* Mark.

That way, he could remove the original Mark, remove the police problems with it and slip straight into the perfect life this Mark had set up for himself.

On that score, at least, this universe's Mark had done well. The man couldn't be relied on to make universe-saving telephone calls. But he'd set up a sweet life, regardless.

And now, Rebecca had poked her nose into things and ruined his chances of taking his place.

Unless…

There was a way out of this. It was messy and unfortunate and not what he'd hoped for. But he was the Mark who made the tough decisions and if messy, unfortunate, unhoped-for decisions were needed, he was the one who would make them.

He continued to stride around the room.

Were there any alternatives? You didn't want to make tough decisions before exhausting all other choices.

Shit.

Why hadn't she just stayed in bed?

AT RICHARD AND JODIE'S HOUSE

"Do you have any idea where they might be?" asked Richard.

"No." Mark continued to walk in circles, mumbling denials. Richard grabbed his shoulder.

"Stop it," he said. "Think. Are you sure you don't know where they are? Where would you take Rebecca if you were running from the police?"

"I'm getting sick of this," said Mark. "Just because we're doppelgangers doesn't mean that we share the same mind. Y'know? For one thing, I don't find it acceptable in any way to shoot people to death."

"Okay, okay. I'm sorry."

"I just… I can't believe any of this has happened. We should never have messed about with that bloody phone."

"Probably not," said Richard. "But regretting it doesn't undo it."

"Could you stop being so sensible about everything for just a minute?" said Mark. "God, you're as bad as your wife."

"She taught me everything I know."

Mark half-smiled.

Richard's phone rang. He picked it up and looked at the incoming number.

"Who is it?" said Mark.

Richard showed him the number. "It's 'you'," he said. He answered the phone. "Hello?"

There was a pause before Richard handed Mark the phone. "He wants to speak to you."

Mark took the phone and a deep breath. He exhaled the latter and raised the former to his ear.

"If you harm a hair on her head—" he began.

"Oh shut up, you pitiful clone. She's fine."

God. It was his own voice. He was talking to his doppelganger. This was too weird. "She'd better be," he said.

"Or what?" said The Other Mark. "Look, just calm yourself down. There's no need for hysterics."

Mark took another deep breath. "Fine," he said. "Where are you?"

"You're a hard man to get hold of," said The Other Mark. "I tried your phone, got an engaged signal." He laughed Mark's laugh. This was too creepy. "Weird times, huh?"

"The weirdest," said Mark. "Where are you?"

"Then I tried Jode. Some detective answered, so I hung up on him, quick smart."

"Oh shut up," said Mark. "Where are you?"

"Fine. I'm at the Thompsons' old farmhouse. Remember the Thompsons, Mark?"

"Yeah," said Mark. "Best foster-parents I ever had."

The Other Mark snorted. "If you say so," he said. "I was never partial to them myself. Maybe something to do with the fortnightly drunken beatings."

Mark's phone began to ring. He looked at the number. It was Jodie. He turned it off and returned his attention to The Other Mark. "What?" he said.

"Thommo didn't beat you?" said The Other Mark. His voice sounded surprised.

"Of course not," said Mark. "And he didn't touch alcohol."

"Huh," said The Other Mark. "Maybe that's where you and I differ."

"Oh, *that's* where we differ."

"We're not that different, Mark. I'm just a little more determined to keep hold of the important things. Y'know, not let the universe collapse in a mass of self-contradictory time looping."

"At least I didn't kill my dog."

"Oh, shut up, you idiot," said The Other Mark. "Of course you did. If I hadn't shown up, you would have killed your dog and everybody else in the universe. Sometimes you need to look at the bigger picture."

"Well, then," said Mark. "I suppose we owe you an enormous debt of gratitude. Please. Continue to run rampant through our reality, kidnapping my fiancée, murdering innocent people."

The Other Mark laughed. "Okay," he said. "To descend completely into cliché, it's clear that there's not enough room in this reality for the both of us. So let's fix that, huh?"

"How?"

"You come to the farmhouse. Alone. Two of us go in. One of us comes out."

"That's it?"

"That's it," said The Other Mark. "But the key word here is 'alone'. If I see the police or if I see Jode or the big Dick, I'll gut Bec with a knife."

"If you touch her, I'll kill you."

"Oh, shut up. I don't want to hurt her. I'd much rather walk out of here, girl in my arms, hero of the day and so forth. So just come alone. Okay?"

"Okay."

"And be here within the hour," said The Other Mark. "Or I'll kill her anyway."

"Within the hour?" said Mark.

"It's doable. Might have to break a few speed limits on the way. But you can make it."

"Fine," said Mark. "I'll be there."

"You'd better be. I know how you are with deadlines." He hung up.

Mark threw the phone back to Richard. "I've gotta go," he said.

"I'm coming with you."

"You can't. He told me to come alone."

"You're not seriously going to take him on alone, are you?"

"I don't have a choice. If I don't face him one on one, he'll kill her."

"Yeah," said Richard. "But if you do face him one on one, he'll kill *you*."

"Maybe," said Mark. "Maybe not."

"I've been watching news reports all afternoon, Mark. This guy's a killer."

"Thanks for the pep talk."

Rich smiled. "Look, I know you two are essentially the same person, but I think, somehow, he might fight just a wee bit dirtier than you. Jesus, Mark, have you ever even been in a fight?"

"Ah," said Mark. "That reminds me."

AT THE POLICE STATION

Detective Jackson returned to the interrogation room. Jodie looked up.

"You'll never guess who just called," he said to Jodie. He held her phone aloft.

"Stevie Wonder?"

Detective Jackson smiled. "Mr Campbell."

"My next guess," said Jodie. "What did he say?"

"Not a lot. We called him back. He didn't want to talk."

"Hardly surprising."

"No. We also found his abandoned car," said Detective Jackson. He put down his coffee mug. "I have to be honest, Mrs Flannery. I thought you were trying to protect him. But everything you've told us has checked out."

"I could have told you that," said Jodie. "In fact, I'm pretty sure I did tell you that."

"You're free to go," he said. "Obviously, if he tries to make further contact with you, please let us know."

"Of course." Detective Jackson handed her phone to her. "Thank you," she said.

She stood up to leave the room. Could it really be this easy?

AT THE FARMHOUSE

Rebecca could hear The Other Mark talking on the phone.

Where was *her* Mark? She needed him. Where was he?

And then, as if she was standing right beside her, she heard Katrina's voice. Katrina's disapproving voice.

"You don't need a man to save you," said the voice. "You are a strong, amazing woman. You can look after yourself."

She was obviously more badly hurt than she thought if she was hearing voices. She probably had some kind of head trauma.

But the voice had a point. She had to look after herself. Now. While he was distracted. This was her chance to get out of here.

She had no idea how, exactly. But she needed to work it out quickly.

She looked up at the bathroom window again. It was too small for her to fit through. But what choice did she have?

There were no weapons in here. No guns. No knives. No flame-throwers, bazookas or nunchakus. She could throw a phone battery at him. That was about it.

The door didn't lock. And, even if it did, she had little doubt The Other Mark could break it down.

No. He was going to return and there was no way she could fight back when he did.

So flight was the only option.

And the tiny window was the only way to do it.

She pushed herself up on her good hand. She refused to look at the other one. It was yammering away at her. Yak, yak, yak. *I hurt so much.* We know, hand. Can't do much about it while trapped in a bathroom with a psychopathic doppelganger of my fiancé in the next room, can we? Let's get out of here and then we'll talk.

Talk to the hand?

Probably less crazy than talking to an imaginary version of her cousin.

Or was it?

She decided to give herself permission to talk to whoever or whatever she liked. Just as long as she got the hell out of here.

She stood on the bathroom seat and pulled the window open.

She was never going to fit through this gap. She wasn't a midget. Her head might squeeze through, but her shoulders and hips couldn't possibly.

No.

Negative thoughts weren't going to help.

Positive thoughts, Tyler. Positive thoughts.

She *was* going to fit through this gap.

She *was* a midget.

AT THE POLICE STATION

Detective Jackson watched as Jodie filled out the last of her paperwork. He smiled and thanked her for all her help, before watching her leave. As she hailed a taxi, he picked up his phone and dialled.

"We've let her go," he said.

"Okay," said Agent Innes. "Let me know if she contacts him."

"Will do." He gestured to one of the other policemen to get the car ready. "Any leads from the car?"

"Nothing," said Agent Innes. "We're doing a doorknock but it's a long shot. If he was here, he's long gone, and no clues to what direction he might have gone." His voice suddenly grew emphatic. "So don't lose her."

"We won't."

AT RICHARD AND JODIE'S HOUSE

"Whose car is this?" said Richard, as they walked down the driveway.

Mark ignored him. He walked around to the boot and opened it. "This guy's," he said.

Richard walked around to the back of the car and looked in.

"Who is this?" he said.

"The owner of the car," said Mark. "Tch. Pay attention."

Richard sighed. "Please tell me you didn't beat up a man, lock him in the boot of his own car and then steal that car to get here."

There was a pause. "Okay."

"You did do that?"

"He started it."

Richard raised his eyebrows.

"He did," said Mark. "I was just minding my own business, avoiding the police, when this moron appeared from nowhere and started hassling me about all the, y'know… All the stuff The Other Mark had done."

"Okay," said Richard. "Whatever. What are we going to do with him?"

"*I'm* not going to do anything with him," said Mark. "I've got a ridiculously short amount of time to get to my foster-parents' old farmhouse. I'm going to need your car, your phone and… Do you have a gun or anything?"

Richard stared at him. "If I had a gun, would I have come after you armed with a golf club?"

"Good point," said Mark. "Okay, just your car and your phone then."

There was a momentary pause.

"Your keys?" said Mark.

"Oh," said Richard. "Of course." He grabbed the keys from his pocket and tossed them to Mark. "And I have to deal with—" he gestured to the man in the boot— "this."

"Sorry," said Mark. He slammed the boot down. "Here are the keys to his car. I'd recommend just parking him around the corner somewhere."

Richard sighed. "Fine," he said. "Good luck."

"Thanks," said Mark. He opened the car door of Richard's Ferrari. "Look after Jode."

"Will do," said Richard. "Look after yourself."

But Mark was already backing down the driveway.

AT THE END OF THE STREET

She knew it.

Katrina slammed the steering wheel of her car.

Rich, you lying bastard.

No sooner had she pulled up at the end of the street than she saw Rich and Mark coming out of the house. They'd opened the boot of the car, looked in and discussed something. Then Mark had taken Rich's car and driven off.

And now she didn't know what to do. The obvious course of action was to follow Mark, call the police and get the asshole arrested.

But, on the other hand, what were they looking at in the boot?

She watched Rich looking all around the street. The poor guy had guilt written all over him. He was clearly up to something he didn't want to do.

Actually, knowing Rich and Mark and their relationship, he was probably only helping him because Jodie had asked him to.

Still didn't make it right, of course. But she could feel some sympathy for him. Rich wasn't a bad guy. She'd known him for, god, three years now. He was one of the good guys.

But she didn't have time to think about that. Richard was helping Mark. Mark was a dangerous murderer who almost certainly had something to do with Rebecca's disappearance. She had to stop him.

A horrible thought occurred to her.

What if?

What if it was Rebecca in the boot?

Now the thought was out there, she had no choice.

She had to stay here and check.

Especially as Rich seemed to be taking the car somewhere else. He climbed into the car, pulled away from the kerb and drove off.

Slowly, and ever so quietly, Katrina followed.

AT THE FARMHOUSE

Rebecca paused. Now what?

She had the good arm out the window. It hung down, trying to find a gripping point on the outside wall. She also had her head through the window. Just.

It was a tight squeeze. She saw no possible way of pulling the other arm through. Particularly as she was now on tiptoes on top of the toilet. To get any further she needed the good arm to support most of her weight. And pull her through a window which had no more room to get through. It wasn't going to happen.

Positive thoughts, Tyler. Positive thoughts.

It *might* happen if she could just push her head far enough to one side of the window. She jammed her neck against the edge of the window. She just needed to make enough of a gap to squeeze the shoulder through. Once she got the other shoulder past the window, she could almost fall the rest of the way.

That would hurt. But it would hurt a lot less than hanging around with The Other Mark.

She pushed her shoulder into the window. It didn't fit.

God. Why did they make these windows so damn small?

She pushed her neck even harder against the side of the window. She was sure she could feel the pulse in her neck diverting around the pane. She tried again with the shoulder. This time it squeezed into the gap.

She wriggled it forward a little.

Just have to get the shoulder all the way through. Everything's easy after that.

(Except for the boobs and hips)

Ignore the negative thoughts. Boobs and hips will be fine. Just get the shoulders through.

She pushed off from the toilet seat. Her shoulder squeezed a little further through the window. She now dangled from it. Using her good hand hanging outside the window, she pulled down. Hard. Her shoulder squeezed through the window a little more.

She was so close. One more heave and she'd have both shoulders through.

She took a deep breath and pulled again with her good hand.

Her shoulder didn't move.

She was stuck.

IN THE TAXI

Jodie settled into the back seat of the taxi and told the driver where to take her. She then pressed the speed dial on her phone. Mark answered it.

"Jode?" he said.

"Marcus?" said Jodie. "What are you doing with Rich's phone?"

"We swapped."

"Okay," said Jodie. "Any particular reason?"

"The Other Mark couldn't call me on mine. He spoke some gibberish about an engaged signal."

"Hmmm. I suppose that makes sense," said Jodie. "So you've spoken to him?"

"Aye."

"And?"

"I have to go confront him to save Rebecca."

"Where are you going?"

"I have to confront him alone."

"This some macho bullshit?"

"I wish," said Mark. "Where are you?"

"I'm in a cab," said Jodie. "You?"

"Rich's Ferrari."

"His phone. His Ferrari. You're doing well."

"Sure. I'm racing off to confront a murderous evil doppelganger. I'm doing swimmingly."

"Well," said Jodie. "I'm pretty sure the police are following me."

"Yeah?" said Mark.

"Yeah. It's the only explanation for the ease of my escape."

"The Force will be with you," said Mark.

"Always."

"So what are we going to do now?"

"Don't worry," said Jodie. "I'll think of something."

Mark looked at his watch. "You'd better make it quick."

NEAR RICHARD AND JODIE'S HOUSE

Richard pulled up around the corner from their house. This was crazy. He could go to jail for this shit.

Let's see. Accessary to murder. Accessary to kidnapping. Accessary to stealing a car.

Quite a crime spree he was embarking on here.

He got out of the car. Should he be wiping fingerprints off or something? He looked around. No neighbours were looking at him. (Although who knew how many were peeking out from behind the curtain.)

He put his hands inside his shirt and wiped the steering wheel. He closed the door, leaving the keys in the ignition.

Was that a crime? Leaving somebody else's car in a position where it was easy to steal?

Probably not. Still didn't feel right, however. But what else was he going to do? If he kept the keys, it would prove very easy to trace his role in whatever car-related crimes he'd just committed. But he wasn't going to throw the keys away. Leaving the keys in the ignition seemed the safest course of action. At least, that way, when they found Boot Guy, he could (theoretically) drive away without bothering anybody.

Would he do that?

Almost certainly not. But there was a chance.

There was also a chance somebody might steal the car and leave Boot Guy somewhere far, far away. That was too nice a thought to even dream about.

He wiped the door clean with the inside of his shirt.

No fingerprints. At least, he assumed there were no fingerprints. Who knew whether wiping a car door with a shirt cleaned these things off or not? Part of him almost wished he'd watched one of those god-awful CSI television shows.

But only a small part.

Okay.

That was it. The guy in the boot could breathe. Plenty of air vents there. He wasn't going to die. Sooner or later somebody would find him and let him out.

Suspicion might be cast on him at that point. Seeing as how Boot Guy would explain that Mark put him in there. And for him to be found just around the corner of Richard's house was too big a coincidence to explain away.

But by that stage, the whole good Mark-evil Mark thing should be sorted out anyway. They could come up with sensible stories then.

Or, if not 'sensible' stories, at least stories that would cast all the blame on somebody else.

He looked around one more time.

Still nobody looking.

Okay. Time to get out of here.

He walked slowly away from the car. Don't look back at it. Pretend it's nothing to do with you. All will be well. Nothing at all to worry about.

As he turned the corner, Mark's phone rang.

AT THE FARMHOUSE

Oh come on, Tyler.

Your butt is not that big. If the rest of you can squeeze through this tiny window, then your hips and butt can too.

She just had to change the angle. Instead of trying to barge everything through head on, it was best to wiggle through a bit at a time, like she did with her shoulders. This was a little trickier, though, since she had nothing to hang on to. The top half of her body dangled out the window, held aloft only by her constrained hips and butt.

Once that came through, she was going to tumble the remaining few feet to the ground. The important thing there was to make sure she didn't land on the sore hand.

'Sore' hand.

Not 'crushed' hand. Or 'fractured' hand.

Just 'sore'.

What a stoic little trooper she was.

What a stoic little trooper with newly discovered child-bearing hips.

She wriggled one hip through. Almost there…

Gravity started to help. Then, in the manner of gravity, started to accelerate its help.

Before she could properly brace herself, she was through, falling to the ground. She broke the fall with her good arm, and its associated shoulder.

A jolt of pain went up that arm too. Perfect. Now both hands were going to be smashed. She pushed herself up with the good hand. No. It was okay. Just a thud on the shoulder. Things could have been a lot worse.

At that moment, she noticed the applause.

It was slow. Deliberate. Sarcastic.

She turned and saw The Other Mark, standing behind her, at the corner of the farmhouse.

"Truly a magnificent escape," he said.

"How long have you been there?"

"Oh, since about the time you got your second arm through," he said. "I didn't think you were ever going to get your butt through. In fact, I'm amazed you got out through that window at all. It really is a remarkably sm—"

Rebecca grabbed a handful of dirt and threw it in his face.

The Other Mark turned his head and swivelled some kind of karate kick into the side of her head.

Rebecca stumbled over. She didn't even have time to wonder when this Mark might have learned karate before the follow-up punch sunk deep into her stomach and she went down.

AT THE HOTEL

"Hi babe," said Jodie. She accepted the change from the taxi-driver and nodded thanks.

"It's me," said Richard.

"I know it's you," said Jodie. "I don't usually greet Mark with a 'hi babe'."

"No?"

"No. He gets more of a 'hey, what's up?' or a 'how much have you had to drink?'"

"I see," said Richard. "So you've obviously spoken to him."

"Yeah. I tried to call you when they released me. Imagine my surprise when Marcus answered."

"It's a long story," said Richard.

"I can imagine," said Jodie. "Hold on a second."

She spoke to the concierge and asked for them to bring her car up. The concierge made eye contact with the sole remaining police officer who returned a small nod.

Jodie smiled, gave a small 'thank you' wave to the police officer and turned her attention back to the phone.

"You understand now why I told you Mark wasn't dangerous?" she said.

"Yeah."

"And why you shouldn't call the police?"

"Okay, okay," said Richard. "But how was I supposed to know he had an evil doppelganger?"

"You could have listened to your wife." She started to walk across the foyer, away from the police officer. "Mark and I have talked things through. We think we have a plan."

"Oh, good."

"Don't take that tone," said Jodie. "Our last plan was working fine too, until you came along and messed it up."

"You're never going to forgive me for that, are you?"

"Forgive? Sure," said Jodie. "Forget? I don't think so."

"Fine," said Richard. "So what's the plan?"

"I'm going to pick you up in about ten minutes," she said. "You'll have about twenty seconds to load the car—"

"Load the car?"

"Yes. Load the car," said Jodie. "Now, listen up. Here's what we're going to need."

NEAR RICHARD AND JODIE'S HOUSE

Jesus! Here he came. Katrina lowered her head, as Richard came running around the corner. Because a car being driven by someone whose head you can't see is always inconspicuous.

Inconspicuous enough for Rich, anyway. He walked past her car, eyes straight ahead. Ears glued to the phone.

He was back quickly. She'd been expecting to follow him for… well, she didn't know for how long, but more than thirty seconds would have been a starting assumption. Long enough for her to slip into third gear, let's say.

And yet, here he was. Walking back. He can't have gone far. What on Earth was he up to?

At least he hadn't seen her. Who was he talking to? Mark?

More importantly, where had he dumped the car? It can't have been far. She turned the corner.

There. Just the other end of the road. She wouldn't need that third gear after all.

She pulled in slowly behind the parked (abandoned?) car.

Why would he park (abandon?) the car just around the corner? What was going on here?

It didn't matter. What mattered was getting Rebecca out of the car.

She ran to the driver's side of the car. Tried the door.

Unlocked?

Why would he leave it unlocked?

And why would he leave the keys in the ignition? Where was Rich's head at?

Didn't matter.

She found the boot release and pulled it. She heard the clunk of it unlocking.

She jumped off the seat and ran to the boot.

"Rebecca?" she said, as she opened it.

Her mind took a moment to process the truth.

"Andrew?" she said. "What the fuck?"

BEHIND JODIE'S CAR

As Jodie left the hotel, Detective Jackson reported in.

"Okay, she's left the taxi now and has returned to her own car."

"Which way's she heading?"

"I'm not sure. Probably…" He consulted his map. "Probably back to her house."

"Let's hope she's not just heading home for a nice, hot dinner and an early night."

"She was on the phone to somebody in the hotel foyer, while she was waiting for her car to be picked up."

"Campbell?"

"Possibly."

"Or possibly not," said Agent Innes. "Okay. Fine. Don't lose her. Keep me updated on where she goes."

"Will do."

OUTSIDE MARK'S OLD APARTMENT

"I'm sorry," said Agent Benson, to the security guard. "You don't get a say in this. We have a warrant to search Apartment 5."

The security guard looked over the warrant. "I'll just have to call Mr Campbell and get his approval."

"If you get hold of him, let us know," said Mills. "Mr Campbell is wanted for questioning over a double homicide. That's why we have the warrant. We believe there may be evidence in that building that explains the motive behind his actions today."

The security guard didn't know how to respond to this. Several different questions were struggling for priority. None of them were a convincing winner at this stage.

"Now," said Benson. "You can either unlock the doors and let us in. Or we're going to break them in. But, either way, we're going in."

"Once we're in, you can call whoever you please," said Mills. "A lawyer might well be a good idea."

The security guard finally found voice.

"Shit," he said. And started rifling through his keys.

ON THE ROAD

Mark screeched to a halt. Shit. Almost missed the turnoff there.

He looked behind him. Nobody there. He put the car into reverse and made his way back to the turnoff.

It had been so long since he'd even thought about the Thompsons. Which was sad. That old couple had single-handedly prevented him from heading down some bad paths. When he'd first met them, he was a stereotypically angry, troubled young teen. By sheer weight of compassion, they'd helped him get his life together. Made him feel like he had a family.

When Mrs Thompson had died a few years back, he'd sobbed for days. When Mr Thompson went a couple of months later, he wasn't surprised. Somehow it had seemed fitting.

He'd left the farmhouse abandoned, while he worked out what to do with it. He'd been surprised they'd left it to him. Touched, too.

And, at some point, the problem of what to do with it had just dropped to the bottom of his to-do list. He hadn't even thought of the farmhouse in years.

He turned the corner and sped up.

He checked his watch. This time he was going to make it in time.

He knew, however, that he was driving to his almost certain death.

His doppelganger had shown no qualms about killing people (and dogs) to get his own way. And the obvious way for him to elude the police was to give them a different Mark Campbell. And the only way he could do that was to give them a dead one. Because an alive one would probably, y'know, spill the beans about the whole evil doppelganger thing.

And that would just get messy.

Of course, supplying a dead Mark Campbell was also the solution to *his* problems, as well. It would just as effectively get the police off his tail.

So, either way, there was going to be a dead Mark Campbell by the end of the evening.

It was just a matter of which one.

Assuming he was the one who survived, Jodie had a 'plan' to sort things out from there. He'd been kinda hoping she'd come up with a plan that kicked in a little bit earlier. Gave him some kind of guarantee that he'd be the survivor of this little face-off.

But nope. He was on his own.

It was times like these—driving to a deserted farmhouse for a one-on-one fight to the death with his evil doppelganger from an alternate reality—that he really wished he'd stuck with the Tae Kwon Do as well.

AT THE FARMHOUSE

Rebecca opened her eyes. She was still sprawled on the ground behind the farmhouse. She lifted her head off the ground and spat out the dirt in her mouth. Oh, good. There was blood in her spit as well. She dabbed her throbbing lip with her good hand and examined it.

A split lip. Just what she'd always wanted. She looked up.

The Other Mark continued to stand over her.

"I'm so sorry," he said.

Rebecca lifted her head slowly. Glared at him. "Yeah," she said. "I could tell you were sorry earlier. When you shattered my wrist. And let's not forget when you kicked me in the side of the head. A very apologetic kick that one."

"I couldn't let you escape," he said. He half-smiled and half-shrugged. "I'm sorry. I wish things hadn't turned out this way. This wasn't what I wanted."

Rebecca continued to glare at him. "Who are you?" she said.

"I'm Mark," he said. "Not your Mark, granted. But I have the same feelings for you. I love you. Just as much as he does. More."

Rebecca wiped some more blood from her mouth. "Again, the beatings clearly prove that," she said.

"I never wanted to hurt you," he said. "You must know that. And I never wanted to hurt Chewie."

"Chewie?" said Rebecca. "What have you done to him?"

"Nothing," said The Other Mark. "Well, not now. I dunno, it's confusing. In one reality, I dropped him off that cliff."

"What?"

"Don't look at me like that. The universe needed a version of me to make that call," he said. "He wasn't up to it. I was. That's why the universe created me. I'm the one here to clean up the mess he created. If I didn't do the things I did, the universe would have collapsed."

"Do you know that?" said Rebecca. "Do you really believe one little missed phone message was going to destroy the entire universe?"

"It's not a risk we want to take, is it?"

"So you just started shooting anybody who got in your way?"

"Of course not," said The Other Mark. "Things just went… wrong."

Rebecca pulled herself up onto her good elbow. Her lip throbbed. Her head throbbed. Her wrist throbbed. She was a throbbing machine at this point. "So what are you going to do now?"

"I'm going to fix everything."

"Like the way you've been fixing everything else?"

The Other Mark snorted out a small laugh. "In a way, yeah." He reached into his back pocket and pulled out the gun. He rolled the gun over in his hand, playing with the safety. "The police are looking for Mark Campbell. They're very interested in arresting him for murder. And they're probably not going to give up on that, unless…"

"Unless?"

"Unless they find him dead, at an old abandoned farmhouse, the result of a grisly murder-suicide."

Murder-suicide? But that meant…

"You're going to kill both of us?" she said. Her voice was a whisper.

The Other Mark laughed. "Both of *us*?" he said, pointing the gun back and forth at Rebecca and himself. "No. Your Mark's on the way. He'll be here within the hour. Then I'll kill both of *you*."

"Oh my god," said Rebecca. This was really it. She was going to die tonight.

"I am sorry, Bec," he said. "If you hadn't checked your phone messages, I could have finished him off, tidied up this entire mess and we could have got on with our lives, living happily ever after. It would have been so neat. So perfect."

"Oh my god," said Rebecca again. He was serious. He was going to kill her.

"I'm sorry," he said. "I really do love you very much. But if I let you live…"

"Wait," said Rebecca. She held up her smashed hand. "Please don't kill me. I don't want to die. I'll never tell anybody about you, I promise. I'll keep your secret. Just don't kill me. Please."

Her pleas trailed into tears. Her entire upper body heaved up and down with ever-increasing sobbing.

The Other Mark rubbed his forehead. "Please don't cry, babe," he said. "I hate it when you cry."

"D-don't kill me." She looked up at him. Her tear-filled eyes met his. "Please. I'll never tell anybody. I swear."

The Other Mark smiled sadly. "I'm sorry," he said. "I wish I could believe that."

CHAPTER TWELVE

"We've got him."

This was a better reality for him.

"It will be awkward if they're just off on a romantic getaway."

"Homer and Krusty."

NEAR RICHARD AND JODIE'S HOUSE

ANDREW STIRRED INTO consciousness. Somebody was hitting him. He held up a hand for protection.

"What are you doing here, you shit?" came a voice.

He opened his eyes. It was some crazy woman with an enormous honker. Why was Little Miss Bignose abusing and hitting him?

She hit him again. "I said, what are you doing here, Andrew? Are you involved with this?"

Andrew squinted and looked more closely at her. How did she know his name?

"Stop hitting me," he said.

"Where's Rebecca?"

"How should I know?" He pulled himself out of the boot, while Little Miss Bignose stood back, watching him. "Thanks for the help," he said, once out.

"Where's Rebecca?" she said.

Andrew took a closer look at her. Oh god. He knew who this was. Christmas, two years ago. Little Miss Bignose—Kathryn?—had got drunk and started crying under the tree. Large pools of snot from her even larger nose had formed makeshift booger-tinsel on the bottom branches of the tree.

What a beautiful celebration of the birth of Our Saviour it had been.

And now she was here? Looking for Rebecca, too? Perfect.

"I don't know where she is," he said. "Do you?"

"No," she said. "But I know who does."

She turned and started to stride back towards Richard's house.

"Wait," said Andrew. "Fill me in. What's going on?"

"Don't have time to explain."

Andrew ran up to her and grabbed her arm. "Kathryn. Stop."

She turned and stared at him. "Katrina."

Shit. "Katrina, right. Sorry."

"Forget about it." She turned away. Andrew stopped her.

"Look, Katrina," he said. "I don't know how much you know. But the little bits I know suggest we're dealing with a dangerous person here."

"I know—that's why I have to find Rebecca."

"It won't do you much good to find her if you get yourself killed in the process."

Katrina hesitated. "What do you suggest?"

"Look. The guy beat me up and stuffed me in the boot. And I'm a lot bigger than you are."

(Apart from the nose.)

Katrina raised an eyebrow at him.

"Let's work together," said Andrew. "We both want the same thing."

Katrina shook her head. "I don't want anything to do with you, Andrew."

Jesus. What was up her butt? "Hey!" he said. "What's your problem?"

"I know how you treated Rebecca."

Andrew rolled his eyes. "Jesus," he said. "Ever heard the notion of there being two sides to every story?"

"I don't want to discuss this. I just want to find Reb—"

A car flew past them.

"I want to find Rebecca too," said Andrew.

"Shut up," said Katrina. "That was Rich and Jodie."

"Who?"

"I bet they're going to meet up with Mark and Rebecca."

Andrew looked around at the receding car. "We need to follow them," he said. He ran towards the driver's seat. "Where are my keys?"

"They're in the ignition," said Katrina. "I'll follow in my car."

"I'm not waiting for you," said Andrew. "I'm not going to lose them." He plonked in the seat and turned the key.

Katrina looked down the road, then back to Rich and Jodie's car as it turned a corner.

"Shit," she said. She ran back to Andrew's car and clambered into the passenger seat.

He accelerated away as she closed the door.

SLIGHTLY FURTHER FROM RICHARD AND JODIE'S HOUSE

"Was that—?" said Richard. He turned and looked back over his shoulder.

"Hmm?" said Jodie.

"I think that was Kat back there."

"Okay."

"What's Kat doing here?"

"Looking for Rebecca?"

"But we don't…" He stopped. "That's where we're going now, isn't it?"

"Aye."

"What happened to Mark's 'I must confront him alone' thing?"

"He's still confronting him alone," said Jodie. "But on the off-chance he survives the confrontation, we're gonna be there to help clean up the mess."

"And if not?"

"If not, then I'm quite sure the police who are following me will be happy to help us lock that son of a bitch away."

"The police are following us?" said Richard. He turned and looked around. "Where?"

"They're being subtle about it," said Jodie. "But they're there."

"Is that them?" said Richard. He peered more closely. "That's Boot Guy's car."

"Who the hell is 'Boot Guy'?"

"You don't want to know," said Richard.

"But he's following us too?"

"Seems so."

Jodie shrugged. "Engh," she said. "The more the merrier."

Richard turned around to the front of the car again. "So…" he said. "Are you going to tell me the plan at any point soon?"

"Sure," said Jodie.

BEHIND RICHARD AND JODIE

"Here," said Andrew. He handed a card to Katrina.

"What's this?" she said.

"It's the number for the detectives on this case," said Andrew. "You need to call them and tell them where we're going."

"Do you know where we're going?"

"North."

"Oh, good," said Katrina. "I'm sure they'll appreciate the tip."

"Call and tell them we're heading through whatever the hell suburb this is, heading north," said Andrew. "Then give them updates until they catch up with us." He turned and smiled. "Do you think you can do that?"

"God, you're a dick," said Katrina. "I don't know what Rebecca ever saw in you."

"You just answered your own question."

Katrina digested the comment and wished she hadn't. "Ugh," she said. "You're gross."

"Yeah," said Andrew. "You're a bucket of charm yourself. Now just call the cops."

Katrina sighed and pulled out her mobile phone.

AT MARK'S OLD APARTMENT

Agent Benson continued poking around the lounge room. He opened drawers. He opened fridges. He opened wardrobes. There was nothing. The place was empty.

"This place is a dead-end," he said.

Agent Mills picked up the phone.

"Anything?" said Benson.

"Nope," said Mills.

"No messages?"

"No messages. Just a normal dial tone."

"Great," said Benson. "After all the shit we went through to get the warrant, the place has nothing."

"It must have something," said Mills. "Otherwise, why the regular phone calls between their old apartments?"

"I give up. I have no idea," said Benson. "Maybe he's just insane."

"He's insanely rich. He's doing something. We just can't see it." Agent Mills circled the room.

"How are you doing this, Campbell?" he suddenly yelled.

Agent Benson's mobile phone rang. "Maybe that's him," he said. He answered the phone. "Benson," he said.

"Agent Benson?" came a woman's voice.

"Can I help you?"

"My name's Katrina Tyler," she said. "I'm in a car. We're following Richard and Jodie Flannery to where Mark Campbell is holding Rebecca Tyler."

"Where are you?"

"Passing through the Hills district, heading north."

"Okay," said Benson. "Hold the phone. Don't hang up. We're on our way. Do not lose them."

"We won't."

He pulled the phone from his ear. "We've got him," he said, to Agent Mills. "Let's go."

The pair of them left the room, slamming the door shut behind them.

They ran down the hallway, down the stairs, past the stunned doorman.

BEHIND ANDREW AND KATRINA

"She's still heading north," said Detective Jackson. "She stopped to pick up her husband and now they're both in her car."

"Where are you?" said Innes.

"We're a few cars behind," he said. "I don't think they've noticed us."

"Perfect. What suburb are you passing through?"

"Castle Hill."

"Okay," said Agent Innes. "I'll join you as soon as I can."

APPROACHING THE FARMHOUSE

Richard's phone rang. Mark looked at the number. It was 'him'.

"I'm coming, I'm coming," he said. "I'm almost there."

"Mark?"

"Rich."

"Yeah."

"Sorry. Thought you were the other me."

"Ah, no," he said. "Just wondering where you were?"

"I'm about ten minutes from the farmhouse," he said. "Where are you?"

There was a pause. Then Jodie's voice emerged. "We're about twenty minutes behind you," she said. "And we're leading a convoy of interested spectators."

"Oh, good."

"So our timing's going to have to be perfect," she said. "Will twenty minutes be long enough?"

"Should be," he said. His mouth suddenly felt dry. "One way or another. You got everything?"

"Yep," said Jodie.

"Okay, then," he said. "I guess I'll see you in half an hour or so."

"You'd better," said Jodie. "Give this asshole hell."

"I'll do my best."

"Look after Rebecca until we get there."

Mark swallowed hard. "Yep."

"Marcus?"

"Yeah?"

"Everything's going to turn out okay," said Jodie.

"I know."

"No. Listen to me," she said. "You can take this guy. You *will* take this guy. You'll save Rebecca. We'll swoop in. Clean up the mess and we'll all go back to our lives. Live happily ever after."

"Okay."

"That's the way it's going to happen."

Mark nodded. "Thank you."

"See you in half an hour."

AT THE FARMHOUSE

The Other Mark sat on the bed. He wore only his boxers.

He stared at the clock. Not long now. He held the gun in his hand and caressed it slowly.

The television prattled in the background. There had been no more news reports about him. Instead, he'd been treated to a repeat of *Frasier.*

If only that federal agent hadn't been so pushy, this whole situation could have worked out so much better. He could have taken his time, hired Bruce or Marty or one of the other guys he knew to knock Mark off, then re-emerged as the one and only Mark Campbell. Minimal mess. Minimal trouble.

Instead, everything had turned to shit.

But he could still salvage it.

He rolled the gun through his hands.

It was messier this way. But he could still get away with it. Get back to a normal life.

This was a better reality for him. He just had to slot into it.

And any minute now he was going to get the chance to do so.

Chewie began to bark. The Other Mark heard him and turned the television off. He walked to the window and pulled back a curtain. He peered out.

Mark had just pulled up in Richard's Ferrari.

Showtime.

BEHIND DETECTIVE JACKSON

"I don't believe it," said Benson.

"What?"

"That's Innes' pet detective in the car ahead," he said.

"Jackson?"

"Yeah."

"Well, how did they get here?" said Mills.

"They must have received a separate tipoff."

"Well… shit," said Mills. "There goes our arrest." He picked up the phone and spoke to Katrina. "Did you guys call any other police officers?"

"No," said Katrina.

"Well, there's one right behind you."

Up ahead, they saw Katrina turn around. She turned back. "The green car?"

"Yeah. The Ford."

"They've been behind us for a long time."

"They're following you to Campbell."

AT THE FARMHOUSE

Mark got out of the car. His head was pounding. He could feel the pulse in his forehead throbbing away. Was that normal?

He walked towards Chewie, who was thumping his tail into the ground.

"Hey mate," said Mark. "How are you?"

Chewie thumped some more.

"Did the evil version of Daddy tie you up?" he said.

More thumping.

Richard's phone rang. He looked at the caller ID. It was 'Mark' again. He answered it.

"Hello?"

"Leave Chewie alone. He's got a bone. He's happy."

Mark looked up. He saw his doppelganger peering out the window at him. His head continued to throb. "Why'd you tie him up?" said Mark. "He hates being tied up."

"I don't have time to explain that," said The Other Mark. "Take all your clothes off."

"What?"

"I'm not going to let you smuggle a gun or a knife in here. Take your clothes off." There was a pause. "Don't worry," he said. "You don't have anything I haven't seen."

Mark sighed. He undressed himself. He stretched his arms out wide and did a pirouette. He put his phone back to his ear.

"Fine," said The Other Mark. "Pull your boxers up and come in. Bring your clothes in with you."

Mark did so.

IN JODIE'S CAR

"He's probably there by now," said Jodie.

Richard looked at his watch. "Yeah," he said. "Do you think he'll be okay?"

"Do you want my honest opinion?" said Jodie.

"No."

"I think he'll be fine."

There was a long moment of silence.

"When do we lose these guys?" said Richard, giving a nod back to their vehicular posse.

"Not until we get closer to this farmhouse," said Jodie. "We only need to be a couple of minutes ahead of them. Mark thought we might gun it from the top of ah… Somerbury?"

Richard consulted the map. "Salisbury."

"Salisbury Road."

"Okay," said Richard. "Until then we just continue along sensibly?"

"Aye," said Jodie. "And hope he doesn't get himself killed."

INSIDE THE FARMHOUSE

Mark closed the door behind him. In front of him stood The Other Mark, also stripped to identical boxers. The Other Mark pointed a gun at him.

"We meet at last," said Mark.

"That we do." The Other Mark tossed him some clothes. "Put these on."

"Where's Rebecca?" said Mark.

"Put the clothes on and I'll show her to you."

Mark looked around the room. "Is she in the bathroom?" He raised his voice and yelled. "Rebecca!"

The Other Mark waved his gun at him. "She's not going to reply. Just put the clothes on and I'll show her to you."

"Is she okay? You haven't hurt her, have you?"

The Other Mark waved his gun again. "Just put the fucking clothes on."

Mark sighed. He began to dress. "Why are we—"

"Switching clothes?" said The Other Mark. "Just an insurance policy."

"But these clothes are the same as mine."

The Other Mark looked at them. "Huh. So they are," he said. "I guess that makes sense." He waved the gun again. "Put them on, anyway."

Mark shuffled uncomfortably. Chewie began to bark. The Other Mark continued to speak.

"Y'see. If I know how you think—and, let's face it, I do—you haven't come alone at all. Jode's probably hidden in the car somewhere, waiting to spring to your aid."

Mark did his belt buckle up. "I came alone," he said. "Just like you said."

"Liar," said The Other Mark. "You're not— *We're* not that stupid."

"I wasn't going to put Rebecca in jeopardy," said Mark. "I came alone."

Chewie continued his barking.

The Other Mark snorted. "How's your head?" he said.

"My head?"

"Yes. Your head. The thing that holds up your hat," said The Other Mark. "Y'know, assuming you wore a hat. Which you don't. But if you did, how's your head?"

"Fine," said Mark. "How's yours?"

"Don't have a headache?"

Mark sighed. "Yes, I have a headache," he said. "You?"

"Yeah," said The Other Mark. "Annoying as anything, don't you think? Especially with Chewie yapping on like an idiot."

"You think the headache's being because we're close to each other?"

"I think the headache's a clear sign that we shouldn't both be here." He pulled the curtain back on the window and looked out at the car again. "Did you really not bring Jodie with you?"

"I really didn't."

The Other Mark snorted. "Boy, you are the stupid version."

Chewie barked some more.

"She *is* coming, though, isn't she?" said The Other Mark. "Maybe following behind ten, fifteen minutes away?"

Pause. "Of course not," said Mark.

The Other Mark smiled. "Liar," he said. "She's coming. Good."

"She's not coming," said Mark. "I came alone."

The Other Mark ignored him. "Regardless," he said. "By the time she gets here, you'll be dead. And I'll be you."

"Maybe," said Mark. "Maybe you'll be dead. And I'll be me."

The Other Mark laughed. "I don't think so," he said. "Besides, I'm the one who deserves to live. I'm the one who saved the universe. You're just the one who almost fucked everything up."

"You're a real hero," said Mark.

"This is what I've been trying to tell people," said The Other Mark. "But, of course, nobody outside the four of us knows the truth, do they?"

"Whatever you say," said Mark.

"And that's kinda why I'm relying on you to bring Jodie here. You'll be dead by then. I'll be you. She'll help me escape from the police. Which, let's face it, won't be difficult, because by that stage they'll have closed the case on yet another grisly murder-suicide."

He shuddered in mock horror. Mark rolled his last sentence over in his mind.

Murder-suicide? Did that mean…

"What?" he said. "Where's Rebecca?"

"Oh," said The Other Mark. "Didn't I mention? Rebecca's dead."

BEHIND ANDREW AND KATRINA

"Y'know," said Mills. "If those two aren't leading us to Campbell, a lot of people will have wasted a lot of time and petrol."

Agent Benson snorted. "Yeah," he said. "It will be awkward if they're just off on a romantic getaway."

"Nothing like several law enforcement officers and a couple of random citizens to lift the romantic mood."

Agent Benson's voice grew serious again. "They're leading us to Campbell. All we have to do is make sure we don't scare them away."

Lights flashed from behind. Agent Mills turned around.

"Oh fuck," he said.

"Is that…"

"It's Innes."

"Oh, for fuck's sake."

INSIDE THE FARMHOUSE

The pounding in Mark's head grew even stronger.

He was lying. He was just trying to throw him off. He could not possibly have killed Rebecca.

"Where is she?" he whispered.

"I'm telling you," said The Other Mark. "She's dead. I didn't want to kill her. But I had no choice."

"You're lying."

"I wish I was," said The Other Mark. "Go. Look for yourself." He waved the gun to the bathroom.

Mark stumbled towards the bathroom. His head pounded. He had to be lying.

He opened the bathroom door. Nothing.

Empty.

A little blood on the floor, but otherwise empty.

"She's not in here," he said. "Where is she?"

"She's not there?" said The Other Mark. "She's got to be there."

Mark heard his footsteps approach. They stopped a few paces from the bathroom door.

"Oh, that's right," said The Other Mark in mock relief. "Try looking out the bathroom window."

Mark closed his eyes. This was it. He leant over to the window and looked out.

There was Rebecca. Dead on the ground. Blood coming out of a pair of bullet wounds in her head.

He reeled back from the window.

This was not happening.

He heard The Other Mark behind him.

"Hasta la vista, doppelganger."

APPROACHING THE FARMHOUSE

Jodie had slowly widened the gap between them and their posse over the past few kilometres. They were still within viewing distance, but were now a lot further back. They were no doubt hanging as far back as possible so as not to let Jodie and Richard know they were following.

Salisbury Road was coming up. Almost time to break free and head to the rescue.

Just needed Mark to have lived up to his end of the bargain. Defeating the villainous evil doppelganger. Rescuing his fair maiden and the like.

"It should be around the next corner," said Richard.

"Okay," said Jodie. "You ready?"

"As I'll ever be."

Here we go.

She turned the corner. There it was. Salisbury Road. She turned onto it and accelerated to top speed.

We're coming, Marcus. Please be okay.

IN THE FARMHOUSE

Mark had seen the bottle of Domestos when he first came in. As far as weapons went, it seemed to be the only one available. He'd twisted the lid loose before The Other Mark had entered the bathroom.

Now, with The Other Mark about to shoot him, he grabbed the bottle, turned and threw it.

He sure hoped it wasn't empty.

It wasn't.

The Domestos flew into The Other Mark's eyes. He recoiled, one hand clutching his eyes.

The other hand fired the gun wildly.

Mark had dropped to the ground as he'd thrown the bottle.

The Other Mark stumbled backwards out of the bathroom. He shot again. Missed again.

Mark followed him out. He grabbed a lamp from the bedside table. He smashed it into The Other Mark's face.

The Other Mark dropped the gun. Mark jumped for it.

The Other Mark swung his free arm wildly. It skimmed off Mark's cheek.

Mark ignored it. Gun, gun, gun. He needed the gun.

The Other Mark's hand grabbed his shoulder. He shoved it away and picked up the gun.

He kicked at The Other Mark's shin and stepped away from the bed.

The Other Mark fell off the edge of the bed.

Mark paused. Took a deep breath.

Time slowed.

He squeezed the trigger.

The Other Mark fell backwards as the bullet hit him in the chest.

Mark took another deep breath. Time was still very, very slow indeed.

He aimed. Shot again. The Other Mark took the bullet in the chest again.

Deep breath.

One final aim at his dying evil doppelganger.

He shot him in the head.

He put the gun on the bedside table. Time returned to normal speed. He walked over to his gurgling counterpart and kicked him.

"You stupid murdering fuck," he said.

He kicked him again.

Then again.

Then again.

"You stupid fuck."

He fell down on the bed.

OUTSIDE THE FARMHOUSE

Jodie screeched the car to a halt. "You got everything?" she said, opening the door.

"Yep." Richard had the bag over his shoulder. He jumped out of the car. The pair of them ran towards the farmhouse door.

Jodie looked back. Screaming police sirens were coming down the road. They probably had a minute—two at the most—until the police got here.

It was not a long time to work with. But it had to be enough. This was it. Either everything fell apart here. Or everything turned out okay.

She knocked on the door. "Marcus?"

No response. Three seconds wasted.

"We're coming in," she said.

She opened the door and walked in. Richard followed her, carrying the bag.

There was one Mark, dead on the ground.

Another one was sobbing on the bed.

My god. They *were* doppelgangers. The dead one was in his underwear. The sobbing one was fully clothed. That was the extent of the differences. Apart from the bullet hole, obviously.

There. Beside the sobbing Mark. A gun, just sitting on the bed. She walked slowly over to it and picked it up. The sobbing Mark did nothing but turn his head slightly.

The sirens grew even louder. Richard looked out the window. "They're thirty seconds away," said Richard. "A minute at the most."

Jodie pointed the gun at the sobbing Mark.

"Are you my Mark?" she said.

"He killed Rebecca," said Mark.

What?

"Oh, shit," said Richard.

Jodie blinked hard. She opened her eyes and aimed the gun tight at Mark again.

"Are you my Mark?" she said. Because if this was some sick trick, this goddamn doppelganger was going to get a bullet in the face and to hell with explaining his existence to the cops.

Mark nodded.

"Give me the code," said Jodie.

"What?" said Mark.

"The code we worked out earlier. Give it to me now."

"Homer and Krusty," whispered Mark.

Jodie dropped the gun. "Oh thank god," she said. She ran to the bed and hugged him.

"We don't have time for this," pointed out Richard. One of the sirens stopped. "They're here."

"Okay," said Jodie, pulling back from Mark. "Marcus, I'm sorry to do this. But… you've got to get out of here."

"She's dead," said Mark. "What does it matter?"

Richard helped him to his feet. "Mark," he said. "I'm sorry. But please, you have to go."

"Marcus. Please," said Jodie. "Just go to the cave. Hide out there for the night. We'll be back tomorrow."

Richard handed Mark the bag. "There's a sleeping-bag and a torch in there," he said. "Some books and food also."

"Please," said Jodie. "Go. We'll pick you up tomorrow."

Richard opened the back door. The three of them ran down the back steps towards the scrub at the back of the farmhouse. "We love you," said Jodie. She kissed him. "Everything will be okay. I promise."

Another siren stopped. Car doors slammed shut. Footsteps from the front of the house.

As Mark disappeared into the scrub, Jodie turned and saw Rebecca's body.

Oh, god. How had it come to this?

He had killed her.

Poor Marcus. How must it feel to know that a version of you was capable of killing the woman you loved most in the world? And now he had to spend the night in his childhood caves. Hiding out. Alone.

She could not imagine a worse night.

She hugged Richard tight, burying her head into his chest until Detective Jackson came around the corner and ordered them to raise their hands.

They did so.

Damn it. This was not how this was supposed to end.

CONTINUUM

EPILOGUE

"None of it makes any sense."

"No more fucking about with the space-time continuum."

TWO DAYS LATER, AIRPORT

"THIS LOOKS LIKE it," said Andrew. He checked his boarding pass again. Gate 23. Boarding in five minutes. Perfectly timed. He sat his bag down. "You going to be okay?" he said.

"Sure," said Katrina. Her eyes were red from two days of near-constant crying. She sniffed. "You?"

Andrew doubted he'd ever get the vision of Rebecca's corpse out of his mind. Every time he'd closed his eyes in the last forty-eight hours, her dead body had appeared. "Yeah," he said. "I'm good."

"You sure you don't want to stick around for the funeral?"

"I'd feel weird being there," he said. "Ex-boyfriend and all. And… y'know." He didn't want to spell out the rest of the thought. Heck, he didn't want this conversation to progress in any way, whatsoever. "Besides," he finally said. "I need to get back to work."

"Sure," said Katrina. She sniffed some more.

Dear god, this was awkward. He needed to get away. He felt trapped. For fuck's sake, let's just start boarding the plane already. He should not be punished any longer for one grief and alcohol-fuelled mistake.

"I might go through Security and wait in there," said Andrew.

"Okay."

"I'll call you," he said.

He had no idea why he said that.

Katrina beamed. "I'd like that," she said.

"Goodbye," he said. He leant in, tilted to avoid her enormous nose and kissed her.

When they broke it off, he could see she was crying. Again.

"Be strong," he said. "Rebecca would have wanted it that way."

Katrina started to cry again. Andrew gave her a final squeeze of the shoulder and made his way to Security.

This trip had been a bad idea.

THE NEXT DAY, AGENT BENSON'S OFFICE

"None of it makes any sense," said Mills.

"Hmm?" said Benson, looking up from his coffee.

"The Campbell case," said Mills. "It makes no sense."

"Oh god," said Benson. He put his coffee back on the table. "Let it go. It's over."

"It wasn't a murder-suicide," said Mills. "Both Campbell and Miss Tyler had more than one bullet in them. That's fine for the murder portion, but… overzealous for the suicide part."

"We know it's not a murder-suicide," said Benson. "Mrs Flannery confessed to killing Campbell in self-defence."

"And you believe her?"

"Why would she lie?"

"She didn't have time to kill him," said Mills. "We were right on their tail. How did she get the gun?"

"I don't know."

"Campbell was shot with the same gun that killed Miss Tyler," said Mills. "Forensics tells us Tyler had been dead for roughly twenty minutes before we showed up. Therefore, the gun was Campbell's."

"So how did she get the gun?"

"Right," said Mills. "There was no time for her to face him, be attacked by him, somehow get the gun and shoot him."

"But her prints were on the gun."

"But she had no gunshot residue. And the angles were all wrong. She would have had to have shot him from the bathroom side of the room, not the front door side of the room."

"So?"

"There's just not enough time for her to get in there, circle Campbell, relieve him of his gun, shoot him, put the gun back near the door, then run out the back door to find Miss Tyler." Agent Mills' face grew more animated. "And that's another thing. Why would they shoot one of their friends, who they spent so much time protecting earlier in the day, *before* they found out that he'd killed Miss Tyler?"

"Do you see now why I'm suggesting we drop it?" said Benson. "I don't think we're going to solve this one. And it's not our jurisdiction anyway."

"But it makes no sense."

"Should we do a sweep of the surrounding area for grassy knolls?"

"And we still haven't uncovered how they were beating the share market every week. Or what the weekly phone calls had to do with it."

Agent Benson smiled a weary smile. "Sometimes, my friend," he said. "You need to let these things go. We're not going to solve this one. Let it go."

"I just want to understand what happened."

THE NEXT DAY, MARK'S HOUSE

Mark sat at the table. He flipped through an expensive comic book his brain was not processing. Chewie sat at his feet. His chin rested on Mark's foot.

"Knock knock," said Jodie, poking her head around the corner. Chewie ran over to her, barking.

Mark looked up. "Hey," he said. He forced out a smile.

"How are you feeling?"

Mark shrugged. "I don't know. I just… I just can't believe she's gone." He sighed. "How are you going?"

"I'm all right. It looks like they're not going to press charges against me for 'killing' you."

"No?"

"He was a murderer. They're willing to buy our self-defence angle. I think they just want the case to disappear."

"That's good news," said Mark. His voice contained no enthusiasm.

"The beard's coming along."

"It's just at that annoyingly itchy stage. Y'know?"

"Not really, no," said Jodie. "But I'll take your word for it."

She smiled and put a hand on his shoulder.

"What about the phones?" said Mark.

"Oh," said Jodie. She paused. "Well, they still don't know about them. They pressed a bit on the share market stuff. I told them you were the brains behind the operation. The rest of us just shared in the money."

"So, that's it?" said Mark. "It's over."

"I think so. Look, we'll lie low for a while. Live on our cash reserves. And when we start it up again, we'll make sure we program in bad decisions as well as good ones. Do our best not to stand out as much as we did last time."

"I don't want to do it again," said Mark.

There was a long pause.

"I'll do it," said Jodie. "I'll leave the messages."

"No," said Mark. "No more time-travelling messages."

"We'll be more careful. We'll sleep there overnight if we have to."

"No. No more. Rebecca is dead. No more fucking about with the space-time continuum.

"Okay," said Jodie. "We'll leave it."

"I'm not going to change my mind."

"Okay."

"I'm going to take Chewie for a walk."

"Okay."

Mark got up. Chewie, whose ears had pricked at the word 'walk' began to jump up and down excitedly. Mark attached his lead.

"Oh," said Jodie. "Almost forgot." She handed Mark an envelope. Mark opened it and peered inside. "Your new identity. Birth certificate. Passport. Driver's licence. Credit card. Bank account. You're ready to start a new life, Mark Byrne."

"Thanks."

"You've got no idea how hard it is to find this stuff. You don't exactly find identity fraud providers in the Yellow Pages."

"I can imagine."

"Any time you're up to it, we'll book a time with the bank and we'll add you to the trust."

"No rush," said Mark. "I trust you not to screw me over."

There was an awkward pause.

"Things will get better," she said.

"I know."

She hugged him. Chewie barked with excitement.

"Okay," said Mark. "I'd better walk this one."

"Okay. Catch you tomorrow?"

"Sure."

HALF AN HOUR LATER, BACK OF THE PROPERTY

Mark hurled the ball. Chewie chased it. Caught it. Returned it. And readied for a repeat. He hopped from front leg to front leg in anticipation.

Mark threw the ball again. Chewie flew off after it.

"Why so glum?" came a voice from behind Mark.

He whirled around.

It was Rebecca.

She was alive. She was smiling. She was here.

He'd clearly gone mad. But, hell, what a way to go. He dropped the ball scooper and ran over to his hallucination of Rebecca. He hugged her. He kissed her, then kissed her again.

As far as hallucinations went, this was his favourite one ever. He squeezed her tight. Tangible for a hallucination also.

Chewie raced over to join the joy. He barked and leapt up at Rebecca, trying to get her attention.

"There's my boy," she said. She picked him up and cuddled him.

Chewie squirmed out and danced around Mark again, looking for another throw. Mark kicked the ball away. Chewie gave chase.

Mark stumbled through his entire vocabulary, looking for the best possible word. He went with "How?"

"The phones," said Rebecca.

"I don't—"

"He was going to kill me. I knew that. He said he loved me, but he couldn't risk me turning him in." She looked up at Mark. "He said he wasn't going back to prison."

"Prison?"

"He was so like you in so many ways, babe," said Rebecca. "I think he just made some… some bad choices somewhere along the line."

"I still don't understand," said Mark.

"Well, I knew he was going to kill me," said Rebecca. "He was too strong. Too vicious. So I did the only thing I could think of. I told myself that in three days I was going to leave a message on your machine."

Mark looked at her, stunned. He began to get it.

Rebecca continued. "It's like Jode said. As soon as you *decide* to call, that sets the chain of events in motion. That causes the message to be left."

"You decided to leave a message," said Mark. He shook his head. Unable to believe the reality of this.

"Right," said Rebecca. "And once the message was on the answering machine, the universe had to make sure I was there to make the call three days later."

"I don't believe it," said Mark.

"Yesterday, I appeared in front of the phone and left the message that I'd thought of before I died."

Mark raised his head to the sky. He laughed in triumph.

"I love you, Mark," she said. She smiled at him. "That was the message."

"Oh my god," said Mark. "I love you too." He looked up at the sky and shouted again. "You're alive!"

"Yep," said Rebecca. "Turns out, every now and then, ruptures in the space-time continuum can work for you."

They kissed again.

If this was a hallucination—if he *had* gone mad—then he didn't want to ever sane up.

They broke away from the kiss. "You're all stubbly," said Rebecca. She rubbed his cheek.

"Yeah," said Mark. "Preparing for my new identity. How do you feel about being Mrs Rebecca Byrne?"

"Byrne?"

"Byrne."

"I had been looking forward to being Mrs Rebecca Campbell," said Rebecca. She smiled that smile that kicked Mark's heart into overdrive. "But I can live with Mrs Rebecca Byrne. Just as long as we're together."

"Always."

"Excellent."

"Come on, Chewie," said Mark. "We're going home." He scooped up the ball.

She was alive. It was a miracle.

He put the ball scooper over his shoulder and pulled Rebecca towards him. Arms wrapped around each other, they headed for home.

Not until they were about halfway back did he even notice the size of this new Rebecca's bicep.

AFTERWORD

Thanks for reading. I hope you enjoyed *Disconnected*. If you did, please consider leaving a review at Amazon or Goodreads or your blog or wherever else seems appropriate. I'm always on the lookout for beta readers for upcoming books and people who leave interesting reviews tend to become frontrunners.

If you'd like to connect with me, you can do so at www.akadler.com. Or, if you prefer, you can follow me on Twitter (@akadler) or Facebook (www.facebook.com/akadler).

Okay, that's all. Be fun.

A.K.

ACKNOWELDGEMENTS

Thank you to Bronwyn Liebke and Sandi Dufficy for their feedback and criticism (and one notable plot hole discovery). Thank you to Morgan Dodge for making the outside of the book look beautiful. And an extra special thank you to Morgan Richter at Luft Books for feedback, criticism *and* making the inside of the book look beautiful. Triple threat!